I0547126

Secret Passions
by Loribelle Hunt

Though Sara Beth Reynard shuns the spotlight, her sensual animal nature always draws unwanted attention. On the rare occasions she leaves fox territory to supervise a construction project, humans are her number one hassle.

When the discovery of human/animal DNA makes her a sleazy tabloid's lead story, Sara finds the whole thing laughable. Right up until some goon attempts to kidnap her. Worse, her alpha sends her to the wereeagles, clan of her childhood nemesis, for help.

Patrick Aquila takes one look at the grown-up version of "Foxy," and wants to peel away all her layers of uptight and proper. His attempt to show her a night of lighthearted fun turns into an off-the-charts explosion of passion. But romance among weres is never that simple.

Patrick is in a race against time to convince Sara Beth they belong together, and find the snitch who is feeding information to not just one stalker, but two. The reporter who wants to hang her out to dry, and a hunter who wants to hand her over to her worst nightmare.

Illicit Passions
by Crystal Jordan

Tori Haida was born a stereotype—a pretty swan shifter—and has spent a lifetime living it down with an in-your-face attitude and a zero-tolerance policy for stupidity. Which makes her attraction to the werewolf Alpha's heir more than a tad inconvenient.

Bastian Lykaios is just the kind of dominant male who drives her crazy, and not in a good way. And yet, she can't help wanting him in the worst way.

The moment he arrives at the Refuge Resort, Bastian is in lust. The were-leopards' administrative assistant is a study in contrasts: a cheerleader-perky blonde with a body built for sin, the mouth of a sailor, and a lead foot for her classic car.

Unfortunately, there's no time to indulge in an affair, not while a werekind traitor is leaking information to the human press. But when Tori is kidnapped by a pair of scientists to use as a live specimen, Bastian's plan for damage control turns into a rescue mission. One where all means of rescue are on the table—including betraying his own kind.

Forbidden Passions, Vol. 2

Crystal Jordan
&
Loribelle Hunt

Forbidden Passions, Vol. 2
Print ISBN: 978-0-9860944-5-3

Secret Passions Copyright © 2018 Loribelle Hunt
Illicit Passions Copyright © 2018 Crystal Jordan

CONTENTS

Secret Passions

Loribelle Hunt

CHAPTER ONE

Sara Beth Reynard had been on edge since leaving her house that morning. Her apprehension had eased when she reached the job site and was surrounded by the work crews, but as everyone began to leave for their lunch, the feeling intensified so much she decided she'd better finish and leave too, rather than be the last on site. She loved the house she'd designed and its country setting, but it had never felt so isolated before today.

It was that damned tabloid reporter's fault. Somehow a handful of scientists had gained access to blood and tissue samples from werekind. Sara Beth didn't believe for one second it had happened by accident—someone inside the community had to be responsible. The world's shapeshifters had kept their existence secret far too long for a small group of humans to accidentally discover them. Most of the scientific and news communities had dismissed the findings, but Jeff Nichols, the crackpot journalist, was all over the story.

Worse, he'd identified her as a werewolf. *A werewolf!* The wolves were descendants of King Lycaon, who, along with his sons had been granted the ability to shift by the Greek god Zeus. They were completely unrelated to the foxes, who'd been created by ancient Germanic gods as warriors. Their common ancestor was Reginhard. As the legends and fables were passed from generations and crossed cultures, Reginhard became the surname of the werefox alpha, Reynard.

She had no idea how Nichols had stumbled on her, but he could at least get the story straight. She was a fox, dammit, not some overgrown, bad-tempered puppy. Her clan thought it was hilarious. The whole mess appealed to them. After all, foxes were known as pranksters in most mythology and felt honor bound to live up to their history. Of course, they weren't the ones with their faces plastered all over those awful rags, were they?

She heard a truck crank up and—glancing out the window—saw it drive away. She finished washing the grout off her hands and hurried upstairs. The house was almost finished. She'd come to see how the final stages were progressing and had been roped into assisting with tiling the kitchen backsplash. Truthfully, she didn't mind. It was the kind of thing she loved and also the reason she'd got degrees in architecture and design. After school, she'd joined the family construction business. She'd only been in charge of the residential side of the company for three years, but she'd been working in it since she was a kid.

The stairs opened onto a large landing that had been designed at the client's request as a library/lounge area. The second story had natural teak floors, which contrasted nicely with the crisp white built-in bookcases that surrounded the landing. The bedrooms on either side of the library differed only in color. She went through the guest room before moving to the opposite end of the landing to the master suite. She'd given the client exactly what he wanted and had to admit the man had good taste.

The back wall was all windows and French doors that led to a balcony, which stretched the length of the house. The room had a sitting area in an alcove that managed to feel private even though it was open, and the bathroom was to die for. She took her time checking it out. It was done in warm earth tones, had a huge walk-in shower and a tub she was convinced would hold four. It was positively decadent. Sighing, she flipped off the light switch and went back downstairs.

In contrast to the traditional upstairs, the first story looked like something out of a slick urban magazine. The floors were polished concrete and the front half of the house was an open living, dining and kitchen area. A small guest bath was tucked into a short hall which led to the final room. The house featured the first studio she'd built for a working artist and so far it was the least-finished room. Only the floors and walls were complete. She had an appointment with the artist later in the week to discuss work surfaces and storage areas.

She heard the front door close as more of the guys left and hastened to follow them. As soon as she stepped outside, she felt watched. Damn, she was getting sick of this. She let her fox side rise to the surface and sharpen her vision, but she didn't see anything or anyone who didn't belong when she looked around. Was danger really lurking or was she just paranoid? It seemed ludicrous to believe someone was watching her, but she couldn't shake the feeling. She decided to swing by her parents' house. One of her brothers was bound to be there for lunch. It would be easy to rope one into having a look around.

She stepped off the porch to the sidewalk, giving the area another visual sweep. Nothing looked suspicious. There were a couple of guys getting in a truck and another couple on the far side of the yard, packing up the tools by the new retaining wall. She waved as she headed toward her own vehicle. She'd arrived late and had to park a bit down the street.

It was broad daylight, bright and growing chilly as the first storm of the season moved in. She felt like she was walking through town alone at night, though. She dug her keys out of her pocket, eyeing the tree line beside her, and activated the remote when she was in range. By then her senses were screaming. She took a deep breath to test the air. At first all she scented was woods, the last honeysuckle of the season and fresh cut grass. Then there was the faintest hint of man. When the scent's owner stepped out from behind a tree, she cried out, more from surprise than fear.

She was damned glad she had when she met his gaze and took another deep breath. His scent was putrid in a way she'd learned to associate with violence. Malevolence. His eyes glittered, his expression anticipatory. He was several inches taller than her, bulky the way bodybuilders were, balding and scary as hell. Then he lunged for her. Her heart thudded in her chest and she backpedaled, just managing to stay on her feet and pivot to run away. She had agility and a shifter's heightened speed on her side, but if the last two guys on today's crew—both werewolves—hadn't been so close she would have been caught. She felt something sting her shoulder through the thin long-sleeved shirt she wore. The two shifters, raced toward her in human form, yelling her name. She made it another couple of steps before her knees went out and her vision dimmed.

The yelling woke her, but it took several minutes before the conversation sounded like more than jumbled syllables. The words came together slowly, one here and there. Attack. Daughter. Tranquilizers. She frowned—at least she thought she did—as she struggled to make sense of the fog in her brain. She forced her eyes open and then turned to shield her face from the glare of the overhead light. The room reeked of fear and fury, and it took a minute to get her bearings. She was in her old bedroom at her parents' house, and they weren't yelling as she'd thought. They stood by the door talking with Michael, the werewolf alpha.

Shit. What had happened? She sat up, ignoring the dizziness that rushed over her, and struggled to remember. She'd been checking out a house that was almost complete. No, she'd been leaving and a man had stepped out from the trees and had tried grab her. She rubbed a sore spot on her shoulder and remembered feeling a sting before she passed out. Someone in the room had mention tranqs. Had the man attempted to drug and kidnap her? It wasn't the skeevy reporter. She'd recognize him. Maybe it was just a random incident. She knew it couldn't be, though, and dismissed the idea about the time the others noticed her sitting up. Scents assailed her. Anger, relief. Fear. She groaned. Well, hell. She was so screwed. It had taken years to wrest her independence from her father. This would make him impossible.

"How do you feel, baby?" her mom asked, rushing to her side.

"Fine," she croaked, and reached for the water bottle on the table, surprised at how parched she was. "What the— heck—happened?"

Her mother cussed almost as much as she did, and her father always griped at them about their language. Her mother hadn't missed the almost-slip and winked as Sara Beth's father and Michael, the werewolf, approached and stopped toward the bottom of her bed. Michael held up a small dart. She scooted forward to take it from him, then brought it up to her nose and sniffed. It was a common animal tranquilizer.

"Did they catch him?" she asked. She remembered the two werewolves racing to her rescue.

Michael shook his head. He didn't look particularly worried, but an expression that crossed his face made her nervous. It was almost expectant, anticipatory. What the hell was that about?

"Well, it wasn't the sleazeball reporter," she said. "This guy was a lot bigger and meaner looking."

"Which is what concerns us," her father said, his voice trembling in anger. Will Reynard glanced at the others, and Sara Beth got the feeling they'd made some decision she was really going to hate. While her father was alpha of the small local fox clan, the clan itself was under the protection of the much bigger werewolf clan. Michael's word was law, whether she liked it or not. And she really didn't.

"Michael believes until we find out who the guy was and eliminate the threat, it's best if you go into protective custody," her father said. "I agree."

Oh he did, did he? This was worse than she thought. She turned, narrowing her eyes on the werewolf, wondering how it benefitted him if she disappeared for a few days. Michael never did anything without ulterior motives.

"I don't think that will be necessary. I was surprised today. I won't be again and I'll make sure I keep my pistol with me." She was the best shot in the clan, but she rarely carried the weapon anywhere but the range. "I have too much to do to take a forced vacation. Besides, I might be able to help. I got a good look at him."

She wasn't the best artist, but she was confident she could sketch an accurate likeness.

"You do most of your work from your home office, Sara Beth. And there is no way you're getting more involved in this," her father pointed out in a tone that told her just how determined he was to protect his adult daughter. "You can take everything you need with you."

She sighed. She knew when she was facing a losing battle. "And where am I going?"

"To the eagles. They have the most secure lands," Michael said. He sounded innocent enough and maybe that was the problem. Sara Beth got the feeling from his voice he was only interested in her as an excuse to visit the eagles. But why did he need one?

She supposed it didn't matter. She hadn't seen Ajax or her girls in a couple of months so a short visit would be nice, and she knew from experience she wouldn't have any problems accessing the internet or phone lines. But that wasn't why she still resisted the idea.

"Okay," she said, giving her father a stern look. "But only for a couple of days."

"This isn't up for debate, Sara Beth," Michael said. His words were pure alpha and set her teeth on edge.

She nodded acquiescence and prayed to the gods she could avoid the one person on the eagle's mountain who posed any danger to her. Patrick Aquila. She hadn't spoken to him in a decade, though she caught the occasional distant glimpse when he came into town. But she hadn't entered his territory in years and he was one of Ajax's advisors. What were the odds he wouldn't get told about this? Hopefully, their paths wouldn't cross. Given half the chance, he'd steal her heart and soar away with it. And he probably wouldn't even realize he was doing it.

Thankfully, he was Ajax's First Consul. He'd be the last choice for bodyguard duty.

CHAPTER TWO

Patrick Aquila was looking forward to finishing this last minute meeting and getting back to Guard headquarters on top of the mountain. He'd been accused of being antsy and claustrophobic, but neither was an accurate description of his mood. Feeling confined wasn't what caused his impatience. This was more like apathy, and hell, going back probably wouldn't help. He'd come down because he'd been bored training new members of the Queen's Guard.

He needed something to shake things up. A little excitement. He was tempted to blame it on his ancestry. Wereeagles had been granted the ability of flight by Hermes, after a runner carried word to Athens of the Greek's victory over the Persians at Marathon. The urge to soar was part of his DNA.

He glanced over at Nico and Ajax, the wereeagle queen. Her head was bent over reports, but her mate was bouncing Alex, their one year old daughter, on his knee to the girl's delighted chortles. Ayla, her four year old sister, in eagle form, was wildly careening around the ceiling. Every few minutes she'd dive at Patrick so he'd pretend he was afraid of the elder royal daughter. He grinned as she made her next pass. There was never a dull moment with Ajax's daughters. He didn't want that much excitement, but he had to admit the girls kept things interesting.

"Why are we here again?" he asked Ajax. "I thought we were through catering to Hector Leonidas's whims. No offense, Nico," Patrick added, not *quite* apologetically to the former wereleopard leader's son.

Ajax laughed. "As long as he's holding Ayla or Alex, you can insult him all you want. And I don't know any more than I've already told you. Hector says Michael is bringing someone he wants us to protect."

Ajax didn't say it, but Patrick knew he'd be the one to get stuck with babysitting duty. This better not be about werewolf or wereleopard politics. Though since the four Leonidas brothers had mated—two of them to wolves—the hostilities between the two species had cooled so much he often thought nothing of it to see them together. But he still didn't want to get stuck on a protection detail. He had every intention of pawning it off to one of the squads in the Guard.

And he'd like to get on with it. What was taking so long? He stood and ducked as Ayla dived once again. He paced to the window. There were no roads up the mountain so the residents used four-wheelers for guests or transporting things from the mountain base. As he watched the dirt path Michael would use, he heard the faint hum of the vehicle approaching. Finally, Michael, Hector and the stranger came into sight and parked under the house. Patrick didn't get a good look at the occupant, who wore a coat and hood. Since his first duty was to protect the royal family, he stepped out to intercept the newcomers. He hadn't been briefed, had no idea if the mystery guest was a threat.

The balcony circled the house. He had to walk around to meet them at the stairs.

He froze when their unexpected visitor took the first step. She was a female fox. Her scent was intoxicating—sweet with a hint of fire—and she was irritated. He would be too, after who-knew-how-long with Michael and Hector.

He held his breath as she came around the curve in the stairs. She carried a backpack and small duffel bag and was wearing an unzipped cream-colored, faux fur lined coat with a tight pink shirt under it. He grinned at the glittery hammer emblazoned across her chest. Her jeans were form-fitting, and her scuffed work boots obviously saw hard use. When she looked up, still several feet below him, her big brown eyes flashed with recognition but it took him a second to figure out how he knew her. She threw back the coat's hood and rich, dark auburn waves spilled around her shoulders with streaks of white framing her face. Her scent should have been familiar, and when he took a deep breath he recognized the girl he'd known.

"Well hello, foxy," he drawled when she stepped onto the balcony.

Damn, she had pretty eyes. Her chilly gaze should have left him a pile of ice on the floor, but it started an entirely different kind of reaction. He blocked her when she tried to step around him, prompting a subtle, almost imperceptible change to her scent. Fear. Not only was it a slap in the face, it provoked protective instincts much deeper and darker than he'd known he was capable. He couldn't stand for her to be afraid of him any more than he could let her run from him.

As Michael and Hector came into view, quietly arguing with each other, Patrick took Sara Beth's hand and gently tugged her farther onto the balcony and closer to Ajax's family. He walked backward so he could keep an eye on her, though if he was honest, he'd admit he watched her so closely because he couldn't stop drinking her in. So he saw her nostrils flare, saw the way she relaxed when she realized he was taking her into a crowd. He wanted to pull her close and shelter her from whatever had scared her. The girl he'd known was fearless, and as he watched, she conquered her fright and looked more like the fox he remembered.

He smiled, hoping to put her at ease while wondering how long it would take before he convinced her to let him hold her and stroke all those lush curves she didn't bother to hide anymore.

"You've grown up," he teased.

She rolled her eyes. "You haven't."

"Oh, foxy," he said, looking her up and down. "We've *both* grown up."

He could hear her grind her teeth and hid his grin. He knew she hated being called that, which was why he'd used it when she was a young teenager trying to follow around the older kids. The nickname pissed her off, had made it easier to keep her at a distance. A three year age difference was no big deal now, but it had been in high school. He'd been drawn to her even then. But damn, the woman had grown into the name. Whether she liked it or not, it suited her now.

He realized she didn't know that though. He'd given her the perfect opportunity to flirt back, but she didn't respond to his teasing. Instead she withdrew, despite her scent taking on a subtle hint of longing, and her eyes were suspicious— like she questioned his interest, didn't believe it. She didn't have the air of a woman confident in her sensuality. It made no sense. Were the foxes and wolves in her life idiots? It didn't matter. He wanted to be the one to show her. Didn't want to share her. Emotion gripped him and twisted his insides. He was amazed at the unexpected possessiveness and forced himself to shut down and step back. He'd never been possessive of a woman and he wasn't sure what to do about it.

He led her into the house and moved into the background. Ajax and Sara Beth had been friends since they started walking, so Patrick knew his queen was perfectly safe with her. Nico, arms now free, stepped up to his side.

"Where's Alex?" Patrick asked.

"Nap," Nico answered. "One minute she's babbling away and the next she's out cold."

It might have sounded like a complaint but it was impossible to miss the fatherly pride. Patrick smiled. Alex charmed everyone who knew her.

"Not who I was expecting," Nico said, nodding toward their visitor. Patrick couldn't keep his eyes off her. He wondered if he'd ever get over the compulsion.

"Sara Beth Reynard," he answered. "She's the werefox alpha's daughter."

"Ajax's school friend. She never comes up here."

No she didn't, Patrick acknowledged, and realized Nico must have met her someplace else. He knew his queen and Sara Beth saw each other in town on rare occasions, but mostly communicated by email and phone. Patrick had never wondered why before but with each hostile look the werefox gave him, his curiosity grew.

"She's very pretty," Nico said noncommittally.

Though the two of them had worked out their distrust of each other years ago, Patrick had a damned hard time not lunging for his friend. Nico had the gall to laugh.

"Well, isn't this interesting?" Nico drawled.

"It's nothing," he snapped.

"Really?" Nico cocked his head to the side, a gesture like that of a cat. "So I should call one of the soldiers to handle this protection detail?"

"Do it and I'll break the no killing the consort rule," he growled.

Nico laughed and clapped him on the shoulder. "Yeah, that's what I thought."

"I have no idea what I'm doing," he muttered, knowing he was acting out of character.

He should let Nico call someone else in. His response to her presence was too intense and inexplicable. She was hot but he knew plenty of hot women. What was it about this one that was so different? The more he thought about it, the less he cared. They were both adults. She glanced over at him, heat flaring in her eyes. There was no way he was letting her out of his sight, and hopefully his bed, until he figured out what it was that drew him so strongly.

"Damn," he murmured.

Nico stepped in front of him, blocking his view of the women. Patrick would have snapped if not for the serious look on his friend's face. "What?"

"You can work out seduction plans later. Right now," he said with a glance over his shoulder, "we need to find out what's going on. What happened that they had to send her here?"

That question sent the closest thing to panic he'd ever known shooting through him. Sweet Hermes, how had he forgotten that? He followed Nico to the sofa where the women sat in time to overhear the end of the conversation.

"I can't stay here, Ajax. You have a family to protect."

"Our lands are the safest in the country."

Patrick watched Sara Beth press her lips together and give a small shake of her head. "Still, I won't take that risk."

"Don't worry, foxy," he said, stepping closer. "You won't put them in danger. You're coming home with me." He looked up as the door opened and Michael and Hector stepped inside. "Now would someone please tell me what I'm protecting you against?"

Instead of answering, Sara Beth opened her backpack, pulled out a sketchpad and tore out a page. She handed it to Ajax. "He tried to kidnap me this afternoon."

It took a second for her words to register and when they did Patrick wasn't sure if it was wrath or fear that filled him. He felt like a vice had clamped around his heart. He was torn between rushing out to find the monster or grabbing her and running to hide her away. When he realized his hands were shaking, he took a deep breath and regained control.

"And before anyone asks," she said, "we have no idea who he is. But it isn't the tabloid reporter who's been writing about me."

Ajax handed the sketch to Nico. Patrick stepped up next to him to look. The first thing he noticed was Sara Beth was quite good at capturing the menace in the man's eyes. They were a little crinkled, lines on the side indicating he was older, but she'd somehow put a mean glint in them. Patrick would put him in his early fifties. His features were just shy of too sharp. He looked distinguished and cold.

"I'll run it through the facial recognition program," Nico said. "Hopefully we'll get a hit."

Sara Beth told them exactly what had happened, and when she finished, Nico turned to Michael. "Did your wolves see how he got away? A vehicle?"

He shook his head. "No, but we emailed the sketch to the pack. If anyone sees him, we'll know."

A sudden gust of wind buffeted the house. "That's my cue to leave," Michael said. "I need to get home before snow closes the road up here."

Hector accompanied him and a few minutes later, when Patrick guided Sara Beth out to go to his place, the werewolf and wereleopard were still huddled together at the ATVs whispering.

"It's weird enough they're friends," Sara Beth muttered. "Now they're keeping secrets? That can't bode well."

It was a damned strange friendship, werewolves and wereleopards having been enemies for centuries. Patrick had become accustomed to them though, so he almost dismissed Sara Beth's comment as coming from someone who just hadn't seen them together much. On closer observation, however, there was definitely a furtiveness to the other men. He wondered what they were discussing. If it was anything to do with Sara Beth or the pack, he needed to know about it. Unfortunately, they noticed they were being watched and before he could butt in, they mounted the ATVs and left. He shrugged off the odd behavior—frankly, it wasn't that odd— and turned her toward the path home.

CHAPTER THREE

Ten minutes later, Patrick ushered Sara Beth into his home. He was on edge, his body tense and ready for action. He wasn't sure if it was from fear for her or fury at the people stalking her. But he was damned sure of one thing: nothing and no one would threaten her again as long as he lived. The need to ensure this was a living crazed beast in his chest. He wasn't sure how he breathed. And he hadn't even fucked her yet. He was nowhere near having that kind of trust from her. Tonight he'd be happy if she'd just let him hold her. He wanted a lot more, but this wasn't really about him, was it? Not after what she'd been going through.

"Nice place," she said.

She was focused on her surroundings, but he wasn't sure if it was because she was truly interested or if she was trying to ignore him. As they'd talked with the others, he'd felt an attraction growing with her but it had seemed one-sided. Maybe she wasn't as unaffected as she pretended, but he was pretty sure pushing her was a bad idea for now. He followed her lead and looked around his place, prepared to give her the grand tour, such as it was.

The house, like everything on the mountain slope, was built high in the trees. It was where he stayed when he was down slope, but it wasn't his official residence as the Queen's First Consul. He'd never felt at home there. It was huge. It was meant for a big family that had friends stopping by all the time.

"It's mine," he said self-consciously. "But it isn't my official residence. When I take a mate, we'll have to move in there."

"Hmm," she murmured. "What a shame. There's a lot to be said for small and cozy. But I guess someone in your position doesn't get to choose, huh?"

He cocked his head and watched as she walked around. The house had only one bedroom and the rest of the space was an open kitchen, eating and living area. It was about nine-hundred square feet, but since there were few walls it had always felt bigger to him.

She trailed her fingers along the back of a sofa and finally looked over at him with a serious expression. "You don't live here. Not really."

"You're right. It's mine but I don't spend a lot of time here." He paused, wondering how to draw her out, expose the real woman she'd so far kept well hidden. "You design the houses your family builds, right?"

"Yep."

"You think a person's house says something about them?"

One corner of her mouth kicked up, a half smile that made his heart stutter. "Yes, I do."

"What does mine say about me?" he asked.

She shrugged. "Like I said, it may be yours, but you don't live here. White walls, beige carpet, brown leather furniture and nothing personal. You really expect me to believe Mr. Flamboyant lives here?"

He wasn't sure if he should be insulted or amused. "I prefer to be on the mountain with the rest of the Guard, but my place is by my queen's side."

Sara Beth gave him that adorable frown again. "Why aren't y'all up there? After what happened to her father and with her cousin, I'd expect Ajax to keep her babies as secluded and safe as possible."

He was a little surprised to hear that from her. Sara Beth's father was an alpha. Alphas didn't back down or retreat. As for Ajax, her father had been assassinated when she was young, and her cousin had tried to kill her a few years ago, but he was no longer a threat to anyone. And Ajax didn't have a submissive bone in her body. "You'd have her retreat?"

Sara Beth shook her head. "Protecting your children is not retreat."

He had to give her that, but he also needed her to understand she was entering a more dominant world. Something told him she could hold her own, no problem.

"We would all prefer the princesses were up there with the Guard. Their father is more comfortable with them closer to the ground though."

She frowned. "They're eaglets. Height isn't a problem."

"Nico is a leopard. Explain that to him," he said dryly.

"I bet that was a shock for him. Eaglets instead of cubs," she said, amusement in her voice and lighting her eyes.

He got the impression she and Ajax had already laughed over this a time or two.

"What would we have, do you think?" he asked before he could stop himself. He'd surprised himself with the question, was even more surprised at how much he wanted to hear her answer. His eagle side seemed to wait in hushed silence. Anticipating, eager.

She snorted. "A fox and an eagle? Are you nuts? We're natural enemies, remember?"

"You're only part fox and I'm only part eagle. And my queen is mated to a leopard," he reminded her.

"Yeah," she muttered. "He's a bit higher on the food chain."

"Does that worry you, foxy?" he asked, letting his voice deepen and his desire seep through. He refused to let anyone else guard her, but he wasn't sure he'd survive such close proximity, himself. Certainly not without touching her, without claiming the woman he wanted to be exclusively his.

He stared at her with sudden clarity. This wasn't just great chemistry in the making. The instinct that drove him to get to know her better would only intensify and could only mean one thing.

But what the hell did he know about being a mate?

Someone had to die, but she couldn't decide who should go first. The list was growing. Some asshole had attacked her. Her father and Michael had insisted she come here. And now Patrick, the grown-up teenage crush from Hell, was…she wasn't sure what. He wasn't exactly flirting, was he? But he seemed to be trying to engage her on a personal level she knew she shouldn't allow. If he wanted to hop into bed, she was *so* there. But she wasn't about to get emotionally involved with an adrenaline-junkie eagle.

On second thought, sex was probably a bad idea. She might not be able to protect her heart if he touched her, if she gave in to the desire to feel him over her—moving in her. It would probably be a colossal mistake.

She was a fox, for crissakes. She did home and hearth and she did it damned well, thank you very much. She wanted comfort and warmth and a man who was devoted to her because of it. Patrick would never be that man, which was a cryin' shame, but as her favorite aunt always said, "Life's a bitch and then you die."

The hell of it was Patrick was the only man who'd ever tempted her wild side. He hadn't noticed her since the day he'd gone off to college, three years before her. She hadn't been as blind. And this was who she got stuck with as a bodyguard? Hell with that. Two days tops and she was going home. She'd hire someone if she had to. There were plenty of werewolves in the personal protection business.

Actually, if she'd been thinking straight, that would have occurred to her earlier. She was an idiot and irritated with herself so she might have been a bit testy when she asked about sleeping arrangements. It all went downhill from there.

"Where is the guest room?"

"There's only one bedroom in the house," he said. "We'll be sharing."

Oh fuck no. She might think about trying him on for size, but she knew the danger to her heart. "I'll take the couch."

"The hell you will," he snapped.

"Does that mean you will?" she asked, sweetly even though she could tell by his scent and expression he intended to sleep with her. More than sleep. His arousal was rich and masculine. Seductive.

"You're pushing it, foxy."

"Don't call me that," she bit out. Gods, she hated that nickname. "Frankly, it's insulting. You called me that when I was an unattractive kid you wanted to get rid of. It isn't getting you anywhere now, I promise."

She just wanted to go home. For some reason, her ego was more bruised now than right after the attempted kidnapping. It took every ounce of her control not to respond when he stepped closer and stroked his hands up her arms.

"You were beautiful. Why do you think I called you that? So sensual, so sexy and so damned young," he whispered. "You scared me. You made me feel things I wasn't supposed to feel. You were too young for me then."

She wrenched out of his grasp and knew her smile was saccharine sweet, totally fake. "I'm still too young for you. You can take the couch."

She tried to stalk away before he could protest, but she wasn't fast enough. He stopped the bedroom door from shutting with ease, slapping his palm against it as she tried to push it closed. There was no way she could compete with his

21

strength and she didn't see the point in embarrassing herself by trying. She set her hands on her hips and used the look her brothers called the death glare. Unfortunately, it didn't have much effect on a tall, well-built wereeagle. And why the hell were eagles so damned tall when she was cursed with shortness?

"What's that look for?" His expression may have been calm, but she was pleased to hear the exasperation in his tone.

"Do you have to keep looming over me?" She waved her hands in a shooing motion. The sun had set hours ago. She just wanted to change and curl up in bed. "Go away. It's been one annoying thing after the other today and you're making it worse."

He arched an eyebrow, pale blond and as perfectly sculpted as the rest of him. His hair was pulled back, but she guessed it was about shoulder length loose. And those eyes…bright, shocking blue. He was tall, his body roped with muscles she wanted to explore. He was disgustingly good-looking and if he got serious about seducing her she knew her resistance would turn to dust with the slightest effort on his part. It wasn't fair, was it?

"First of all, I don't loom," he said. "Second, I am not leaving you alone."

She wanted to scream. Or throw something at him. "Why am I with you anyway? You're Ajax's senior advisor. Bodyguard duty isn't exactly in your job description, is it?"

"No one else can keep you as safe as I can," he said, arrogant and haughty.

"Wow. Does that hurt?"

He looked confused. "What?"

"Carrying around a head swelled that big."

At first he looked stunned. She doubted anyone ever gave him grief over anything. Then *he* stunned *her*. He laughed, deep and full, totally genuine. When he reached for her, it didn't occur to her to dodge. He held her close with one hand on her ass and the other on the back of her head. As she became aware of every hard inch of his body, he fell silent.

"You are something else, baby," he whispered.

His eyes darkened to a stormy blue, the skin around them pinched tight as if he was under a great strain. His head lowered, his lips moving closer to hers slowly enough she could turn her head and struggle free. If she'd had an ounce of self-preservation, that was exactly what she'd have done. She had more curiosity, though. She'd imagined what his kisses would be like, and even though she had no knowledge, she'd compared the kisses of other men to her fantasy. Now was her chance to find out.

She closed her eyes and felt the softest touch against her lids before his lips touched hers. His tongue stroked the seam until she opened for him. She wasn't sure what she'd expected. It wasn't the slow, tender exploration she got.

"We shouldn't do this," she murmured a protest, even though she yearned for deep, drugging kisses.

"Why not?"

"We don't know each other. We're practically strangers."

"That's crazy, Sara Beth. I've known you your whole life," he said.

"Not well enough for this."

"What is it you think this is, baby?" he asked so gently she thought the pressure on her chest would make it cave in.

Patrick didn't hang on when she pulled away. She walked to the window, crossed her arms over her chest, and stared outside. Her posture was solitary, almost sad. He couldn't stand it.

"I don't do casual sex," she said suddenly. "One night stands, weekend flings. I don't do that kind of thing."

Now he was insulted. He knew they were meant to be together. How could she not? Okay, he'd only just come to that conclusion. Maybe she didn't see it yet. He knew it didn't work the same for every couple. Some mates knew each other when they met. Others took longer to realize or accept it.

"That isn't what we're doing, foxy," he said, intentionally using the nickname to rile her. He wanted to see the fight he sensed was a part of her. He wanted her to fight for them.

She looked over her shoulder with a hot glare. "Are you trying to piss me off?"

"Is it working?"

Never let it be said he didn't have a snappy comeback. He hadn't felt so much like a grade-schooler since, well, grade-school. He took a deep breath and tried to read her scent. She was a jumble of emotion and sensation. Lust, regret, anger, a lingering hint of fear. That touched him in a way a woman's fear never had before. He didn't know how to make it go away, which might drive him to madness.

"Yes," she said.

It took a minute for him to remember where the conversation had been going. He felt bad for getting distracted but not bad enough to let it go. He didn't want her to have any doubt about his interest. Had no intention of walking away from her.

"There is nothing casual about this, Sara Beth," he said, trying to pour all the sincerity he felt into the words.

He could confront her. He could demand his mate, and his more primitive instincts were clamoring for just that. He was a dominant predator. If he let that side of himself free, her instincts would make her bend to it. But that wasn't enough. Forcing her to his will would never satisfy him. She had to stay with him by choice. Mate with him because that was what she wanted.

She turned around, tucked her hands into her pockets and gave him a wan smile. "It's been a really long day, Patrick. I just want to curl up and sleep for eight hours."

He nodded. He could see her fatigue, but he knew she wasn't a woman accustomed to violence and danger. He didn't think she'd sleep well unless she knew she was in safe arms.

"I know, baby. And that's why I can't—why I won't let you sleep alone tonight. We won't do anything you don't want to. I would never take advantage of you, but at least give me the privilege of watching over you."

She scowled, her brows drawn together in confusion. "I don't get you. You've changed."

He gave her a half smile and shook his head. "No, I haven't. You just didn't know me as well as you thought." He'd always been a protector.

She huffed. "If you say so."

A sudden gale battered the house. He'd wanted to get up the mountain before the storm reached them, but he was glad he hadn't got the chance. He'd much rather be here with her, and if he'd taken her to the Guard's compound he wouldn't have an excuse to keep her so close. The bedroom was on the small side—the king-sized bed took up most of the space and faced a big fireplace. The lights flickered and he knew the power would go out soon. He stepped toward the door and nodded at the bag she'd dropped on the floor.

"You should get ready for bed before we lose power. I hope you brought something warm to sleep in." Not that she'd need it. "Can you light the candles?" There were several on the mantle. "I'm going to bring in more firewood and I'll make some sandwiches for dinner if you can get the fire started."

There was a pile of wood waiting, but he knew from experience he didn't want to have to go outside for it in the middle of a blizzard. The storm wasn't forecasted to be that bad, but he'd had the sense all day the weather men were wrong. He stepped over to a small closet, pulled out two heavy quilts and set them on the end of the bed.

She was looking at him like he was crazy.

"Sara Beth?"

"You can't stay in here with me."

"You'd rather I freeze to death alone in the living room?" he teased.

She bit her bottom lip and he managed to repress a groan. He wanted to do that. He wanted to bite a lot of spots on her delectable, curvy body.

25

"It'll be easier to keep the heat in here. It's a much smaller space."

She gulped. "Of course. Go on. I'll get things ready in here."

She moved to the mantle and lit the candles first, then gave him an impatient look as she bent to start the fire. "Well?" she asked in that grumpy tone that just made him want to grin.

CHAPTER FOUR

What was it about her? Every mood, every shift of emotion, and he was completely charmed. He decided the why didn't matter as he left the room. He brought in all the chopped wood from outside. Some he piled in the grate in the bedroom, the rest by the fireplace in the main living area. It would be easier to transport from there. Then he set about making a simple dinner of ham and cheese sandwiches. He brought those, chips, bottled water and a couple of beers to the bedroom.

Sara Beth sat cross-legged on one side of the bed. She had the candles lit and a fire roaring. She'd spread the two extra quilts over the mattress and put on a long flannel nightgown. Her hair was tied on the top of her head and her computer was on her lap. She gave him a distracted frown when he entered with his haul.

"This storm went from a few inches to a blizzard in a matter of hours. They're saying it's one of the worst snow storms in years. It might be days before we get out of here."

He shrugged. "That's living on a mountain. We're well supplied."

She looked horrified. "I can't work without power."

"Once it clears, we'll have limited power. Not enough to run the heat, but enough for some lights, to charge your laptop and limited stove use."

She tilted her head and accepted the sandwich he handed her. "Solar?" she asked.

He nodded, swallowed a bite. "A generator too, but I'm not here much so it hasn't been refilled in awhile. It might not last long."

He wasn't worried about that. He'd be able to produce enough power to cook—she could have a couple of hours a day on her laptop, and a light or two when it got dark. He wanted the rest of the time for himself. This sudden storm was the best thing that could have happened.

"At least we won't starve or freeze," she muttered, bending her head back to her computer.

When she opened her email program, he picked up the remote from his night stand and turned on the television mounted above the fireplace. He doubted the power or satellite would remain on much longer, so he might as well give her a bit of space to get used to his presence, right? He found a football game and settled back to finish his dinner and beer, but the longer he didn't speak the more he felt her nervousness grow. Then the power flickered a couple of times before going out. She heaved a sigh, shut down her computer and lowered the lid.

"The net is out."

He nodded. "No power for the router."

She stood and carried her laptop to a small table in the corner. When she faced him again, she twisted her hands anxiously and bit her bottom lip. He'd never felt such a mixture of tenderness and lust. He gathered the remains of their dinner, stood and carried it to the door.

"Why don't you get under the covers, baby? Even with the fire, it's going to get chilly in here."

He didn't wait for a response before leaving the room. In the kitchen, he tossed the leftovers and got his satellite phone off the charger. Chances were good it wouldn't work most of the storm. If they lost power later, charging the phone could be a challenge. He called to check in with Nico.

"Y'all okay over there?" he asked when the consort answered.

"Fine. We've got the girls in our bed and the fire going." Nico paused. "What about you two?"

"We're set."

"Be careful," Nico warned, and Patrick knew he wasn't referring to the storm or Sara Beth's stalker.

He should have been offended Nico was worried about how he'd handle the woman, and that he *wasn't* offended told him more than he wanted to know about his state of mind. He took a deep breath. She was his. He might push her, but he'd never endanger her or hurt her.

"I've got it under control," he said.

He hung up without saying goodbye and hoped like hell he knew what he was doing with Sara Beth. She wasn't waiting in bed when he returned to the room. He was surprised at how disappointing that was, but he didn't chase her down. He knew where she was. She hadn't pulled the bathroom door all the way closed, and the flickering candlelight gave away her presence as much as her enticing scent. He wondered how long she planned on hiding. Sighing, he went back to the kitchen. In the pantry he found an electric camp light and a pack of spare batteries. He paused in the living room to grab the new spy thriller he'd just bought, then returned.

He set up the lamp, pulled down the blankets, and had started to strip when it occurred to him she wouldn't appreciate the way he usually slept—naked. He wanted to challenge her, to intrigue and tempt her, but she was skittish enough he didn't dare push his luck. He found an old pair of sweats in the closet and pulled them on. He blew out the candles, then sat on the bed, piled some pillows behind him and picked up the book. There was no willing away his erection, but the pile of quilts would conceal it well enough.

It seemed like forever before she came out. He was relieved to have an excuse to put the book down. He'd read the same page three times.

She didn't say a word as she climbed into bed, lay on her side facing him and pulled the blankets up to her chest. She held them close as if afraid someone would steal them. No, that was wrong. It was like she considered them a shield. He turned off the electric lamp and mirrored her actions, except for the blankets. He kept them at his waist and was pleased when her gaze drifted over his torso. Her nostrils flared and her eyes were wide. She couldn't hide her arousal no matter how hard she tried. But other than that he couldn't get a read on her.

He was surprised that she had faced him, but she hadn't decided if she could trust him yet. He wouldn't turn his back on a potential enemy either. That irritated him as much as it made him proud.

"So what have you been doing the last, what? Fifteen years?" Patrick asked.

A half smile curled her lips and her eyes sparkled in amusement. "Seriously? Should I give you the long ten minute version or the short two minute?"

"Give me the really long version," he said, serious where she'd joked. Her brows drew together in a scowl.

"Why?"

He shrugged, his instincts telling him to downplay his curiosity. "You have something better to do?"

"I guess not," she conceded wryly. "It's not exciting anyway. I finished high school, went to college and came back here to work in the family business."

He couldn't decide if she was trying to hide something or really believed she was that uninteresting. What the hell kind of men had she had in her life?

"No friends? Boyfriends? Vacations?"

"What's with the inquisition?" she snapped. He wondered if her contrariness was habit or because of some past experience. She *was* an alpha's daughter. She probably had people poking their noses into her business all the time. He wasn't just anyone, however.

"Just passing the time, foxy. Quit trying to change the subject."

She glared. "I work a lot. I bought a house a few years ago and restore it in my free time. There really isn't much more."

"When was your last vacation?"

She snarled. "I go the beach with some college girlfriends every summer."

"That's it?" He cocked an eyebrow.

"Weekend trips sometimes. Biloxi. Savannah."

He grinned. "I'm sensing a water theme here."

Her shrug was self-conscious. "So I like the beach."

And he could imagine her there. Slick with lotion. Lazy and relaxed on white sand and under a hot summer sun. He wondered if he could talk her onto jet skis or deep sea fishing. Did she gamble?

"You like the casinos in Biloxi?"

She laughed. "I go for the beach and the sun. My father doesn't pay me enough to throw money away," she joked.

He smiled. She was starting to relax. "Have you been out west? Lots of sand there," he joined in.

Her smile faded and she shook her head. Why the sudden acceleration of her pulse? The subtle scent of anxiety?

"I prefer to stay closer to home," she said softly, but it was only part of the truth. There was more she wasn't saying. He let it go for now, but he was determined to find out everything about her.

"You've probably been everywhere," she countered.

"It's in the job description."

He was a wereeagle. They ran the Messenger Corp, carrying information and correspondence for all the shifter species all over the country.

"I haven't traveled in years, to tell the truth. I have to stay close to Ajax." He couldn't remember the last time he'd had a vacation, actually. "A weekend on the beach sounds pretty damned good," he admitted.

Her expression was incredulous. "I can't imagine the guy I knew being happy with that."

He reached over to finger a loose tendril of hair. "I was a Messenger for a few years. We all have a turn at it. Honestly? It's exhausting. You're always gone. You don't get much time for friendships or relationships. It was a relief to transfer to the Guard, and I always knew I'd serve Ajax when she took the throne."

Her scent was heavy with disbelief. Her expression scoffing. What the hell?

"What is that look for, baby? What doesn't ring true?"

"I've never known an eagle who wasn't an adrenaline junkie," she replied.

There was some truth to that, but it wasn't the whole story. Sure, he'd been reckless as a teenager, had sought out danger even into his mid-twenties. He'd long since decided courting death was stupid, though.

She snorted. "You agree with me. I don't even need to use my senses. It's clear on your face."

"Okay, fine, we have our share of thrill seekers," he said, exasperated. "What does that have to do with anything?"

What does it have to do with us? he wanted to ask.

She gave a slight shake of her head. "Nothing. It's just not like me so I don't really get it."

"Wait a minute," he interrupted when she opened her mouth to elaborate. He thought he was figuring out why she was holding back and he didn't like it one damned bit. "You're fighting this thing between us because you think I'm an adrenaline junkie and I want the same thing in a woman?"

Her smile was big and relieved. "Exactly. I knew you'd understand."

Oh, he understood her reasoning. It was just wrong. But first…did she realize she'd made an admission? He grabbed her under the arms and pulled her with him as he rolled to his back. There was no way she could miss his erection as she sprawled over him. Her eyes widened and he felt a surge of satisfaction. There was surprise in her gaze, yes, but also anticipation. Heat. He held her to him with a hand on her lower back, cupped the back of her head with the other, urging her close enough to kiss.

"So you acknowledge this thing between us?" he murmured against her lips.

She stared down at him, fear in her eyes making his heart ache. "It's just lust. It doesn't mean anything."

She was wrong. It meant everything and was so much more than lust, though there was plenty of that. She wasn't ready to believe him yet, but he wasn't giving up. She was his and he intended to keep her.

"I know what I need in a relationship, foxy. Maybe one day you'll figure it out," he whispered.

Her. All he needed or wanted was Sara Beth. She pressed her fingers to his lips when he would have kissed her, her expression bewildered.

"Tell me," she demanded.

"I want you just as you are, Sara Beth. I wouldn't change a thing."

"I don't believe you."

He nodded. "I know. But you will." He nipped at her bottom lip, wanting so much more.

"Pretty conceited, aren't you?'

He gave her a slow, lazy smile. "Confident," he countered.

And he was done talking. Words wouldn't convince her of anything tonight, but he could sure as hell demonstrate how perfect, how explosive they would be together. He didn't wait or ask for permission, just took her mouth in a demanding kiss.

CHAPTER FIVE

Sara Beth had no idea what to make of his declaration, and he didn't give her the chance to scoff. His kiss was nothing like the first one. The tender seductive man was gone. The lover who replaced him was dominant and sensual. His tongue stroked over hers, his teeth nipped at her bottom lip. She felt like he was trying to inhale her, to consume her, and she was more than happy to go along for the ride.

The sane, practical part of her voiced misgiving, but she ignored it. She'd probably never have this opportunity again, and after years of fantasies, she couldn't stop. It felt too good being held in Patrick's arms. He growled, flipped them over, then braced on his elbows and broke the kiss. His eyes were hot with a dangerous glint that excited her.

"I want you skin to skin," he said in a voice guttural with lust. It was all she could do to nod. He reached for the hem of her gown and yanked it up, never pausing as he pulled the fabric over her head and tossed it aside.

"Dear gods," he muttered half a second before leaning down and sucking one hard nipple into his mouth.

He nudged her knees apart and settled between them. She whimpered at the sensation of his soft sweats rubbing against her pussy. She was embarrassingly hot and wet. He moved to the side a bit and cupped her sex with his palm while licking her nipple. She tried to arch into his touch, rolled her pelvis against his hand. Desire and need made her desperate. She wanted to be penetrated, taken hard and fast.

He didn't give her what she needed. Instead he kissed a trail from one breast to the other and lavished attention on her neglected nipple.

It felt so damned good that when he tried to switch again, she threaded her hands through his hair and pricked his scalp with her nails. His growl was more a satisfied rumble than objection and he pressed one finger inside her. Gasping, she matched the easy thrust-retreat rhythm he set until a second finger joined the first, and his thumb brushed over her clit. He rubbed the hard nub while sucking harder on her nipple as she felt the first spasms in her pussy. She couldn't have held back the orgasm if she tried. It took hold and shook her, leaving her weak and replete when it finally passed.

When she opened her eyes, he loomed over her. He'd got his sweats off without her noticing then the head of his cock nudged her entrance. His eyes were clear and intense.

"You're so beautiful, Sara Beth," he whispered as he pushed inside her. "And you're mine."

She would have objected, but he kept their bodies connected and sat back on his heels, then pulled her so her butt rested on his thighs. He kept a firm grip on her hips and started moving in slow deep strokes that stole her voice. His eyes bore into hers in a silent demand she couldn't interpret, but one which made her heart race and filled her with yearning. She lifted her hands to stroke his chest, flicked her nails over small hard nipples. The skin drew tight over his face and he clenched his jaw.

"What is it? What's wrong?"

"Not a fucking thing, baby," he practically snarled. He took one of her hands and moved it to where they were joined. "How could you ever think something was wrong with this?"

Heat flooded her face, but she didn't protest when he moved her fingers to her clit.

"Touch yourself for me. I want to watch you come again," he said.

She caught her bottom lip between her teeth and did as he requested. She never took her eyes from his face as her embarrassment faded and desire spiked, but his gaze stayed focused much lower, presumably on her fingers as she strummed her clit. His cheeks were streaked red, his eyes hot and clouded, and his rapt attention made her brazen. She'd never been brave enough with her former lovers to make demands in bed. She'd never been wild and wanton, but he was bringing out the urge. She let go of his arm and moved it to cup her breast. His eyes widened and he blew out a shaky, strained breath.

"Oh yeah," he muttered, leaning down to take the nipple she'd subconsciously offered him.

Patrick wasn't sure his heart would hold out. The taste and feel of her nipple—sweet and soft—in his mouth, coupled with the feel of her slick, tight grasp as he fucked her was enough to drive him crazy. He could lose himself in her forever and die happy. He watched her face as he suckled her. Watched as she became lost in ecstasy as her cunt gripped him hard.

He released her nipple, threw his head back and froze, desperately holding back his orgasm. Not yet. He wanted more of this incredible sensation before he let it end, because once it did, she would probably revert to fighting him. When the shudders wracking her body subsided, he stretched out over her and started moving again.

His teeth sharpened beak-hard as he struggled against the instinct to claim her. His bite would mark her for everyone to see. It would connect them so deeply even she couldn't deny she was his. It was a primal instinct, a demand from the eagle part of him that was afraid of losing his mate. He watched as her eyes cleared, as doubt began to enter her expression, and swore a blade twisted in his gut.

"Don't," he whispered, feeling the words wrenched from him. "Don't regret this. Don't fight it."

"I don't know what you want from me," she answered just as softly.

"You'll understand soon enough, baby," he promised. Once she opened her heart and accepted. He vowed not to push her, to give her time to get to know him better, but he refused to fail and he would use every skill at his disposal to seduce her to his cause.

Starting with the beautiful body pinned under his. Unable to resist temptation any longer, he let his control slip and took her the way the lust roaring in his veins demanded. Hard and fast and a little rough. She grabbed his biceps and hung on as he pounded into her. Her cunt grew slicker, hotter with each thrust and he was damned relieved. He wasn't sure he had the power to stop if she didn't come along for the ride. Just when he thought he couldn't hold back one more second, she convulsed around him.

He stared into her eyes for every spasm, snared by the passion reflected back at him. Wild and pure and honest. The sound of his name on her lips as she came broke his last bit of civility. The eagle took over and wouldn't be denied its mate. As the orgasm exploded from the base of his spine and his seed spurted into her, he found the curve of her neck. First with a kiss, then a teasing nip, before he bit down and sucked. He broke the skin and heard the eagle's exultant scream in his mind. The ecstasy of marking her was so intense, he was consumed.

It seemed like forever before he had the strength to let her go. He licked the wound on her neck then pressed a soft kiss against it, before easing from her body. He rolled to his side, even though it was the last thing he wanted to do. She was small and he knew he was probably crushing her. He stared down at her. She was limp and pliant, a subtle curve of satisfaction on her lips. He wanted to see it every time he fucked her.

But he knew that sweet, satiated look was bound to be short-lived and he was right. Her eyes flew open and she lifted her hand to his mark.

CHAPTER SIX

"Have you lost your tiny little bird mind? Do you have any idea what you've done?" she screeched.

Funny. He didn't know foxes could make that noise. Now was probably not the time to point it out to her. He didn't appreciate the aspersion on his intelligence either, but they'd get to that later.

"I knew exactly what I was doing, foxy. Every step of the way."

Or thrust of the way, as it was and he'd done it even knowing she wasn't ready. He should feel guilty but it was hard when she was looking at him with a mix of fury and building desire. He wanted to kiss her until the rage faded and the passion blazed out of control. But damn, the more he thought about it, the more irritated he got. He'd just had the best sex of his life, and he was pretty sure she had too.

He could understand confusion, even ire, but her reaction seemed over the top. They were both shifters, both in their thirties. They understood instinct, and mating was instinct. But instead of trying to get to know him better, she was resistant. It made him angry, but more than that, he was disappointed and perplexed. He hadn't gone looking for a mate, but he'd never rejected the idea of finding one. He'd never imagined turning away from his when he did meet her. He rubbed a hand over his face and tried to figure out what to do next, but he didn't have a clue. Why hadn't anyone warned him claiming a mate would be such a test?

He glanced at her and was struck by how vulnerable she looked. She'd regained enough control the scent of rage had faded, along with any lingering arousal. She smelled like Sara Beth again—sweet with that hint of hidden fire. He inhaled deeply, taking it in, and noticed something else. Something it took him a long time to define.

Pain.

He reached over before he could think about it. She slapped at his hands, but he was bigger, stronger and faster. He yanked the blankets away and ran shaking hands over her, searching for signs he'd hurt her.

"What are you doing?" she snapped.

He met a gaze that was more testy than mad. "Your scent. What's the hurt from, baby? I only left one mark on your body."

The scent grew sharper, but she didn't flinch when he touched the bite.

"Shit," he muttered. She wasn't physically hurt. That was emotional pain. Why? "What's going on, Sara Beth? Did you have a boyfriend I didn't know about? A lover?"

If she did, he'd get rid of him damn quick.

She got out of bed, found her gown and pulled it back on. "You got any beer left?" she asked.

"Ignoring me won't work. I'll keep asking."

She gave him an impatient look until he sighed and stood. He didn't bother with his sweats when he noticed her trying to avoid looking at his body, though. She was very appreciative of his physique and he wasn't above using sex to get her to open up.

"Get back in bed," he ordered. "I'll get you a drink."

He grabbed two beers and hurried back. She held out her hand when he climbed into bed but he didn't give the bottle to her right away. He set both drinks on the nightstand and pulled her into his arms. There was no resistance in her body. He tilted her chin up with a finger.

"This part we seem to do well," he said.

She gave him a half smile. "There's more to life than sex. What happens when the chemistry fades?"

"You know that doesn't happen between mates," he said softly, gently.

He could see she *did* believe it was possible for the desire to die. Who the hell had she been hanging out with, because he'd never seen it. She shook her head and retreated from his embrace. He let her. For now. But there was no way he was giving up on her, or backing off for more than a couple of hours. She needed time to adjust? Fine. He'd give it to her, but he'd never let her go.

He twisted the tops off the bottles and handed her the drink, waiting till she took a long drink before he spoke.

"What now?" he asked.

He'd already taken one decision away from her. He wouldn't take more unless her life was jeopardized. But he was convinced that she would choose to stay with him. He was a predator. He was patient. And if he couldn't seduce his own mate, what use was he?

She laughed. "You're asking me? Isn't it a little late for that?"

"I can't undo it." He wouldn't if he could. He was unrepentant.

"And you don't regret it." Her tone was waspish but he heard doubt too.

"No, I don't, baby," he said, pouring all the sincerity he felt into his answer. He took a drink from his bottle. "What happened to you?"

"Huh?"

"You talk about work and houses and you ooze confidence. You carry yourself like you own the world. You aren't afraid to say exactly what's on your mind."

She was looking at him like he'd grown two heads and he realized she didn't see herself the way he saw her.

"If that was true I would have told Michael and my dad to shove it where the sun don't shine when they insisted I come up here."

He was sure she'd bitten her lip repeatedly to keep from doing so. "They are your alphas," he pointed out. "Or *were*."

He was the more dominant person in their mating. There was no question of her leaving her clan to join his. He was pretty sure that was one thing she wouldn't fight him over.

She didn't. She laughed. "Well, there is a silver lining then."

"There's more than one, foxy."

At the not-so-subtle allusion to sex, she withdrew.

"There you go, doing it again."

"What?" she asked, exasperated.

He watched her carefully. Her eyes were shiny as if she was close to tears and she refused to hold his gaze.

"You're not afraid of sex."

She couldn't have faked her response to him. She glared at him, but remained silent.

"Or me. Or, despite what happened today, men."

"I'm not afraid of anything."

"No. It's more like distrust."

"You're a little paranoid, you know?"

He shook his head. "Nope. But I am relentless. Ask Ajax."

"I'd love to," she muttered. He got the impression she'd like to do it in person and use her old friend as a buffer.

"So what, exactly, is your objection to being my mate?"

So what if his voice was clipped and angry? Hopefully, he'd egg her into a real answer. He needed to know why. He already couldn't imagine not having her in his life.

"For how long?" she snapped back. "How long till you get bored and want to move on? You kind of removed that option, didn't you?"

Okay, that was the last thing he expected to hear and it really burned his ass. He took the beer from her hand, set both on the nightstand and turned to glare at her.

"How could I possibly get bored when you spend all your time trying to piss me off?"

"You should have thought about that before you bit me," she said, her voice sugary.

"Keep it up, sweetheart, and I'll bite you again."

She sucked in a deep breath and it wasn't from fear or anger. Gods, save him. She was hot and welcoming. His *mate*. How could he resist? He didn't want to. He wanted her scent on his skin, wanted her to be so much a part of him no one would ever doubt they belonged together. He set his palms on either side of her waist and lowered himself over her until she lay against the pillows. Her hair spread out around her and she licked her lips, not quite panting. He leaned down to nip the smooth skin under her ear.

"You don't object to that idea, do you, Sara Beth?" he whispered. "You'll take this from me but reject everything else."

"No." She gasped when he sucked her skin. "It's not like that."

He gripped her gown and tugged it up. Over her waist, exposing her breasts. He licked one nipple then the other. She tried to arch into him but he held her still.

"What is it like? Explain it to me."

She stared at him, regret in her eyes.

"I tried. I'm not adventurous or outgoing or…exciting. I'll bore you, Patrick, and one day you'll resent that."

He stared at her a minute, taking in her scent and sudden tension in her body. She really believed that crap and he knew nothing he said would change her mind. She'd have to see for herself she was wrong. That he'd much rather have a mate who stayed home with him than one who wandered the world risking her neck.

"You'll see, Sara Beth. I'm not the man you think I am. I won't live up to those expectations of yours."

"Well," she said, a hint of heat and amusement lighting her eyes. She wiggled around, spreading her thighs so he rested between them. "Some of those expectations *are* pretty high."

She lifted her hands to his chest and scratched. Rolled her pelvis to rub against his cock. She was teasing him. Tempting him. Trying to distract him and it was definitely working. Maybe the trick to convincing her they belonged together was to keep her satisfied, so replete she never imagined leaving his bed.

She thought he would get bored. He grinned.

"What's that look for?" she asked suspiciously.

"I was just thinking," he said, thrusting into her. Her gasp of pleasure filled his senses, her pussy clenched around his cock, and he almost lost his train of thought.

"Thinking what?"

"Boredom will never be a problem. I can be very inventive, baby," he crooned.

Passion clouded her eyes. "Show me."

CHAPTER SEVEN

From the safety of a vacationing neighbor's house, Victor King watched several shapeshifters scurry around like the animals they were. Wolves and foxes who could take human form. He hadn't believed it was possible until he'd seen for himself, and he'd been hunting game since he was a child.

He'd been hired to take the female. Sara Beth Reynard. He had watched her for weeks to get confirmation she was, in fact, one of the shapeshifters the scientists wanted. As soon as he'd seen her change shape with his own eyes, he'd put a plan into action. Unfortunately, he'd miscalculated and she'd escaped to the house he watched now. Her father's. The neighborhood teemed with patrols. Men and women he could only assume were like her. So many. How could there be so many and humanity not know about them?

As he watched, Sara Beth stepped out the front door and walked to a waiting truck. He seethed. He couldn't leave the safety of his hideaway yet. Couldn't follow her, and he was damned sure they were trying to hide her away somewhere. He lifted the camera from the living room table and zoomed in on the faces around her before returning to her.

She was becoming an obsession.

There was something bewitching about her. She was pretty enough, but that wasn't it. She was so much more. It was the way she moved, with an easy sensual and evocative grace. The few times he'd been close enough to hear her voice, he'd been entranced. There was a husky timbre to it, a seduction that almost seemed subconscious. But she was a fox. They were cunning and sly. She had to be aware of her affect on others. It had to be calculated on her part. He'd noted similar qualities in other females of her race, though she seemed different. Somehow she was *more*. Sexier. More alluring. He couldn't explain why, but he intended to find out.

When he went after her the next time, he'd have to be better prepared for her wiles. He could have taken her that morning, but he'd been mesmerized standing so close—then she'd screamed. He'd almost had her in his grasp. If only those last two wolves hadn't been so near.

Next time he would be better prepared. The next time he'd capture her. He simply had to research her connections. Her pack's. He'd figure out where they were taking her, and the opportunity to catch her would arise.

CHAPTER EIGHT

She was going stir crazy. Pretty amusing, actually, since she'd accused Patrick of not being a homebody while claiming she was. Twenty-four hours after the snow had stopped, he showed no signs of cabin fever—seemed totally happy to be cooped up. Of course, he hadn't been idle. He'd had her in every room of the house. He was insatiable. If she didn't know better, she'd think he was trying to convince her they should be mates through pure exhaustion.

She turned from the living room window to study him. He was lying on his back on a thick rug in front of the roaring fireplace. Reading a book. He flipped pages every couple minutes, appeared calm and relaxed. She wondered if anyone else would notice the tension tightening his body. It was subtle, hard to read, but she'd spent a lot of time studying that form in the last day. There was no way to miss his hard-on. Despite that, he was calm and reserved and it just didn't seem freaking fair. He should suffer like she was. He didn't say a word as she approached and straddled him.

He peeked over his paperback. And who the hell read paper books anymore? "Don't you have an e-reader?" she snapped.

"Of course." He cocked an eyebrow. "But I also read paper. And I don't want to waste our limited power on charging the reader right now."

Good point. She'd be screwed in the zombie apocalypse. It didn't improve her mood though. She hated being stuck inside. He just smiled. Or *smirked* might be a better description. Then he flat out laughed. She punched him in the shoulder, though she wasn't sure if she meant it to be jesting or serious. She had to fight her fox side when it came to playing with him. He grinned, knowing and much too smug.

"What's so damned funny?"

"You," he said, rolling over and tucking her under him. "I am perfectly happy being snowed in with you. You're the one going stir crazy. And you call me the adrenaline junkie."

She stilled, not quite sure how to respond to that. She shook her head. "I don't like being cooped inside. Not the same thing." She paused, took a deep breath and smelled no frustration or detachment. "Aren't you bored?"

"Do I look bored?"

He looked too sexy for his own good, but that wasn't the question, was it? He didn't give her a chance to answer. Instead he took her mouth in a kiss so hot her toes curled. They were both panting when he broke away. "I've got all the adrenaline I need right here, foxy. If I was the thrill-seeker you think I am, I'd be out there skiing or snowboarding or hell, even sledding."

As he spoke, her eyes widened and on the last shone with interest. His little fox was more adventurous than she wanted to admit. He lifted her away from him and rolled to his feet.

"Come on, beautiful. Let's get dressed. I bet I know where Ajax and her girls are right now."

Driving the consort crazy. There was a nice little sled run near the Queen's house, and Ajax wouldn't be able to resist it any more than her four year-old daughter. It was a popular spot. There would be several eagles and their children there.

It would be a good place, a casual atmosphere, to introduce Sara Beth to his clan.

Sara Beth bit her lip, worried it. "Where are we going?"

"To watch the kids," he said. Then laughed. "And some of the adults." He tapped her ass as he walked by. "Come on. We don't want to miss it."

He hurried to dress. If he didn't, they'd never make it out of the house. Thankfully, she didn't torment him, but her gaze was curious as he took her hand, led her outside and onto a little-used path. The air was chilly and the forest was hushed, coated a pristine white. It wasn't long before they came to the clearing in a circle of pines and found exactly what he'd expected. Sara Beth released his hand and went to talk to Ajax, who was surrounded by other mothers in the clan.

Patrick sought out Nico. The leopard smirked when he approached, his nostrils flaring as he no doubt took in Sara Beth's scent on Patrick's skin.

"The mighty has finally fallen," he said.

"Oh shut up," Patrick replied, but he didn't put any rancor behind the words. "Have the races started yet?"

"No. They're leaving it to kids right now. It was a nice snowfall, but it warmed up fast and the ground isn't as cold as usual so we figure it will melt off sooner."

Patrick nodded. "Kids should get their fun first," he said.

But he was disappointed. Sara Beth's eyes had lit up when he mentioned sledding. It was an adrenaline junkie kind of thing to do and it could serve as a connection between them.

Nico must have scented his disappointment, because he gave him an amused, knowing look and, after several minutes, stepped into the crowd and announced the hot chocolate and soup had arrived. Patrick hadn't even noticed the set-up going up on the opposite side of the clearing. Nico waved him over to the sleds.

"This is your chance, man," he said softly.

He didn't hesitate, didn't even think about it. He joined Sara Beth, grabbed her hand and a sled. After leading both to the top of the hill, he guided her into the seat.

"Ready?" he asked, grinning at the mix of confusion and excitement on her face.

"Are we racing?"

He shrugged. "We can."

She grinned back. "Let's."

He got another sled and returned to the starting line. Before he knew it, they were joined by other sledders, mostly younger teenagers but a couple of the gutsier grade schoolers too. Sara Beth smirked at him. She knew what position he held in the clan. He was dominant to all these kids, supervised some of their training. Training wasn't just about improving their strengths, but building cohesiveness and loyalty, especially for this group—most of whom would one day join the Queen's guard. A little healthy competition was a good way to foster that goal. As soon as he agreed to race, Sara Beth signaled the kids to take off. She started a split second later. He had to grin. And he heard his mate's laughter all the way down the slope.

She was smiling with the kids when he saw her at the bottom. They were thrilled they'd won against Patrick Aquila. He scented her happiness and her eyes were bright, her skin glowing. She helped a couple of the little ones drag their sleds back up the hill, and he followed slowly, listening to them chat. Her joy was palpable, seemed to be from just being with the children.

"I always thought it was her," a soft feminine voice said at his side. He turned to meet his queen's gaze.

"Are you disappointed?"

Her smile was wide and she shook her head. "Hell no. You can shake her up and she can ground you."

"Do I need grounding?" he asked, cocking an eyebrow.

She pressed her lips together and studied him a moment. "Maybe you both need shaking up. You have been pretty laid back the last few years."

He stared at her, wondering if she and Sara Beth had been talking about him. "She seems to think she's not exciting enough for me."

Ajax blinked. "Oh dear." She turned back to watch her friend, who was now making snow angels with the kids. "I never would have agreed to this if I thought it would be a problem. I figured y'all would meet again and everything would, well, come together."

"It will," he assured his queen. He refused to allow any other outcome. "She just needs time to adjust."

Ajax looked at him like he'd lost his mind. "What?" he asked.

"She's my friend. I don't want to see her miserable."

"I'm working on it." The last thing he wanted was for Sara Beth to be unhappy. Did Ajax see something he didn't? Maybe he needed to up his game. Mind blowing sex was great, but he needed her to be emotionally invested in him.

"You marked her too soon," Ajax accused. "You should have given her more time to get to know you."

No, he was pretty sure Ajax was wrong about that. If he'd waited to claim Sara Beth, she would have thrown every obstacle she could find in his path. He didn't bother explaining that, however.

"She's mine. Don't interfere, my Queen. I wouldn't let anyone stand between you and your consort."

"No, I wouldn't expect you to," she murmured, watching as the kids picked a snowball fight with Nico and he, in turn, pulled Sara Beth into it. "You won't be able to keep her up here much longer. Her life is down the mountain."

"Yeah." He sighed. He wanted her safe, in lands he could navigate blindfolded, and he knew she'd never go for that. "Has Nico found out anything about her stalker?"

Ajax shook her head. "There's no reason for anyone to target Sara Beth, though. We should focus on that. Why Sara Beth? Is it what she is or who she's connected to?"

Damn good questions, but he'd been avoiding them while he could. Looked like the vacation was over.

Sara Beth and Nico approached as the kids returned to the sleds. It seemed the most natural thing in the world to pull Sara Beth to his side and wrap his arm around her shoulders. She tensed for a second before leaning into him.

"What's up?" she asked.

"We were just wondering why you in particular were targeted," Ajax said.

"Jeff Nichols has plastered my picture all over that rag he passes off as newspaper. So maybe that's where the other guy got the idea."

Patrick couldn't fault that logic, but it begged another question. "But why did Nichols latch onto you?"

She shivered. He wasn't sure if it was from fear or cold, but she didn't protest when he held her closer, tighter.

"I have no idea how he came up with my name. It was more annoying than anything else, until the other guy showed up. Maybe they're working together," she mused.

Hell, he hoped not. Then he'd have two to worry about. If Nichols was just chasing a story, he probably wasn't a real danger. But if he'd hired someone to kidnap her? Patrick would kill him after he beat the kidnapper's name out of him. He met Nico's gaze and the leopard gave him a very subtle nod. Permission to do whatever was necessary to protect his woman. Not that he needed it.

"I think we need to pay this Nichols a visit," Nico said.

"Good idea. Can we scare him?" Sara Beth asked.

He was pleased to hear the bloodthirsty edge in her voice, but there was no fucking way he was letting her near the reporter. One look at her face, though, and he knew he would have a fight on his hands.

"We'll talk about it later."

She narrowed her eyes and stepped back. "Don't even think about leaving me behind," she said, much too sweetly. "I'm not helpless."

No she wasn't. But she also wasn't a soldier. She hadn't been training her whole life like he had.

"Let's talk about this at home."

Hopefully he could get her horny and naked before she brought it up again.

"Fine," she snapped and stalked away.

He followed her back to his house, but stayed outside, hoping a few minutes alone would cool her temper. He could still feel her anger and frustration lashing at him. At least she wasn't afraid of him. Finally, he went in. She was pacing. He leaned against the wall and crossed his arms over his chest, wondering what had her more agitated: him and his instinct to protect her, or why she was the focus of a reporter and an unknown assailant.

She stopped on the opposite side of the room and met his gaze. "None of this makes any sense, Patrick."

"You mean the reporter and would-be kidnapper? We really need to find something to call him."

She waved a hand as if she was waving off an annoying fly. "Stick with stalker. Short and to the point. And yes, them. And…"

"Us," he finished for her.

She nodded. Reserved. Wary.

"I want to go home, and I need to be involved in figuring this out."

Fuck. How the hell was he supposed to respond to that?

"We'll probably be able to leave in the morning," he said.

"And the rest?"

He ground his molars together. Logic warred with instincts. "You follow my lead, Sara Beth. If I think something is too dangerous, I want you out of it."

She huffed. "And I'm supposed to let you decide what's dangerous or not?"

"Yes," he snarled, striding toward her. "You don't have my training. You aren't a soldier. And you said yourself, you're not the predator I am, baby."

She opened her mouth as if to argue then snapped it shut. Smart move. But there was a look in her eyes that made him think she was just retreating temporarily, not conceding the fight.

CHAPTER NINE

Patrick wasn't sure what to expect when he entered her home. Maybe cool and modern or stuffy old-school Southern. It wasn't that at all. It was inviting and eclectic. Comfy without being generic. The floors were dark, the trim and moldings crisp white. The rooms were big and had high ceilings. The house had big porches on two stories. The furnishings were a mix of new and antique. The house felt warm, welcoming. He saw her light touch everywhere, and wondered what miracles she could work for his homes.

"Nice place," he said after he'd swept the house for signs of danger while pretending to just have a look around. There was no point in alarming her.

It was neat. Nothing looked disturbed, but he couldn't shake the feeling someone had been inside during her absence.

"Thanks."

She'd taken her coat off and stood in the living room, hands pushed in the back pockets of her jeans. She was nervous and sexy as hell. She worried her bottom lip, turned and walked away.

"Are you hungry?"

Hell yeah, but not for what she was offering, he realized as he followed her into the kitchen. It had a long counter in the center with stools on one side that faced the wall where the stove and other appliances were. He sat and watched as she started a pot of coffee. Then she got eggs and bacon out of the fridge.

"Sorry, this is about it. I haven't been to the grocery store in awhile."

Her voice trailed off when she turned back to face him. Her eyes widened and she took a deep breath. She could scent his arousal just as he scented hers spike in response. He stood and slowly rounded the island, stalked her as she retreated. Until her butt was against the counter and she had nowhere left to go. She looked up, breathing fast. He heard her heartbeat accelerate and her desire lashed at him. Called to him. *His mate.* He knew she was growing weak, desperate with her need for him. He set his palms on the counter, one at each hip, caging her in. Leaning down, he scraped his teeth over the mark he'd left on shoulder. Felt her shiver in response.

"I'd rather have a bite of you," he whispered.

"Oh gods."

She tilted her head to the side, giving him access to her smooth, tender skin and her jugular. A submissive, trusting action. A vulnerability she'd only show her mate. His heart thudded. He pressed his lips over her fluttering pulse, trailed up her neck, then across her jaw to claim a kiss. She was sweet, hot and giving. He'd never get enough of her.

He broke the kiss and shoved up her shirt, released the catch on her bra then palmed her breast, and lowered his head to her nipple. He licked her before closing his lips over the hard point and sucking. She rewarded him with a long, needy moan and dug her fingers through his hair. When he switched to her neglected breast, her nails scraped his scalp. Snarling, he looked up at her. Stared. She was flushed. Her eyes were bright amber, the color of her fox, and dazed.

"Oh gods, Patrick, don't stop now."

He grinned at the desperate plea, pulled her shirt off and went to work on her jeans while she reached for his, but he stopped her. He needed to be in control and her touch would blow it all to hell.

"Not yet, foxy."

He placed her hands on the countertop on either side of her hips then pulled her jeans and panties down. Helped her slip off her shoes. In seconds she stood before him, naked and hot and breathtaking. And he had to taste her. He dropped to his knees, spread her thighs with his shoulders and her sex with his fingers.

Sara Beth stared down at Patrick. How the hell had things gotten this out of control this fast? She wasn't sure she cared. His smile was pure sinful intent. His eyes shone with avaricious hunger. She trembled as he watched her, as one finger slid into her pussy, stroked back and forth once before he lifted it to his mouth and sucked. She would melt in a puddle before him if he wasn't holding her up. And oh, she liked it. She wanted more.

She held her breath when his mouth moved closer to her, jerked when that wicked tongue darted out to stroke over her, and barely grazed her clit. Then it thrust inside her. Slow, teasing. He moved again, this time his lips on her clit, teeth scraping.

"You taste so good, baby," he murmured. "I could lick you all day."

She groaned, recognizing this mood—that tone of voice. He wanted to tease, to draw it out. To make her beg. She'd thought returning to her house would allow her a bit of distance, would remind her why they were so wrong for each other. No chance of that happening. She'd never be able to enter the kitchen again without remembering this moment.

He licked her again as he thrust one, then a second finger into her pussy. She rocked against him, welcoming the invasion with a breathy sigh and a silent demand for more.

Her eagerness, her greed for this man's body and possession overtook her. Demolishing any hope of emotional distance. Ruining any chance of protecting her heart. And at the moment, she just didn't care. He was making her feel too good, winding her body so tight she thought she might break when he made her come.

He sucked her clit and thrust his fingers, curling them so they brushed her G-spot each time. In minutes she was crying out, her muscles locked around him as he continued to suck her. Kept her coming again and again until she was sure she would pass out from the pleasure. She was still shaking when he rose to his feet, shoved his jeans down and lifted her.

She wrapped her legs around his waist, gasping at the sudden hard invasion of his cock. He perched her on the edge of the counter and thrust slowly as he stared in her eyes.

"You still with me, baby?" he asked, voice teasing. "You look a little dazed."

He hadn't stopped moving as he spoke, and at the end of his statement dragged his cock over her G-spot. She couldn't have spoken if she wanted to. Every muscle in her body locked up with the pleasure.

"Hmm, I *like* this look," he said, breaking the spell. She trembled as the release broke over her.

Then he dipped his head, his lips brushing hers, once, twice. She caught his bottom lip between her teeth and tugged until he opened his mouth for her. She gripped his shoulders. Tilted her head to the side for a better angle and stroked her tongue against his. It started out gentle. Tender. He let her explore a few moments before taking over. And she let him. Reveled in his wild claiming.

He moved inside her again, this time harder, faster. The orgasm took her by surprise, fast and fierce and rushing through her. Exquisite pleasure and mind-bending torment. If the sex got any better she'd never survive it. She was so lost in the aftermath she barely noticed Patrick come, paid no heed as his teeth closed over the mark on her shoulder. He held her still as he shook. It seemed a long time before he finally straightened and moved back.

She missed the connection immediately and looked around the kitchen, not wanting him to see a lost expression in her eyes. But he cupped her face in his palms—softly, gently—and held her gaze.

"Are you okay, foxy?" he asked.

She jerked a nod, shoved at his chest until he stepped back and let her jump down from the counter. He watched as she gathered her clothes. She felt raw and exposed and it wasn't because of her nakedness. He saw too much when he gazed in her eyes. She didn't want him to see her as weak or needy, and that was how she felt. She wanted him again already. More than that, she wanted him to just hold her until she felt like herself. Until the world righted itself. This wouldn't do at all. She stepped toward the door, noticed his eyes narrowing on her and suspected he was about to pounce.

"I need to get cleaned up. I have that client meeting in an hour," she reminded him. And she needed to regain her equilibrium. Get back in her right mind before she ran into any of her clan members or family.

He gave her an abrupt nod but didn't approach. "We are going to talk about this," he said, his voice hard and alpha enough to set her teeth on edge. "You can't keep hiding from me."

He might be right, probably was, but she could sure as hell try. She didn't voice the response, though, just turned and left the room while she still could. If she challenged him so bluntly, she knew there would be no escape.

CHAPTER TEN

The meeting with the client had gone well. The artist had walked through the studio space with her so he could point out what he wanted where while she'd made a floor plan. He was exacting, but she preferred that, actually. It was the wishy-washy clients or the ones with only a vague idea of what they wanted that were a nightmare. She walked him out, chatted a moment more and waved as he walked to his car. Sighing, she shut the door and leaned back against it.

She'd had to get bitchy to get Patrick to leave. This was her job, her life, and she couldn't have him hovering all the time. Besides, there was no danger in the middle of the work day with several werewolves in the area. Still his agreement had been a little too easy. Then he laid out his terms. She rolled her eyes. He'd drop her off and pick her up, but at no point was she to leave the house without him. She would have flat-out refused, but he didn't hide his worry for her. It was clear on his face and in his eyes. The man was going to drive her crazy, but what could it hurt to allow him this little peace of mind?

Besides, his absence gave her the perfect opportunity to question one of her tormenters. Her eyes narrowed as she caught the faint scent again. Nichols was close, probably outside the back door, which was where she headed next. He didn't even try to hide as she jerked the door open and glared at him.

"You're trespassing," she snapped.

"Seemed like the only way to talk to you without your bodyguard."

"He'll be here any minute," she said, voice so saccharine he blanched. "So talk fast."

"Someone has been following me. Is it your people?"

She wouldn't put it past Patrick or her father, but if they were, she hadn't been told. She shook her head. "No."

"I was afraid you'd say that. Someone broke into my apartment. I assume that wasn't y'all either?"

She was sure she would have heard about that. "Nope."

"This is the only thing I'm working on," he said. "It has to be connected to you."

Now, that got her full attention. Nichols had been following her for weeks. What about the other guy? "Your turn. Do you have someone watching me when you can't?"

"Hell no. I'm not sharing this story with anyone."

She rolled her eyes. "There is no story. There's no such thing as werewolves."

"I've seen the evidence, Ms. Reynard. They're real. You're real."

"A werewolf?" She scoffed, her derision was probably easy to read though he wouldn't know why. She wasn't a fucking wolf. For a moment, it looked like he might believe her, then he shook his head. Something else was going on here, and since denials weren't getting her anywhere, maybe fear would. It wasn't like he'd have tangible proof if she exposed herself. There were no witnesses. No cameras. She would have scented them.

She let her animal side rise to the surface, let her senses expand and the predator show in her gaze. His eyes widened and he stepped back but she wasn't letting him get away that easy. He was making her life hell. Maybe it was time that she return the favor. She grabbed his arm, her claws piercing the leather of his jacket.

"I was right," he whispered.

"No, Mr. Nichols," she said with a mean smile. "I'm *not* a wolf." She let that sink before continuing. "I want to know why you're so certain I am, however. How did you find me?"

Patrick stood in the shadows and held his breath. He'd scented a stranger as soon as he arrived. He'd followed the smell around to the back porch to find his mate talking to the interloper. His first reaction was fury when he realized who the man was. Patrick had told her to stay inside. Insisted she stay safe. What had she done? Confronted her enemy. But she was getting that enemy to talk and they needed his information. He'd edged closer so he could listen in. When she'd gone fox, his knees had nearly buckled. She was exposed now. There was no way to hide.

But damn, was she magnificent.

He waited to see what she would do next. Waited to see if she needed his help.

"I have a source," Nichols answered.

"The scientists?"

"No. Someone like you."

Patrick stepped forward. If one of theirs had betrayed her, he'd tear the bastard apart limb by limb. "Who?"

Nichols gaze jumped to him and his fear was easy to read. "I don't know," he stammered. "He contacted me. I've never met him face to face."

"And this man gave you Sara Beth's name?" he asked softly, allowing the menace he felt to seep into his voice.

"How did he contact you?" she interrupted, when it was clear Patrick had scared him too much to speak. The reporter's gaze jerked back to her.

"He sent me an email. I'll give it to you."

"Yes you will," Patrick went on in that same lethal tone. "Then you are going away. You won't come back here and you won't write about her again."

He saw the protest in the man's eyes but Nichols was smart enough to keep it to himself. Patrick got the information he needed and sent the man away before leading Sara Beth to the car. She didn't say a word as he held the door for her, but her scent told him everything he needed to know. She was unrepentant but wary. She should be.

As he slid into the driver's seat, he felt a tick start in his jaw from clenching his teeth so hard. She hadn't been in any danger. She could obviously handle the reporter if necessary and he'd been there for backup. But she hadn't known that and she hadn't known she was only dealing with that defenseless weasel. He started the car and put it in drive. After a few minutes, she cleared her throat.

"My house is the other way."

"We're going to meet your parents and Michael."

She groaned. "Not now, Patrick. I haven't told them anything and…"

She trailed off when he growled and turned to look at her. He knew his eyes glowed and he radiated anger and tension. Why wouldn't he? She'd talked to her parents more than once since he'd claimed her and she hadn't told them? Why? Was she embarrassed to be mated to a wereeagle? Or that determined to get away from him? He didn't speak. Wasn't sure he could without yelling. He just followed the directions Michael had given him.

He parked on the curb and turned in the seat to face her, stretching his arm along the back to play the ends of her hair through his fingers. He struggled to contain his anger. It was impossible.

"Why not?" he ground out.

She pressed her lips together and despite his anger, he wanted to tease her, kiss her into talking with the promise of so much more. Her hand clenched on the door handle.

"Because I'm a grown woman and I don't need two alphas trying to interfere with my personal life. And you're crazy if you think my dad is not going to explode. Michael too, probably."

"Why would he object to his only daughter taking a mate? Is it because I'm an eagle?"

She looked at him like he'd grown a second head. "No, it's because no matter how old they get, fathers don't want to give up their daughters, and they sure as hell don't want to admit they're having sex."

Her words stopped his anger cold. That made perfect sense. He didn't have any sisters and his parents were long dead. He'd never been involved enough with a woman to meet her parents. Suddenly, he was nervous—off balance. *Shit.*

Sara Beth smirked at him. "Didn't even think about that did you, hot shot?" She leaned close and nipped his bottom lip before whispering in his ear. "Consider this training for when you have to deal with your daughter mating."

She was out of the car before he could reply. He caught up with her at the door and took her elbow.

"*Our* daughter is never leaving the house, much less dating. Forget mating," he growled.

She grinned and stepped inside. The little minx was enjoying this. He was going to be put on the spot, probably grilled. She knew it, and planned to enjoy the show.

"I ordered you to stay with the eagles," a gruff voice said.

Patrick stepped around the corner to see a roomful of men. Their collective anger was a violent wave. The air thick with hot spicy scent of it. Her father, Will Reynard, and brothers were the major source of that fury, he guessed. Michael was glaring at Sara Beth, but his scent was subtler. She didn't quite meet the alpha's gaze, but she didn't back down either.

"I have a business to run," she said to her father, and jerked a thumb over her shoulder. "And a perfectly capable bodyguard."

Relegated to bodyguard, was he? Not in this lifetime. He stepped up behind her, set his palm on her nape and squeezed as his thumb brushed over his mark. No one missed the possessive, proprietary move. He was suddenly the focus of several angry sets of eyes. Sighing, Sara Beth stepped in front of him. She grabbed his arms when he tried to move around her. Her claws were sharp on skin, just a little more pressure and she would have drawn blood. Her aggression seemed to calm the others in the room, however.

It had the opposite effect on him. He liked her claws, though not necessarily in this context. He wanted to feel them on him when he was fucking her to ecstasy. He pulled her hands away so he could step forward. Didn't flinch under the scrutiny of the other men in the room. She was his mate. He would never back down from that.

Her father stepped forward aggressively, gave his daughter an imperious look. "Step away from him, Sara Beth."

She'd been looking for a way to escape him—them—so Patrick was a little surprised when she shook her head. "I can't. I won't. Sorry, Dad."

So many emotions crossed the other man's face when he looked at his daughter even Patrick had a hard time chasing them. Love, regret, anger, pride. Then the fox alpha turned a hard gaze on Patrick, and Patrick vowed to have no daughters of his own.

"We sent her to you for safety," her father said, disapproval in his voice.

He shrugged. "She's mine. She's safe."

"She's exposed here," the other man snarled.

Patrick resented the implication he couldn't protect his mate. He may not be a king or an alpha but he was more than capable of taking care of his own. There was no way he'd let these men interfere with his life or his mate's.

"She won't be harmed," he snapped. "And she is no longer your concern."

Sara Beth's claws pricked him again before she stepped away, scowling. "I'm not helpless," she reminded them.

She wasn't, and he wasn't sure how he felt about that. He didn't want her defenseless, but he wanted her to know she could depend on him. He wanted her to *need* him as much as he was coming to need her. It was the primal instincts of his eagle side, but he couldn't deny the man wanted the same thing.

"You met with the client?" Will asked, changing the subject to something neutral.

"I did. I'll draw the plans tonight and fax them for final approval. The carpenters should be able to get it done in a few days."

Her father nodded. "There's no need for you to be here for that. You can return to the mountain tomorrow morning."

Will glared at Patrick, daring him to argue, but he wouldn't. Patrick hadn't wanted to bring her down for even two days. As long as her attacker was loose, she was at risk. "Agreed," he said.

This time Sara Beth glared at him and her father smiled. "I have a life here, remember?" she groused.

There was no fucking way he was getting in an argument with her in front of her family. He shrugged. "For the moment, the mountain is the safest place. We have the email address now. It shouldn't take Nico long to track it down."

"What email address?" her father asked.

"From the guy who gave Nichols my name."

"I want that name," her father said, voice thick and guttural with his animal. The other man's eyes glittered a demand for vengeance. That was a fury Patrick shared.

It was Michael's reaction that raised the hair on Patrick's neck though. He didn't think anyone else noticed—Michael's scent didn't change—but Patrick had been looking at him when Sara Beth spoke. The werewolf alpha knew more than he'd said. The knowledge flashed across his face so fast Patrick couldn't be certain he saw it. What the fuck was going on? Patrick didn't like this situation at all, but he had no reason to suspect Michael. No evidence. Just his gut. But hell, at this point, it was possible he was just suspicious of everyone. The last thing he needed to do was cause an interspecies war by making unfounded accusations. He'd wait to confront Michael when he could get him alone.

CHAPTER ELEVEN

"That asshat. I'm gonna kill him," Sara Beth muttered, barely holding back a snarl as she stared at her laptop screen. They'd left her father's house a couple of hours ago and seemed to settle into a companionable silence in her large home office.

"What?" Patrick asked, but he sounded distracted. Or bored. She ignored the hurt that threatened to claw at her heart.

His phone rang before she could respond. He answered, stood and walked into the hall to speak in a low voice she couldn't make out. She glared at the damned screen. One of her pack mates had emailed the link to Nichols's newest story. She hadn't expected him to back off, not really, but she'd hoped for a least a few days of respite. Had she got that? Hell no.

Werefox and were-what? You be the judge!

The bastard had managed to get a photo of her and Patrick. In front of her house. She bet he was still close. The article claimed a source had confirmed she was a fox shifter, but couldn't confirm what species her lover was. Her lover? She was so mad she could spit. Though, looking at the photo again, there was no denying Patrick felt possessive of her.

He'd kept her close, even for the short walk to the door. One hand on her hip, face all hard lines and glittering eyes.

Her phone rang. She looked at the caller ID, groaned, and sent it straight to voicemail. She was so not in the mood to deal with her father right now.

Patrick walked back into the room. They spoke the same words at the same time, reminding her stalkers weren't the only thing complicating her life. There was a small matter of a new mate bond.

"We have a problem."

"You first," Patrick said.

She stood and waved her hand toward her desk. "Nichols isn't done. I say we kill him and be done with." She wouldn't *really* kill him, but it sounded like a damned fine idea.

He sat and growled low in his throat as he read. The sound was angry, should have been menacing, but it didn't scare her in the least. It made her wet. Hungry. His head jerked up, his bright blue eyes clashing with hers, and his nostrils flared. In the time it took her to blink, he was in front of her. Damn, he was fast. It made her wonder for the first time what he was like in eagle form. He cocked his head.

"What are you thinking about?" he asked as his arms circled her waist.

Unable to resist him, falling into his eyes, she lifted her hands. Stroked his chest. "I was just wondering what you're like in your other form," she whispered, standing on her toes to brush her lips against his.

His arms tightened around her, a hard, possessive band. She should have protested. Shouldn't give into him just because he made her hornier than hell. He was a predator—an alpha male to the bone. If she didn't assert some independence, he'd smother her with protectiveness. Her brain knew all that, understood it, but her body didn't care. She felt safe in his embrace. She knew he'd never hurt her. Would stand between her and pain if he could. Protect her from the outside human world that didn't know about them and probably wouldn't accept them.

"What's the other problem?" she asked, voice breathy.

She fought the need beginning to rage in her body and it was so much more than sex now. She'd grown accustomed to having him around. Had adjusted to his energy in her personal space. He'd already become a part of her daily life. His gaze, his scent, his *voice*. That deep, smooth baritone that made her body react even when he wasn't trying.

He ground his teeth and loosened his hold on her. She stepped back reluctantly, but he nudged her toward the couch when she would have retreated to the relative safety of her desk. She could have maintained some distance between them there at least. Instead, he sat next to her, held her hand and brushed her knuckles with slow gentle strokes. It was a soothing touch, nothing sensual about it, and it freaked her out a little bit. What had that phone call been about?

"Nico identified your attacker." He paused and met her gaze. "His name is Victor King. He's a big game hunter."

She blinked. What the fuck? Did he think she was some kind of trophy? No. He hadn't killed her. He'd used a tranquilizer.

"He wants real proof. He wants to catch one of us and expose us to the world," she guessed.

Patrick nodded. "That's what it looks like."

"This is not good. Does Nico know where he is? I'm sure he's still close."

She had felt watched, hunted, before going to the eagles. Now she understood why. The feeling had returned when they came into town, but she'd ignored it. Written it off as paranoia.

"Not yet. But we'll find him, baby." Something dark and determined and lethal moved through his eyes.

"What are you going to do to him when you find him? You can't kill him, Patrick. He's human."

"We can't let him loose, either," he responded.

She knew she wouldn't be able to persuade him. He'd already made up his mind. But dear gods, what if something went wrong? What if this King guy killed Patrick instead of the reverse? Her pulse raced.

"You'll be careful?" she asked, throat tight with the fear she tried to repress. She couldn't lose him now.

"Worried about me, foxy?"

His smile was slow, sensual and seductive, and despite her concerns—despite the serious conversation—she responded. He lifted her hand and pressed it over his heart. It beat in a fast, staccato rhythm like her own. Her fingers flexed, her nails lengthening and curling in a partial shift. He groaned and moved to rip his shirt over his head. He tossed it behind him and pulled her hand back to his chest.

"Now let me feel your claws," he whispered as his lips lowered to hers.

His mouth brushed hers, then over her closed eyelids as he stroked his fingers over her face. Gentle. Tender. *Loving.* Every defense she had against him threatened to crumble into dust. It scared the hell out of her.

He held her chin until she opened her eyes. "No fear, baby. Not with me. Not in this."

How could there not be? He touched her and she forgot every reason why she should protect her heart, mate bond or not. But she nodded acquiescence despite her misgivings. And he kissed her. *Finally.* She felt like she'd been waiting forever. Her lips parted and his tongue stroked in. It was a sweet languorous kiss. A tease, a temptation.

"More," she gasped when he lifted his head.

She wanted so much more. The craving was an ache now. She straddled him, moaned when she rubbed over his cock. She stoked her hands up his chest. Let him feel her claws as she leaned down and kissed him. She didn't ease into it— didn't want to go slow. She heard fabric ripping. Her shirt and bra fell to the floor. Then his hands were on her. Firm and strong. He palmed her breasts. She gasped, breaking the kiss and throwing her head back when he squeezed her nipples. He took full advantage and sucked one of the hard points into his mouth.

She dug her fingers into his shoulder, desperately held back the urge to mark him as he had her. Not yet. She couldn't do that until she was positive he'd never regret mating her. She felt a hint of teeth and looked down to meet his gaze. Hot and intense. A fury of need she shared. She groaned when he released her, but he was only moving to the neglected breast. He sucked her between his teeth, this time hard and possessive. She ground her pussy against his cock. Even with both of them covered, she found just the right friction against her clit. The orgasm hit her so suddenly she screamed. While the aftershocks rippled through her, Patrick dumped her on the couch next to him. Ripped off her jeans, then his.

Patrick covered her. His mate. She stared up at him. Shocked. Dazed. And thank Hermes, still hungry for him because there was no way he could stop now. He moved a hand between them, found her pussy hot and wet. Satisfied she was ready, he pushed into her. Slow, inch by inch, wanting to drag out the exquisite pleasure of taking her. She had other ideas, however. She bit the corner of her lip, gave a slight shake of her head and shoved him away. He was so surprised at the rejection he sat up. He was even more surprised when she straddled him.

"This time I'm in charge," she said, voice husky.

He stared up at her and this time he was the one who was dazed. His little fox was taking *him*. If it was a dream he hoped it never ended. He set his hands on her thighs, slid them to her pelvis to brush softly over the lips of her pussy and spread her. She sucked in a breath and her eyes widened when he gave her a slow smile.

"Is that right, baby? Now that you have me in your control what are you going to do?"

She licked her lips. Uncertainty crossed her face for just a moment before she gripped his cock and guided him to her entrance. She worked the head in, then slid slowly over the length of his dick. He thought he'd die of pleasure.

"How 'bout I do this?" she asked breathily, rising so he almost slipped free of her sweet pussy.

"How 'bout more?" he growled, stroking his thumb over her clit.

He was rewarded by a low, delicate snarl. She grabbed his hands and he let her move them.

"I'm in charge, remember? You agreed."

"Did I?"

Perhaps when he hadn't protested, he'd given tacit permission. Normally he'd never give up control to anyone, much less a woman in his bed. But he was intrigued by this new facet of her personality. Seductive. Aggressive.

"You didn't say no," she said with a sultry smile that was almost shy.

Damn, she was killing him. For now he'd agree to this little experiment. He nodded.

Her smile was brilliant and confident. Then she got down to the business of torturing him. Soft hands stroked his chest and she lowered herself over his aching cock. Again and again. So slowly he had to grit his teeth against the urge to take over and pound into her. But when she came again, her hot little cunt tightening and squeezing his erection, he gave up all pretense of letting her have control. He grabbed her hips and thrust deep. Fast and hard in a steady intense rhythm.

The feel of her, the pleasure rushing through his veins…it was nirvana. He claimed her lips and tried to pour the intensity of his emotions into the kiss. He felt his orgasm build and rush through his body like wildfire. As he came, jets of come filling her, his arms banded around her. He swore he felt her to his soul. He also felt her continued resistance to the bond. It didn't matter. He'd never let her go.

CHAPTER TWELVE

Patrick left Sara Beth at her parents' house after securing her promise not to leave until he came for her. She'd given it too easily, was quiet and subdued. It worried him. If she tried to run from him, he'd chase, of course, but he shuddered to think of the danger fleeing would put her in. Hopefully, she'd do the sensible thing and stay put. He couldn't worry about that now. He needed answers to eliminate the threats against her. He hadn't quite decided what to do about the reporter yet, but the hunter had to die.

Nico was waiting for him in the rear corner booth of the closest Waffle House. Patrick slid in across from the consort, twitching at placing his back to the room. Nico grinned and spread his arms across the back of his seat.

"Sucks, doesn't it? Should have got here before me," he goaded.

Patrick scowled but the waitress arrived before he could come up with a snappy response. She smiled, but when neither man responded to her flirting, took their orders and disappeared quickly.

"What have you found out?"

"Whoever the email is from is pretty careful. There's no name on the account, nothing I can track. The emails were sent on open Wi-Fi, mostly here in town. Could be anyone," Nico said, but he didn't sound too frustrated. "I have the birds watching the places he's used so far. He'll send another email and I'll be waiting. We'll catch him then."

Patrick wanted to know who'd betrayed his mate. Now. But he was more worried about the hunter.

"And Victor King?"

Nico's smile was feral. "We hunt him."

"Leads?" he asked.

Nico waited to answer until the waitress, who'd brought their food, left.

"We've been checking out the hotels in the area. Couple clerks at two different places think they may have seen him."

"You should have started with that," he snapped.

Nico glared back and shoved a fork in his eggs. "Eat first, Patrick. I just got this info when I got here or I would have checked it out already."

Patrick picked up the patty melt and took a big bite. He knew Nico in this mood. The former security chief was pulling rank and as Ajax's mate, most eagles would let him. Normally so would Patrick, but this was *his* mate they were talking about.

"You need your head on straight for this, Patrick," Nico said, keen understanding in his eyes. "She's too important to you and that goes both ways."

His words cut Patrick. He'd never risk his mate, but fury and fear might make him act rashly. Worse, she was his world but he didn't think she felt the same way. Not yet.

"What?" Nico asked. Patrick realized something of his anxiety must have shown on his face.

"She hasn't accepted it yet."

He couldn't believe he'd shared that, and wished he hadn't when Nico grinned.

"She may be little, but foxes *are* predators. You didn't really think she would give in without a fight, did you?"

"Ajax did," he grumbled.

Nico laughed. "No she didn't."

Curious, Patrick tilted his head and studied Nico, surprised at his amusement. Of course, even if Ajax had fought him on their mating, that was a long time ago.

"I didn't know that."

Nico gave him a sharp look edged with humor. "You don't know it now."

"How did you do it?" he asked, too curious not to. Ajax wasn't just his queen. She was his friend. And Nico's answer might help Patrick figure out what to do.

"You're actually asking me for advice?" Nico asked, laughing.

Patrick growled.

"Trust takes time," Nico said softly. "Especially for a strong independent woman used to walking alone."

But Sara Beth wasn't used to walking alone. He shook his head. "That isn't her objection. She thinks…"

Hell, was he really going to talk about this with Nico? Sure, they'd become friends. Hell, he'd mentioned his concerns to Ajax. He was amazed she hadn't passed on the conversation to her mate. Apparently she hadn't. Patrick would take the other man's counsel on any number of other things, but his personal relationships had never come into it. Fuck it. What could it hurt?

"She thinks I'll regret it. She thinks I'll be bored with her."

Nico stared at him like he was crazy. There was a good chance he was.

"You're going to have to explain that one."

He snorted. "Would if I could. She seems to be under the impression all wereeagles are incurable travelling adrenaline junkies," he said dryly. He loved the thrill of flight, but he'd out grown courting danger for the hell of it a long time ago.

Nico's jaw dropped. "Doesn't know you very well," he said.

Patrick wasn't sure if the consort's disapproval was directed at him or Sara Beth, but he sure as fuck didn't like it.

"She needs time."

Nico blinked. Nodded. "Trust."

"Yeah."

Patrick accepted the check when the waitress held it out. "Let's find the bastard that's after my mate."

They paid and were on their way to the first motel, where the clerk confirmed Victor had stayed there, but checked out days ago. The room had been cleaned and rented since, so they decided searching it was probably a waste of time and moved to the second hotel.

"Yeah, I remember this guy. Creepy." The young woman, a werefox—Patrick would guess—shivered. "He checked out yesterday."

She handed over a room key before they even asked. He cocked an eyebrow, surprised at the easy cooperation. "Michael said we should expect you," she said.

Of course. The werewolf alpha was paving the way to protect one of his own. Patrick still didn't trust him.

"Thanks," he said, taking the card from her.

The room was the last on the corner and only took a minute to walk to. Inside, Patrick could see nothing had been touched. Michael's wolves had been visiting hotels with King's picture so the staff had known not to touch the room. However, except for the unmade bed and thrown away fast food bags, there wasn't much to find. It was depressingly drab and run down, the kind of place that had arrangements to rent by the hour for the proper kickback. Nico searched the dressers and Patrick looked under the bed, then between the mattress and box spring. When they were done Patrick had the urge to wash his hands in bleach and he knew he wasn't done yet. That was when he turned to the small trash cans. Nico followed his gaze and heaved a put upon sigh.

"I hate searching people's garbage," Nico grumbled.

Patrick just upended both pails on the bed.

"Easier," he said, shrugging when Nico looked at him.

He found a pen on the bedside table and used it to sift things around. Food wrappers and bags, nothing of interest until he noticed one had addresses written on it. He picked it up by the corner.

"What's this?"

Nico entered them into his phone. "Local public library and public records."

"What's he looking for?"

He already knew where she lived.

"We better find out," Nico said.

They went to the library first, where an old school friend of Sara Beth and Ajax's manned the front desk. She smirked when Patrick approached, leaned back in her seat and crossed her arms over her chest.

"Hello, Anne," he said.

"Patrick. I always knew you had a thing for her."

"Call her and tell her that, will you?" he joked. Hell, it might help him win her over. "This is Nico Leonidas. Ajax's mate."

She nodded. "We met at the wedding. So what can I do for you gentlemen?"

Patrick slid the photo of King over. "Seen this guy?"

"Michael and Will's people have been asking about him," she said soberly. Obviously she'd heard about the attack. "This is the guy, huh?"

"Yeah. I'm sure I don't have to tell you he's dangerous."

"I haven't seen him. One of the girls thought he looked familiar but wasn't sure."

"Any idea what he was looking for?"

Confusion crossed her face. "That's the weird thing. Stacey said he went into the local history section but the only thing on the tables to be reshelved were high school yearbooks."

"Our years?"

She nodded. "Why would he look for those? He already knows who she is."

And he was looking for her friends. Looking for people who might hide her.

"Son of a bitch," he muttered, knew Nico had reached the same conclusion when he pulled out his phone. Patrick did the same. While Nico checked on Ajax, Patrick called Michael and filled him in. The werewolf alpha agreed to find out what King had accessed at the property records office. Thank gods the county refused to upgrade their systems and everything was still on paper. If the hunter had done a computer search, they probably would have found out too late.

"Email me the list," he ordered Michael, not caring in the least he was talking to an alpha and disconnected the call the same time Nico disconnected his. "Ajax and the girls?"

"They're fine. We'll all head to the Guard's enclave when we get back. Go get your mate."

They'd driven separately. Nico turned in the opposite direction, hurrying back to his mate and children. Patrick pulled out his phone again and called Will, just in case Michael hadn't, to tell him to warn Sara Beth's friends and family. King couldn't be sure they were shifters, but he'd use them as bait if he had to. Patrick punched the accelerator, desperate to get her. To protect her.

The scene he walked in was the last thing he expected.

Sara Beth checked her phone for the time, then looked out the living room window, watching for Patrick's familiar truck. He'd dropped her off as the sun was rising, but that was a couple of hours ago. How long did it take to meet Nico anyway? A growl of frustration left her lips and she quickly clamped down on the emotion. She'd wanted a little distance between them, hadn't she? It wasn't fair to complain when she got it.

She went to join her mother in the kitchen. She offered to help with breakfast but got waved off.

"Sit, darlin'. It's almost done."

The house was quiet. Empty. She couldn't believe her father would leave her mother unprotected. "Where is everyone?"

"Your father had an appointment at the lumberyard. The boys went for a run."

Sara Beth walked to the big window overlooking the backyard. They were probably in fox form, which would heighten their senses, and no doubt they were close. She'd never admit it, but that made her feel better. She turned back around to see her mom pull biscuits from the oven and scoop them onto a large platter.

"Do you want to talk about it?"

"What part? Creepy reporter or creepier hunter?" She rubbed her hands up her arms and over sudden goose bumps.

"How 'bout the mate?" she asked lightly.

Sara Beth met her mother's warm loving gaze. "There's not much to say."

"Liar," she responded with a grin. "Make a plate."

She helped herself to eggs and bacon and joined her mother at the table. She only got a few bites before her mother tried again.

"He marked you, but you haven't done the same. Why not?"

Suddenly not hungry, she shoved the plate away. "You're not gonna let this go, are you, Mom?"

Sara Beth could stonewall her father, but never Janelle. Her mother was more pit-bull than fox. Now she smiled, shook her head and pushed Sara Beth's plate back in front of her. "Eat while you talk."

She sighed. Yep. Definitely pit-bull blood in there somewhere.

"I'm just taking my time, Mom. Making sure," Sara Beth said, hoping to give her enough explanation she'd lay off, but instead she got a long hard look for her effort.

"I can't help if you won't talk to me, hon."

Could she help? Sara Beth doubted it, but it might be nice to talk it out. "He didn't hesitate at all. He should have waited to get to know me. To see if we'd…match."

Her mother sat back and arched her eyebrows. "Have you ever known a dominant male shifter to do that?"

"No." She had to concede the point. "And it doesn't make me feel better either."

"You doubt his heart?"

She shook her head. "It's not that. We live very different lives, ya know? He's high in his hierarchy. He's used to excitement, and let's face it, Mom, I'm not very exciting."

Her eyes narrowed. "Did he say that?"

"No. Of course not. But one day he'll realize won't he?"

"I don't think you have to worry about that, darlin. Unless," she said with a wink, "you plan on giving the practical joker crown to your brothers?"

Hell no. She had way too much fun jerking their chains.

"I heard about the pink bedroom," Mom said, the chiding tone ruined by the laughter in her eyes. "I've given up all hope of y'all growing up."

Sara Beth grinned. "He had it coming."

Her brother had taken a trip out of town, and instead of asking her to supervise the remodel of his condo, had just assumed his baby sister had nothing else to do. He'd dropped the project in her lap without even asking. She didn't have it in her to ruin the whole project, but had had no compunction at all about slapping enough layers of bright bubble gum pink paint on his bedroom and bathroom walls that, even with primer, it would take days to cover.

"Well, he won't take you for granted again," her mother said dryly, standing to clear their plates. "Is that what you're afraid of with Patrick? Or is it just risking your heart holding you back?"

She should have known her mother would circle back to Patrick. She rejected the first question out of hand. Patrick was a leader and he took his responsibilities seriously, and that included the mental well-being of those under his protection. As for risking her heart, she may be fighting it but she was pretty sure it was too late for that.

"Speaking of brothers," her mother said, saving Sara Beth from trying to explain why she hadn't claimed her mate yet, when she wasn't sure of the answers.

Sara Beth heard the front door open, scented her siblings before they entered the kitchen. Charles, the brother in question, squeezed her in a big hug and spun her around till she laughed and punched him. "Put me down."

He did so immediately, but only so he could rub the top of her head. She jumped out of the way.

"Don't think I'm not planning my revenge, baby sister. You crossed a line."

She scoffed. "Yeah. Whatever. Bring it on, tough guy."

Noel, her other brother, whistled from where he was filling a plate. "Dude. You gonna let that kind of challenge go unaccepted?"

She watched as a slow smile of pure sibling rivalry crossed Charles's face. "Oh, I accept," he said.

She narrowed her eyes, wondering what he'd come up with. She couldn't plan her retaliation until she knew what he was thinking.

"'Course, she could just get her mate to beat you up," Noel offered helpfully.

She rolled her eyes. "Leave him out of this."

"Leave me out of what?" Patrick asked, tone harsh and hard as he entered the room. She'd been so focused on her brothers she hadn't heard Patrick enter, but she realized Noel had and had spoken for Patrick's benefit. Patrick crossed the room to her.

"Now what?" Patrick practically snarled.

"It's nothing important. Nothing dangerous."

He relaxed until Charles crossed his arms and sent her a mock glare. Patrick, reacting to that look, tried to push her behind him, but she dug her fingernails into his arm until he stopped. Charles grinned.

"How do you feel about pink, Patrick?" Charles asked him.

Oh no, she had to derail that idea before it fully formed. "Mates are off limits."

"You're the only one with a mate. You live with him. You can't place those kinds of limits."

"What the hell are y'all talking about?" Patrick asked.

"You mated into a family of foxes, dear," her mother said. "Pranksters to their core, this lot."

CHAPTER THIRTEEN

Patrick looked down at Sara Beth, intrigued by this new facet. She kept surprising him. Kept showing him something new. "This circular conversation is about a prank?"

She shrugged. "He was taking me for granted. He won't again."

He arched his eyebrows. His sweet little mate had a mean streak.

"Taking you for granted? I asked my designer sister for a little help, was all," Charles said.

She narrowed her eyes. They were all shifters so Patrick knew he wasn't the only one who scented her irritation, but he didn't sense any real anger in it. "No, you dropped a personal project in my lap and assumed I'd help without even asking."

"And you emailed the results to the whole clan. I've been unmanned. Retaliation is absolutely necessary."

The only reason Patrick didn't lunge for him was because he heard the affection and glee in Charles's voice, saw it in his eyes. And it was reciprocated in Sara Beth. Now Patrick was damned curious.

"What did you do?" he asked Sara Beth. A smile tugged her lips.

"I'll show you when we get home."

"We need to head into the mountains for a couple days."

She gave him a sharp questioning look. "Clan business," he said. "It shouldn't take long."

"I'll keep a close eye on your house while you're gone," Charles said solemnly.

Instead of responding with anger, Sara Beth burst out laughing. "Mom, please keep him the hell away from my house."

Patrick turned to Janelle Reynard. He hadn't met her before, but it was clear she was the source of Sara Beth's beauty. She met his gaze a moment and he saw a woman of deep strength and warmth. Then she turned an expression on her children that was half stern and half bemused.

"I think it's time to declare houses off limits. Y'all find another way to torment each other."

Charles and Noel looked aghast and Sara Beth smirked. "Ha! Now what?" she goaded Charles.

Her brother narrowed his eyes a moment before his expression morphed into satisfaction. "Like I'd warn you in advance?"

A few minutes later, Patrick and Sara Beth drove to her house, packed a few things and were on the way back to the mountain. She stared out the window several minutes, lips pursed, before finally pulling out her phone and opening her email.

"What is he planning?" she muttered.

He didn't like being ignored so completely, but he appreciated that her brothers had distracted her from the fear he'd seen too often in her eyes. He reached over and laid his hand on her thigh. Squeezed.

"What did you do to rile him up, mate? What should I expect in return?" He thought back over the conversation. "And what does it have to do with pink?"

She shrugged, but gave into the grin tugging at her lips. "He was renovating his condo when he had to go out of town for a couple weeks. Just tossed it in my lap like I had nothing else to do and told me to do whatever I liked."

"And?" he prodded when she didn't continue.

"The downstairs is lovely and suits him very well. Dark wood and granite, warm colors." She teased him with details, and he didn't rush her because he sensed part of her enjoyment was drawing it out.

"Two bedrooms upstairs." She cocked an eyebrow when he didn't ask for more. Okay. He could play too. And suddenly he got it.

"Pink?"

"Bubble gum pink," she responded. "The bathroom has lime green stripes too. It needed a little oomph."

He stared at her a moment before snorting, not sure if he should be horrified or amused. "How many years has this been going on?"

"Since the time he filled my closet with frogs. He wasn't sure how many I'd need to find a prince," she said.

"How old were you?" He was afraid almost to ask.

"Five."

"How did you retaliate?" That he was *definitely* afraid to ask.

"Hmm. I don't remember exactly. But I'm pretty sure it involved blue dye and a shampoo bottle."

Who knew a five year old Sara Beth had been such a menace? His hands clenched on the steering wheel. "Baby, I love you, but you're a little scary."

He scented her surprise at his declaration, then alarm. Grabbed her hand before she could protest and continued. "We are definitely having eaglets."

"Yes, dear," she said drolly, her panic ostensibly receding.

And he was definitely never going to grow bored with her. That reply, her tone, made him want to pull over, peel off her clothes and show her exactly why they were mates.

"Do you really have clan business to take care of?"

The change of subject was unwelcome. He'd enjoyed the respite—just getting to know her better, seeing what was important to her. And this was a dangerous question. He didn't want to lie to her but he figured she'd fight his need to protect her and go after her stalker himself. Because there was no doubt now Victor King was hunting her.

"Patrick? Please don't lie to me," she whispered. He heard something fragile in her voice and knew if he tried it would be a breach of trust she wouldn't forgive. He sighed.

"I do need to go the Guard's enclave. That isn't a lie."

"So you're going to leave me alone?" she asked. He heard the surprise in her voice, shared it.

"Hell no. Why would you think that?"

"Ajax told me once that no one goes to that enclave except the Guard and royal family."

He took her hand and lifted it to his lips. "And mates and children of her advisors."

"Oh. I didn't realize. Why are we going then?"

"To take Ajax and the girls up."

She twisted in her seat, suspicion lighting her eyes. "Why?"

He clenched his teeth. "Victor King went to the library and looked up our old yearbooks. Then he went to the property records office. I'm waiting for Michael to send me a report on what King was searching for."

"You think he might target my friends?"

"We think he's looking for where you've been hiding."

"He won't find Ajax's name on any records," she reminded him. Her property was held in a corporation, buried under layers of companies and names to protect the royal family.

"He won't," Patrick agreed. "But we're evacuating them just in case. Until this situation is dealt with."

"All this trouble for me."

She sounded bewildered. He kissed her palm.

"Don't worry, baby, I'll keep you safe. And everyone has been warned. Nothing bad is going to happen," he promised, and hoped like hell he was telling the truth.

CHAPTER FOURTEEN

Patrick felt followed, but never saw anyone in his rearview mirror so he wrote the sensation off as paranoia. He began to relax once they reached his house. He looked around the place, seeing how it lacked warmth and personality after a couple of days spent at Sara Beth's. It was time to move on, anyway. The First Consul's house waited.

He dropped their bags in the bedroom. "We aren't staying here tonight, but we can't take anything with us. To get to the enclave, we have to shift."

He was looking forward to it. He hadn't flown in days, but more than that, he wanted to see her in her other form.

"What do we do for clothes if we can't take a bag?"

"Ajax will take care of it. We fly in what we need."

"Bird, plane or helicopter?" she joked, but was obviously curious.

"Bird and helicopter."

He set his hands on her hips and slowly drew her closer, but before he could kiss her or act on his desire, his phone rang. He sighed when he saw the caller ID.

"Yes, my Queen," he answered flippantly. She laughed at him.

"Feeling testy, Patrick? Never mind that. No time. Where are you?"

"We just arrived at my house. Are y'all settled in?"

"Getting there. I had your suite cleaned and clothes brought up for Sara Beth."

"Thanks. We're leaving now."

He turned the phone off and left it on his dresser. "Ready, foxy?"

She grinned and started to strip. He held his breath, mouth going dry as she was bared to him. "Well?" she asked. "I've been on guard so long it feels like forever since I've been able to shift."

Her excitement was a sharp tangy scent that filled the air. He was enthralled. Intoxicated. He wanted to take her to bed and lose himself in her, but he didn't want to see this joy in her eyes dimmed. He would give her the wild and fuck her later. All night long if it was up to him.

He stripped and led the way to the porch, then secured the door behind them. "Change, baby. I want to see my fox," he teased.

She looked a little uncertain, but she nodded, stepped back and knelt. She shimmered for a few seconds—like a mirage—as her body changed, contorted. And then she was a red fox, lovely and striking. He dropped to one knee in front of her and stroked a hand over her head, down her back.

"Beautiful," he whispered, staring into eyes that shone with intelligence.

She stepped into the caress, rubbed her muzzle against his knee. Then she stepped back and yipped at him, a fox's impatient demand to get a move on. He chuckled and straightened, reached for his bird half and changed. As soon as it was complete, she scampered down the stairs. She obviously expected him to follow. He couldn't in his current form so he dove over the side of the porch, slowly circled lower to the ground as he waited for her to catch up. She was there in seconds and followed him when he took off down a commonly-used trail.

With the eagle's eyes, it was easy to track her progress. He'd been worried he might have to temper his strength and speed, but he'd obviously worried for nothing. She was fast and nimble, her small lithe body clearing obstacles with skill and ease. He called to her as he slowed and circled. He signaled a turn in direction and they veered onto a new steeper path. Soon he would have to dive under the branches or she wouldn't be able to see him any longer. He hoped she didn't panic when she saw a full grown eagle coming at her. If he could have, he'd have snorted. Even in their animal forms, he was sure she would surprise him. And then the time for speculation was over.

In a controlled glide, he dropped almost to the ground, swooped around her twice, just long enough to make sure she was still unafraid and continued up the mountain. It was only a few minutes longer and he was unsurprised to rise over the top of the ledge and find a single sentry—Jack—waiting with a pile of clothes. Patrick shifted and started pulling them on. He was snapping his jeans as his fox appeared.

"Leave," he snapped at Jack, his old friend and another of Ajax's councilors. The other man cocked an eyebrow, looking back and forth between him and Sara Beth, who hadn't shifted yet.

"But I want to meet your mate," Jack said with an innocent look Patrick knew was all act. He snarled.

"Later."

"Killjoy."

"Get over it."

With a parting grin, Jack turned and strolled away. Sara Beth shifted and dressed in haste. She looked around, catching her bottom lip between her teeth. Nervous. Patrick finished dressing, then pulled her to his side.

"Let's get inside," he said. They were safe here, but he still felt exposed on the plateau they called the landing area. He headed for the squat building that appeared to be little more than a lean-to against the face of the mountain.

Sara Beth looked around curiously. "What did y'all do? Blow off half the mountain face?"

He chuckled at the guess. "That's exactly what we did. Long ago before this area was populated enough for outsiders to notice."

"How?" A scowl furrowed her brow. "Dynamite?"

"Too early." He shook his head, almost gave her the answer but she held her hand up.

"Gimme a minute."

He was happy to do that. They were fixing to go inside anyway, and then she'd likely revisit the question.

"Black powder," she said just as he opened the door.

He wasn't surprised she figured it out. Before he could confirm her guess, they went inside and she stopped cold. He waited. It surprised everyone the first time they entered this hall. The eagles hadn't just cleared the landing area outside—they'd also hollowed out the top of the mountain and built rooms around the side they'd left standing. The ceiling soared above them. At the back wall of the huge room were staircases leading up to three levels where the eagles worked and lived while here. It wasn't dark because of the huge skylights above them.

"Wow," she whispered.

"Incredible, isn't it?" Ajax asked as she approached.

"It's a treasure," Sara Beth agreed, hugging her friend. "Thanks for the clothes."

"No problem. There's more in your suite."

"I have a suite?"

"Patrick does. He's yours. So…" Ajax shrugged and turned to him. "I got roped into helping with a flying lesson. We'll see y'all at dinner though, in our suite."

He nodded. "Of course."

Sara Beth frowned as Ajax left the building and Patrick led her to the stairs. "Why is the queen teaching a flying lesson?"

"Battle maneuvers," he said. "She's one of the best I've ever seen. It takes a lot of skill and practice, though."

"But a Guard requirement, I suppose?"

"Yes," he said.

They reached the third floor and he steered her to his suite. It was two down from Ajax's. He opened the door and ushered her inside, feeling his need for her rise with each step. He wanted her stripped and under him, panting and crying out his name as he made her come over and over again.

"Damn. More wonders." She walked inside and straight to the French doors, which opened on a small deck with a sheer drop into the valley. "No rails."

"We eagles don't need them," he said.

"And of course, we'll have eaglets," she mused. "Since it seems to be about dominance."

Her words froze him for so many reasons. First, it was the second time she'd inadvertently agreed they were mates and there would be children. Second, she'd acknowledged that he was dominant. That didn't mean she was weak or defenseless, just a statement of fact. But in mixed were-matings, the more dominant partner's genes took precedence. That was the theory, at least. Patrick had wondered more than once if Ajax and Nico had found a way to tamper with nature in that regard. Ajax had to have a wereeagle heir, and had had two. But Patrick had seen the two go head-to-head more than once over the years, and Nico was often the victor.

Sara Beth set her hands on her hips and turned to check out the room. It was a large area combining the kitchen, island bar and living room. It was a plain, ordinary space like his other one she'd seen.

And she was worried about boring him? He was the dull one in this relationship.

"The view outside is great and if I could go shopping, I could do something about the view inside. Since that isn't an option, what the hell am I supposed to do? Normally, I'd have plenty of work but I couldn't bring my laptop."

"Oh, foxy, trust me. I can keep you occupied."

Her eyes widened. "You're insatiable."

He had no argument there. "You haven't been complaining."

"I'd just be punishing myself if I did," she pointed out, a ghost of a smile curving her lips.

"True." He took her hand and tugged her down the hall. "Maybe this time I'll give you reason to complain," he teased, just because he liked seeing the blush heat her face.

The bedroom wasn't much to look at but it had the essentials. Two small nightstands, a dresser, and—most importantly—a bed large enough to share. One wall was glass and she dropped his hand to go look out over the valley.

"Amazing," she whispered. She walked up to the wall and set her hands on it, tilting her head like she was trying to get a better look. She was so beautiful she could stop his heart with a look if she tried. She must have sensed the change in his mood because her head jerked up.

"What's wrong?" she asked.

"Nothing," he said, shaking his head. "Not a damned thing."

He could tell she didn't believe him. "Your pulse just spiked," she countered.

It pleased him she was that attuned to him. "What can I say? You have that effect on me."

She blinked and he could tell she wasn't sure if she should believe him.

"How long are we staying up here?"

"Don't like it?"

"It's incredible, but pretty disconcerting for my fox. I don't really do heights."

That didn't surprise him. "We're only staying the night. I just needed to be sure the royal family got here safely."

"We didn't have to come up for that." She tilted her head. "Are you cutting short your visit because of me?"

Hell yeah. He wanted her all to himself, at his house. There were too many people in the enclave. They'd want to meet her. Would put demands on their time.

"Patrick?"

"I'm selfish. And greedy. I'm not ready to share you yet."

She smiled and slipped into his arms. "I'm not complaining about that."

He kissed her, and that fast he was lost. This, right now, was all that mattered.

CHAPTER FIFTEEN

Victor had expected the shapeshifters to search for him, so he'd changed motels the night before his first attempt to grab the werefox. After that, assuming shifters could access facial recognition programs to be on the safe side, he figured he had a day or two before he needed to move on again. His target had disappeared, but he'd been studying her. He'd found out who her friends and family were, where they lived.

But now she was back and she wasn't alone. Victor had taken up residence in an empty foreclosure across from her house and watched as she exited the vehicle. A tall, powerful-looking white haired man also got out. No, that wasn't right. Victor studied him using a high resolution camera, zoomed in and snapped a picture. His hair was very pale but blond. The stranger hustled the woman inside. Nothing Victor had discovered suggested a boyfriend, but he was certain they were in a sexual relationship. The stranger's hold was possessive. Protective. Victor would either have to take him out first or wait until he left the woman alone.

Maybe the other man wasn't that dangerous though. He'd looked familiar; Victor scrolled through the photos he'd taken of her high school yearbook. He'd been looking for group shots of her and the stranger wasn't in them. He'd have to risk another trip to the library, but it would have to wait. His employers were waiting for an update. They'd insisted on a video conference, which Victor considered a stupid waste of time, but they were footing the bill for this little enterprise. He powered up his laptop and waited for the program to load. A few minutes later, two men in lab coats appeared on his screen.

"We're growing impatient, Victor. Where is our subject?"

"She's just returned to town, but she has a new bodyguard." He shrugged. "I can kill him to take her, but you said no killing."

The two men exchanged a look. "Maybe you should look for an easier target."

No fucking way. He acknowledged his obsession to himself, but he refused to allow the scientists see it. They simply saw her as an experiment. Victor wanted to study the animal. See how human they were, determine how threatening they were.

"The ground work is laid for the Reynard woman. I'll get an opportunity to take her and I doubt it will take long."

"How long?"

He shrugged. He was a hunter. He was patient, unlike these two buffoons. He understood sometimes you had to wait.

"As long as it takes. Days. A week."

The older scientist finally spoke. His gaze was cold and hard but it didn't faze Victor. "One week. If you can't do it in that timeframe, we'll find someone who can."

Victor disconnected without responding. This was his job. No matter how long it took, he'd catch his quarry.

Two days later, he snarled as he watched Reynard and her companion, Patrick Aquila, load bags into their vehicle and leave. He'd gotten the man's name from the library yearbooks. He'd had to slip in and out after hours. The whole town seemed to be watching for him now. But he hadn't been able to get anything else on Aquila. The man was ghost.

As far as Victor's contacts had been able to determine, there was no property, utilities or credit cards in his name.

This time he was able to get to his car without being seen. But he wasn't fast enough. Incredibly, for the second time her protectors managed to spirit her away. Time for a new approach. He'd seen the tabloid reporter's ridiculous new story speculating on Aquila's species. Time to pay the man a visit.

CHAPTER SIXTEEN

"Don't hang up," Nichols said on the other end of the line.

Sara Beth's hand tightened on the phone. *Now what?* Patrick, who was spooned up behind her, tensed.

"Put it on speaker," he growled. She pressed the correct button. "You have a hell of a lot of nerve, Nichols. What do you want?"

"Someone came to see me. He was asking questions about you and Ms. Reynard."

"Like what?" she asked.

"Who your boyfriend is. If I had any idea where he'd taken you."

"And what did you tell him?" Patrick asked in a voice so cold it burned.

Nichols snorted. "That I don't know. I don't think he believed me. He also wanted my source. Since I don't know who it is I couldn't tell him that either."

"Did you give him the email?" she asked. Damn. That could be a problem if the hunter tracked it down before they could.

"Yeah. He's a scary bastard and he had a gun. And since I couldn't trace the email, I figure he can't either," he said softly. "Ms. Reynard, you need to be careful. This guy is seriously creepy. Like fanatical creepy."

"Have a change of heart, Nichols? Little late for that, doncha think?" she retorted.

He was quiet so long she thought the call had been dropped.

"Eventually, you shapeshifters are going to have to show yourselves to the world. Some people are going to consider you more animal than human. I'm not one of them. I'm not your enemy. Be careful."

He hung up before she could reply. She rolled onto her back and stared up at Patrick, who lay on his side, propped on his elbow.

"That was strange. King, you think?"

"No doubt. He's getting desperate. He'll make a mistake soon, and then we'll have him."

"I wish he'd just give up and go away. Both of them," she muttered.

He stroked her cheek with his fingertips. "You know they won't, baby."

"I know." She held the sheet to her as she sat up. "So what's on the agenda today?"

If he thought the subject change was abrupt, he didn't say anything. Instead, he grinned. "I want to show you something."

"What?"

He rolled to his back and pulled her down to sprawl over his chest. Then gave her a long, hot kiss that left her panting and wanting. "You'll see," he teased.

An hour later, he ushered her into a large house. It had footbridges leading to two more buildings in nearby trees. It was only a couple of feet to exit one and enter another. The First Consul's house, she realized. It was wide open and airy, and clean, even if outdated.

"Do you always keep it ready?" Sara Beth asked.

That made no sense if he hadn't planned on using it. He shook his head. "Jack and some of the other Guards cleaned it up when we were at your house."

She felt him watching her as she wandered through the living room and kitchen, and followed the curving hall to see what was in the opposite side of the house. There were two bedrooms connected by a spacious bathroom. She backtracked to find Patrick waiting right where he'd been in front of the door, as if he was barring her escape. But his expression was reserved, maybe a bit nervous.

"What do you think?" he asked.

She looked around the space. "It has a lot of potential. Can you do whatever you want to it or does it belong to the clan?"

"I can change anything, but I wouldn't know where to start."

He was so solemn, so serious, she couldn't help but tease him. "I know a designer who might offer a suggestion or two for free."

He shook his head. "No. I want the whole package. I can pay."

She caught her breath, knew from the seriousness in his voice and expression that he wasn't offering the traditional payment for her design work. "With what?" she whispered.

He approached slowly. A graceful predator on two legs. She stood her ground. Didn't trust her trembling limbs to safely retreat. He circled her, brushing close to sweep her hair over her shoulder. He held her hips as he leaned down to the curve of her neck. Hot breath. The barest kiss. Scraping teeth. She shivered.

"I can pay," he whispered. "Just name your price."

"It's pretty steep." She gasped when he bit her.

"Hmm." He licked the bite. "Put me on the lifetime installment plan then."

His hand slid up to cup her breast and squeezed. Electric need shot straight to her pussy. "That's a major investment," she rasped.

He turned her around and stared into her eyes. "Worth every penny."

"Patrick," she breathed, lifting her hands to grip his shoulders. All he had to do was look at her, give her the most innocent touch and she wanted him with a desperation that made her worry about her sanity. "What have you done to me?"

She shoved her fingers into his hair and tugged him down for a kiss before he could answer. She didn't need to hear it. She felt it in every scorching look, every possessive hold. He was claiming her. Seducing her. Making her fall in love with him. And she didn't have much fight left. If he decided later she wasn't for him…well, she'd figure it out.

But did she really have to worry about that? His scent surrounded her. Hot and rich. Devotion and love and all for her.

She wanted to touch him. Taste him. Claim him. She broke the kiss and sharpened her claws until he released his hold on her hips. She moved to one of the armchairs and sat to pull off her boots. Then she stood and stripped to the skin. Neither spoke as he followed suit.

When he was naked, he crooked a finger at her.

"C'mon, foxy, let's christen the place."

He gave her a smile so carnal it made her toes curl. She could feel his dominance and possession. The demand that seemed to pulse from him to her, that she mark him as irrevocably as he'd marked her. A week ago that desire, that instinct would have sent her into a panic. Now it felt right. But she wasn't giving into him so easily.

"I don't think coming over there is such a good idea."

Oh, but it was. She almost didn't recognize her voice. Filled with lust and so much more. Yearning. The love she could no longer hide. He was in front of her before she could blink, his hand wrapped around her nape.

"Tell me, baby. I can smell the emotion. Put it into words."

There was a part of her still holding back, though. Still defiant. "Make me," she dared him.

If the look he leveled on her was any gauge, she was in serious trouble. Oh gods. He reached for her, but she was a fox. Nimble. Fast. She easily evaded his grasp, but he wasn't angry. His grin was sharp and anticipatory. A raptor on the hunt and she was his prey. Her body pulsed. They were on opposite sides of the couch—not that it provided a real barrier. She didn't really want one. She wanted him touching her, holding her, thrusting inside her. She wanted him to feel as much, to feel everything she did. But that wasn't fair. He loved her. She knew; she'd scented it. What pissed her off was his insistence she say the words when—except for that one time, which hadn't exactly been a declaration of undying love—he hadn't. Which she knew was completely infantile. She'd been holding back for days. Why shouldn't he? How he'd said hadn't exactly been flattering either.

Baby, I love you but you're a little scary.

It was time to make a choice. Claim her eagle or walk away. It would rip out her heart to leave. She couldn't do it. In the end she just had to trust he'd known what he was doing when he mated her. She had to trust him. She made her choice and met his gaze. Somehow he knew.

He angled his head. "Foxy?"

She knew in that moment that she could break them both. If she didn't trust him enough to love her, eventually she'd poison that devotion. The resentment she feared would be of her own making. That wouldn't be fair to either one of them.

"Half-way?" she queried back and somehow he knew exactly what she meant. They moved at the same time, met in the middle of the room over a thick plush rug in front of the fireplace. Suddenly cold, she shivered.

"Does it work?" she asked, glancing at the fireplace.

"Let's find out."

His friends had left it ready for them and all he had to do was strike a match. In moments, a comforting fire filled the hearth. Patrick took her hands and guided her to the rug by his side. He urged her to lie down, then covered her with his body as her back came into contact with the fur rug. He cradled her close.

"Sara Beth," he whispered.

She *felt* the emotion in his voice. The longing and desire. And she understood that the emotional distance she'd aimed for while they got to know each other—while she worried about his ability to be happy with a fox—was useless now. It was no longer necessary. She trusted her instincts. He loved her. He wasn't disappointed in her and he most definitely wasn't the adrenaline junkie she'd accused him of being just days ago. She'd seen that in the time they'd spent together. So she stopped fighting it. He gave her a long, slow blink and yanked her close. She felt a tug on her body and heart that wasn't normal.

"The bond between mates is more than physical. More than emotional."

She jerked a nod.

"You aren't afraid of me," he whispered, kissing her neck. "Choose me, baby."

At the same time, he tilted his head to the side. An invitation. Exposing his jugular to her. His hands molded and shaped her body. His fingers caressed her nipples. She felt her incisors sharpen and lengthen. Scraped them over the smooth skin of his shoulder. A shudder wracked his body as her teeth closed and she bit him.

Then he stopped pretending she had any control.

Patrick snapped. She'd finally done it. Finally marked and claimed him, and that action broke all pretense of controlling his instinctive animal side. He moved down her body. Kissing, licking, biting. He gripped, spread, lifted her legs over his shoulders, and blew a hot breath over her sex. She gasped and dug her fingers into his hair, nails scraping his scalp. He bit the sensitive skin of her inner thigh in retaliation. Looked up to meet her hot, dazed eyes.

"Stop that. It's my turn."

"That doesn't seem fair. Do I get a turn?"

"Oh yeah. Later," he said, gut tightening when he imagined her mouth on him.

He liked teasing her, slow building the pleasure until it exploded into ecstasy, but he didn't have the patience for that right now. He needed to drive her wild, needed her to burn as hot as he did and he knew just how to do it. Using his fingers, he spread the lips hiding her pussy and licked her. Thrust his tongue into her. She bucked against his hold.

"More."

He loved the catch in her breath, the greediness in her eyes and scent.

He found her clit and bit, not quite hard enough to hurt—he knew her body and her responses well enough to know how much she could take—but she froze. He took in a deep breath, searching for any hint of fear or displeasure. There was none. Only arousal and the lush, rich scent of his woman so close to coming apart. His cock throbbed. His eagle side was insistent and demanding. He forced it under control. He wouldn't give into those instincts until she was ready—until her need was desperate. But he didn't have the patience to go slow or easy.

He licked her clit. Sucked it between his lips as he thrust two fingers into her. Her fingers tightened in his hair, her hips rolled up to meet his thrusts, and he feasted. She tasted like heaven. The air around them was heavy with the scents of emotions. Love, desire, trust. Acceptance. Deep and total, his fox had accepted him. He couldn't wait. He had to be inside her. With a final bite on her clitoris that made her cry out for more, he pried her fingers from his hair and slid up her body. He didn't thrust into her until she met his gaze. He could only imagine she saw the dominance and possessiveness that gripped him when she looked in his eyes.

"Yes," she hissed. "Take me."

He wasn't gentle. He didn't have it in him right now. Couldn't hold back and would definitely not last long. He reached a hand between them and found her clit as the speed and depth of his thrusts increased. He was determined she come with him. The touch was all she needed. He stared at her in wonder as she shattered, so happy she was his. When his orgasm rushed through him, he didn't hold back the eagle's exultant cry.

A long time later, she lay quiet in his arms before the fire. He'd considered taking them to one of the spare bedrooms in this part of the house but just felt too damned good to move.

She spoke. "You want me to move up here, don't you?"

"It's safer. And I have to stay near Ajax."

For the first time in his life, his eagle half stilled. Questioned that lifelong, previously unquestioned loyalty. Its mate came first—Ajax would be the first to tell him that. His heart stuttered at the offer he knew he had to make.

"I could go with you," he said softly. "Jack could take over my duties."

He felt her shock. She leaned up over him, eyes wide and wondering. "You would do that?"

He rolled them over, holding her close to his heart. "I'll do whatever you want, baby. As long as we're together."

She lifted her hand to his lips and shook her head. He nipped the finger tracing his mouth.

"You belong here," she said. "I work for the family business, not the clan. I can continue that from anywhere."

A part of himself he hadn't been aware he was holding in reserve relaxed.

"The rest of this house is in the other two trees."

"I figured." A smile teased her lips. "Do I get to see them?"

"Maybe later," he murmured, leaning down to claim a kiss. Much, much later.

CHAPTER SEVENTEEN

A week later, she was ready to use her claws on him and Patrick knew it, but he couldn't seem to help himself. He hadn't been able to leave her in peace. He'd hovered and kept her trapped in the house. And now he had to leave her alone. He wasn't sure if he'd get a snarl or triumphant cheer when he told her. He found her at the kitchen island, sketching her plans for the house that was now hers. She ignored him.

"I need to carry a message," he told her. For the first time he wished she was a bird. She could come with him in that case.

She frowned at him. "You're commander of the Guard and First Consul. Why do you have to carry a message?"

A few weeks ago he would have considered the question impertinent and refused to answer. But she was his mate.

"Peace treaty for some bear clans up north. It's sensitive material and no one else is free right now. And you're safe here. There hasn't been any sign of King."

She just looked at him. There was wariness and growing anxiety in her eyes, in her scent. He knew she wondered if her earlier concerns were true. She wondered if he was bored and clinging onto any excuse to leave. He wanted to shake her. The last thing he wanted was to leave, and not just because they hadn't found Victor King yet. He didn't want to sleep alone in some strange bed and there was no telling how long this would take. As a Messenger, he was neutral, not a mediator, but he was damned tempted to change that role now.

"We can't send a junior messenger on this," he explained. "And they need someone now. This has nothing to do with us."

She didn't believe him and hell, frustrating as that was, he couldn't blame her. He'd kept them both confined to the house and though he loved being with her, needed her safe, even his eagle was beginning to chafe. It was past time to strangle his protective instincts.

He walked to her and stared at the drawings she made. It was more than just furniture layouts. She'd used color on the walls, couches and beds, drawn planks or squares on the floors. When she was done, the house was going to look incredible, but what fascinated him were the differences between the private and public living areas. Technically his house was three buildings. One held a kitchen, living room, and two guest rooms. The other was the family quarters. And the third served as a kind of headquarters for him and Ajax. The residence hadn't been used in years. Sara Beth liked the idea of keeping clan business out of their private spaces and he agreed. But she hadn't treated this area of the design in a cold, businesslike way.

He trailed his fingers over the page. The design was for the smallest of the three buildings, the one that would be accessible to the clan. It was almost all open—the only privacy the bathroom, which had a shower for convenience. Since they usually shifted nude, she'd also added a long wardrobe on one hall that could store extra clothes. Smart. Of course, she was a fox. Then there was the full, expanded kitchen. Before it had been small almost useless space. Her design added a full sized fridge and large pantry. It made sense. Made clan business much easier to conduct if it could all be in one place.

"What do you want to do first?" he asked.

She tapped her finger on the page that had caught his attention. "The clan room. I value my privacy too much to invite anyone I don't know into our areas." She shrugged. "And the rest is livable. It can wait."

He set his palm on the nape of her neck, unable to resist standing so close without touching her. He made a decision he knew might break him, but he needed to see the light returned to her eyes. "I'll be gone a couple days. You should go into town, pack the rest of your things and order what you need for the remodel here."

She didn't show any surprise at his capitulation, and it *was* capitulation. The primal, animal part of him screeched its frustration. But he wasn't all eagle and he wouldn't treat her like he was. She stood and moved into his arms. He held her tight enough she complained.

"Be careful," he whispered. "Take Nico or Jack when you go into town and don't growl when they stop to check on you."

And they would, without him even asking. They were his friends. She was his mate.

"Maybe one of your brothers could come stay a couple days," he suggested.

She growled at him. Or not.

"Don't push it. I'll be fine." She shoved her hands into his hair and pulled him down. "How long till you leave?"

"I have an hour," he whispered. And no need to pack. He was going too far to carry anything.

"But you'll be back." A statement. No fear in her scent. She was beginning to believe in him, in *them*. His chest clenched at her show of trust. He started pulling off her clothes.

"Couldn't keep me away if you tried," he whispered when she stood bared to him.

His mate.

His life.

He proceeded to show her that with every trick up his sleeve.

CHAPTER EIGHTEEN

Sara Beth couldn't help grin as she ran smack into her brother, Noel, outside the furniture store. He smiled back as he steadied her.

"Well, you look happy," he said.

She was happy. It bubbled within her, threatened to erupt and infect everyone around her. He slung his arm around her shoulders and walked her into the parking lot.

"I am."

"So we don't get to kick the eagle's ass?" He sounded so put out, she laughed.

"No. He's mine. You have to treat him like family now."

He looked even crankier at her demand. She almost laughed but took pity on him instead. She stood on her toes to kiss his cheek before she got in the car. He stopped her before she swung the door shut. "You going to see Mom?" he asked.

She shook her head. "I went this morning. I need to get home."

Patrick hadn't taken a phone of course, but he'd borrowed a computer to send her email. He'd be home tonight. She couldn't wait to see him. Was amazed at how much she'd missed him even when he was hovering.

Noel looked like he wanted to protest but he just kissed her forehead, stepped back and shut the door.

She didn't pay much attention as she drove away. Since they still weren't sure where the game hunter was, Michael had arranged for her to borrow a truck. No one outside the local clans would know or expect her to have it, and she hadn't felt any undue attention in the last two days. But when she pulled into the small lot that served as parking area for several families this side of the slope, the hair on the back of her neck rose.

She kept the doors closed and tried Patrick, even though she knew he couldn't be back yet. When that call went to voice mail, she hung up and she tried Ajax. No answer, and then the automated system to leave a message played.

"Ajax, it's Sara Beth." She huffed. Hesitated. What if she was just paranoid? Hell. What if she wasn't?

"I'm in the parking area and something feels wrong. I don't see or scent anything—it's just a bad feeling." She sighed. "This is stupid. Just ignore the ramblings of the crazy lady."

Still, she exited the cab of the truck and carefully smelled the air. There was nothing there that shouldn't be. So why the fuck was she so uneasy? She dropped the keys in the floorboard and started to remove her shoes and clothing. Her senses might not be able to pinpoint the danger but she *knew* it was there. It would be easier to evade and hide in the skin of her fox. She tossed all her things into the truck and locked it, then shifted.

As a fox, she didn't have the advantage of strength and power a wolf or big cat did, but she was limber and fast. She could fit through spaces and contort her body in ways a human never dreamed. Once she changed, she darted into the shrubs. And then she smelled the dogs.

A part of her, her human side, froze in disbelief. Insulted. Dogs? Really? Her fox side was just fucking pissed off. She snarled. She could handle the dogs. She smelled two, and they'd recognize the human in her. Would accede to her dominance. But how could she hold off the hunter? Patrick and Ajax would come, she knew that. She just had to survive long enough for them to help.

First, she had to deal with the hounds. She scented them close, far in front of their master, and led them into a patch of bushes and briars. Once she drew them in, she whirled around and pulled her lips back in a snarl. The dogs skidded to a stop, stared at her a second, then whimpered and lay on their bellies, snouts on the ground. They wouldn't follow her and she took off again, suspecting her time was short when she heard soft steps behind her.

She took off, sliding under bushes and logs, knowing the damned hunter had spotted her. She needed to do the unexpected. She had to climb. Not something she was suited for, but she could make do. The trick was to find steps and slopes. Trees that had fallen or were falling would get her high above the ground. The first wasn't hard to find and she jumped to another fallen trunk that gave her access to branches in a tall pine. By the time she found a high perch, she felt Patrick drawing close.

Below her, the hunter lurked, and she had no way to stop him. Her helplessness rankled. She couldn't expose herself without risk. She didn't have a death wish and knew the loss of his mate would destroy Patrick. She wouldn't do anything to hurt him, even though she wanted to fight. She wouldn't win this one though, and she knew it. Instead she found a place high in the trees and waited.

Patrick hated to stop. He just wanted to get home to Sara Beth, but he couldn't ignore a signal from another Messenger. Jack. He knew it must be urgent because the eagle dove straight to the ground, pulled up sharply and shifted.

Patrick was right behind him.

"Sorry," Jack started. "Ajax wanted you to have warning."

111

He went cold. "What happened?"

"We don't know. Sara Beth left her message. Ajax said she sounded freaked out. She left the truck in the parking area and disappeared. Her clothes and keys are inside. She probably shifted."

Patrick saw red. "That damned hunter. She's in danger." And everything male in him screamed a protest.

"Maybe. But she's a fox."

"What the fuck is that supposed to mean?"

Jack just cocked an eyebrow. Then he grinned. "Man. She got you good, didn't she?"

"She's my mate," he snarled. "What aren't you saying?"

Jack slapped Patrick's shoulders, the grin not slipping an inch. "She's a fox, man. She'll use her strengths. She has to know that not only you and Ajax will come for her, but Nico too. So, think like a fox and tell us what to look for."

He was right but his words didn't calm Patrick. If his eagle knew how to hunt a fox, so would a human hunter. And she knew that too.

"She'll take to the trees," he said softly. "It isn't natural for her, which is exactly why she'll do it."

Understanding spread across Jack's face. "Let's go," he said a split second before shifting.

Patrick easily overtook him. They were close to their lands—fifteen minutes if he pushed hard. He resented the delay, but was glad of the warning. A fierce nervous excitement filled him. The threat to Sara Beth would be destroyed once and for all and no one would know. The idiot had dared to cross onto shape shifter land. Worse, eagle land. They were more territorial than anyone else. No one went on eagle land without permission. King would just disappear, no one the wiser. But first Patrick had to find Sara Beth and make sure she was safe. He prayed to the gods they weren't too late.

He flew harder than he ever had before.

He was still far away when he felt her alarm. The bonds that connected them were strong. He knew she was afraid. It was a bitter acid on his tongue. He dove into the canopy. He couldn't pinpoint her exact location but he knew she was close, scared and cornered. He used his senses—sight and smell—to evaluate the situation. He was right. She'd climbed into the trees. Very unusual for a fox, but she also had the mind of a woman. And she knew her mate would come for her. The hunter was still beating the bushes, unfortunately, and he saw Patrick coming.

Though the attack was so fast it must have been a blur, the man got a shot off. Patrick veered out of the way and the bullet hit a tree to his side, sending shards of bark flying at him through the air. Fire and pain throttled through his wing. It hurt like a bitch, but he could scent Sara Beth now. Scared and bleeding. Rage propelled him toward King. His talons tore through the man's heavy jacket and Patrick smelled blood. King screamed, reeked of fear and fury, but it could in no way match Patrick's.

He was turning for another pass, this time aiming for the human's jugular, when a sleek deadly leopard joined the fight. King watched wide-eyed, seemed to realize at the last minute that he didn't have a chance in hell of surviving both cat and eagle attacks. He scrambled back to avoid Patrick's talons, but it was too late. He and Nico, the leopard, struck at the same time. Patrick ripped into his neck and Nico took him to the ground.

Several other eagles flew into the clearing at the same time. He barely managed to pull out of his dive and circle around to the high branch where he scented his mate. The fox glared at him a few seconds before shifting into Sara Beth.

"Idiot," she snapped. "He could have killed you."

He wrapped his talons around the tree's thick trunk and looked down. Victor King was no more. Nico was already barking out orders to dispose of the body. Patrick, still in eagle shape, looked at his mate. She was safe. He nodded and let go of the branch, spreading his wings and spiraling to the ground. The injury hurt like a bitch, but he managed his way down, Sara Beth following him after she shifted back into a fox. She averted her eyes from the fallen hunter. Her focus zeroed on Patrick. Part of him preened. She was his mate. Why shouldn't she pet and stroke him? But what the hell had happened?

She shifted and rushed to him. He tried like hell to pretend none of the other males landing in the clearing saw her. She was *his*. And he didn't share. Shape shifters were used to nudity and he'd never considered it a problem before. Then again, none of those women were his.

"You need to shift," she said softly.

Many times shifting helped heal. Not this time though. He felt the bark fragments in his wing. He stretched it out, hoping she would understand. She lifted her fingers and caught her breath.

"Can you fly home? I need tweezers."

He might be able to fly from here. He needed to. Needed to make sure no one saw any weakness. Getting purchase off the ground was not so easy though. Then Nico approached and held out his arm. A perch. A launching post. Patrick was much bigger than a natural bald eagle in this form. It was a lot of weight for the leopard to take, but Patrick knew he could. His respect for the man rose and he wished he could thank him, but he couldn't shift fully until the fragments were removed. He could do small shifts. Teeth, claws, eyes. But he couldn't leave a wing as wing and the rest of him a man. His mate understood, however. She nodded.

"If you could, Nico," she said. "I need to get him home."

Then she shimmered, changing back to the fox and took off. He hopped onto Nico's arm and even with the agony tearing through his left wing, launched and flew home. Ajax shadowed him. He knew she was just worried about him but it fucking pricked at his pride to be babysat. Better to focus on something else. He reached the house and used his senses to track Sara Beth.

She was in the area she'd deemed public. He landed, Ajax at his side. Then Nico was there and holding out his arm again. Patrick accepted the lift. By then, both women were inside and Sara Beth had a First Aid kit unfolded on the counter. He didn't remember one in the house's inventory, so she must have gotten it while he was gone. As if she knew they'd need it. Given his position in the clan, it was a logical assumption. If he'd been in human form, a feral grin would spread his lips. This was his woman.

Nico set him down on the counter. He kept his injured wing close to his side. Fought the instinct to fight when Sara Beth reached for him. She gave him an exasperated look.

"I need to get the fragments out," she said softly. "It won't heal if I don't."

The eagle had taken over and it only knew two things: hunting and protecting. It didn't know self-preservation. But despite that and against all instinct, it knew this woman, its mate, could be trusted. She might cause hurt, but it would never be on purpose. He spread his wing and with a set of tweezers, she set to work.

CHAPTER NINETEEN

She had no idea how she did it. How she remained calm in the midst of chaos. When she got the last, tiniest piece out, he shifted. She could see the anger and terror in his eyes but she just didn't fucking care. He was her mate and she needed to be held. She lunged forward and he caught her.

Gods. She'd been terrified. She still was. The hunter had found her. Would he be the last? How many more would come?

"We have company incoming," Nico warned softly. "You should get dressed."

She hurried away because she scented what he didn't say. Her father and brother were close. Also Michael and Hector. She went to the family quarters, Patrick at her back. He locked the door behind them. It was only then she realized she might be in a more serious kind of trouble than she'd ever imagined. His gaze was so intense it burned. Hot, angry, possessive. Scared. She knew that fear was for her and a part of her melted at his protective streak, but the other part rebelled. She was no one's pet.

And they didn't have time for that conversation. He stalked her slowly. For a bird, she sure was getting a lot of four-legged danger vibes off of him. It didn't really surprise her anymore. A lot of people, shifters included, thought birds were helpless. They were so, so wrong. She felt exposed. He'd never allow pretense between them and if she was honest, she didn't want that either.

"You're okay," he said.

He could see she was. His gaze swept over her again and again. Was she imagining that touch or really feeling it?

"I'm fine," she said through dry lips. He gave her the slow wicked smile that made her melt.

"Oh yes, that you are," he agreed.

He was going to reach for her any second now and she wouldn't fight it. Hell no. She wanted to cling to him. Wanted him inside her, making her forget the danger she'd just been in. Before either of them could move, however, she scented more people arrive. Patrick groaned and crushed her lips against his for a minute before stepping back.

"Later," he promised.

She dressed quickly. He pulled on a pair of jeans and started to put on a T-shirt when she shook her head. He would heal fast, but there were dozens of ugly scratches on his arm.

"We need to clean that and bandage it for a couple of days."

He carried the shirt and followed her back to the others. He sat on the stool near the First Aid kit and waited while her family fussed over her. They meant well so she gave them a couple of minutes before extricating herself and returning to Patrick. There were peroxide wipes in the kit and she ripped one open.

"What happened?" Patrick asked as she started cleaning the wounds.

"He was waiting for me in the parking area. I have no idea how he found it."

"We found a tracker on your car," Nico said. "He must have put it there yesterday when you were in town. All he had to do after that was set up an ambush."

Fear was quickly overcome by fury. Her growl was sub-vocal, but Patrick knew. He lifted his uninjured arm to squeeze her nape. The contact calmed her.

"We need to make sure there are no signs he was ever in the area," Patrick spoke to Nico, who nodded.

"Already on it. We have his vehicle and it shouldn't take long to find out where he was staying."

"This isn't over, is it?" she asked. The idea filled her with dread. "I mean, Nichols isn't going to give up. And what if there's another hunter out there looking for a half-human trophy?"

Anger scented the air and growls rumbled around the room.

"We have to begin preparing everyone for exposure. It's inevitable," Michael said.

"I agree," Hector said.

And that made her damned suspicious. She could tell by Patrick's expression he felt the same. Michael's words too closely mirrored Nichols. Surely Michael hadn't given Nichols her name? He was the werewolf alpha, protector of them all.

"The reporter can be silenced." Ajax spoke so coldly, Sara Beth shivered.

Patrick pulled her back into the V of his thighs and wrapped his arms around her.

"You can't kill him," Hector said. "The hunter might not be missed. Nichols will. But if we can control the story…"

He let the thought trail off but everyone in the room knew where he was going with it. Not just exposure, but coming out of the shadows on their own. She stared at him and Michael. Someone had given her name to Nichols, which left her open to King and gods knew who else, and she'd bet the entire contents of her bank account that someone was right here.

"Have you gotten anywhere with that email address?" she asked Nico, not taking her eyes off Michael. If he was guilty, he hid it well.

"Not a damned thing," Nico said. "Whoever it is, hasn't contacted Nichols again."

Nothing in Michael's or Hector's expressions gave them away—the two shifters were thick as thieves, if one knew something, she'd bet the other did too—but the suspicion nagged at her. It sucked not to be able to trust her alpha.

"There has to be a way to contain Nichols," Ajax insisted. "And let me remind you, gentlemen, you are here as a courtesy. I rule this land and I don't answer to anyone."

"A fox is the target. That is my business," Michael countered.

Sara Beth had had enough. "No. It isn't. My mate is not in your clan, and I choose to stay with him. I'm no longer your concern, Michael."

She had stunned Michael speechless. It was her father who spoke. "Sara Beth, you don't have to do that."

She had the feeling it might be the only way to stay alive. "Yes, I do, Dad."

She held his gaze, willing him to see her resolve, and finally he nodded. "I understand." He kissed her cheek, grabbed her brother but stopped at the door. "Make sure you call your mother."

She nodded. "I will."

Thankfully, Michael and Hector left with her family. She was left with Patrick, Ajax and Nico, and Jack. Everyone was grim-faced. It felt like a damned war room.

"Those two are up to no good," Ajax said darkly. Sara Beth agreed. There was something just off about how Michael and Hector had behaved.

"No doubt. One of them gave Nichols my name, I'd bet on it."

Nico prowled the room while the eagles stood very still, eyeing the man who seemed more cat than man. If the situation weren't so dire, Sara Beth would have found it amusing.

"My father is an ass, but I can't believe he'd expose one of our women." Nico shoved his hands through his hair. "Hell, who am I kidding? Of course, he would do it if he could justify it to himself."

"We can't prove it," Sara Beth said. "Even if we could, what would you do?"

Patrick was all controlled fury behind her. If he ever found proof, she knew he'd kill Hector and Michael for putting her in danger. Or at least try. She couldn't allow that. She set her palms on his thighs, and the contact seemed to calm him.

"We couldn't kill them," Jack said, the voice of reason. "Even if you could make it look like an accident, the repercussions throughout the shifter world might very well destroy us all." He paused and looked at Nico, then her. "Unless you think Jason and Bastian can hold the leopards and wolves in check?"

"Jason is already doing that," Nico said. "And my brothers will help him."

Then they all looked at Sara Beth. Were they really standing here talking about assassinating the werewolf alpha and the former wereleopard alpha? It was insane.

"I don't know Bastian very well."

"Better than the rest of us, baby."

True. "He's strong. Well liked. Loyal." She shrugged. "He's the heir. As long as he wasn't implicated in his father's death, the clan would follow him"

"Your clan too?" Patrick asked.

"Of course. But y'all seem to be forgetting something that *I* shouldn't have to point out."

"What's that?" Ajax asked.

"You're neutral. And you aren't assassins. You want to cause upheaval in our world? Break either of those covenants."

Ajax scowled. "Well, there went my chance of getting rid of Hector."

Nico laughed and slung his arm around her shoulders. He tugged her back to his chest. "You know he's not that easy to kill. And Sara Beth is right."

"Well shit," Ajax muttered. "We can't do nothing. Not with this."

"Baby, aren't you friends with Celeste?" Patrick asked Sara Beth. Celeste was Michael's human step-daughter, and Jason Leonidas's mate.

"Why?"

"Just curious," he said, much too innocently. She wasn't buying it for a minute, but she played along.

"Yeah. I haven't talked to her since we mated. She'll be pissed if she hears about us from someone else."

"That is sneaky and underhanded," Nico said. "But it'll work without breaking the rules."

She understood. Anything she told Celeste—including suppositions—would get passed onto her mate, Jason, the wereleopard leader. Sara Beth wasn't sure if she liked the solution, but she did agree with the others that everyone should be warned. Once it leaked, the Messengers would have a legitimate reason to spread the rumor.

"And Bastian?"

"Celeste will fill him in, I'm sure, if Jason doesn't contact him personally."

"Well, that's settled then." Ajax stood. "We're going to have to take a new look at our security, but that can wait till tomorrow."

"See you in the morning," Patrick said as the three eagles left.

Sara Beth turned in his arms. Finally. Alone with her mate. He wasn't smiling, though, and she thought she knew why.

"I'm fine," she said. "I knew if I hid long enough, someone would come."

"It's going to be a long time before I get over that terror."

"Me too. He tried to kill you."

He took her hand and led her back to their room. "I think we should stay in bed for a week."

"You have a meeting in the morning," she reminded him.

"*We* have a meeting in the morning."

She frowned. She appreciated being kept in the loop, but… "I'm not part of Ajax's council."

"This is more of an inner circle meeting, and as my mate, you belong there. By my side."

He gave her a look so scorching she forgot how to breathe. Then he crooked his finger.

"C'mere."

She shouldn't give in so easily. He'd come to expect it all the time. But she saw the lingering fear in his gaze, felt her own. That bullet had come so close. She went to him.

"I could have lost you," she whispered, tears pricking her eyes. How would she have survived the loss?

"Hey, hey. It's okay, baby," he said, pulling her into his arms. "I'm right here. A little scratched up, but I'm fine."

It was the wrong thing to say. The tears fell and a sob caught in her throat. She clung to him, and despite his injured arm, he carried her to bed. Somehow he stripped them both without letting her go which made her cry harder. He didn't say a word, just held her while she completely melted down. Finally she was out of tears, throat raw, and embarrassed as hell.

"I'm sorry. I never do that."

He rolled over her and glared. "Don't ever apologize for loving me, Sara Beth. I couldn't stand knowing you regretted us."

"Idiot." She smiled. "How could I regret something so wonderful?"

The corner of his mouth kicked up in a half smile. "That's what I've been trying to tell you." He kissed her breathless. "A little less excitement than today though, okay? Torment your brothers instead. I can handle that."

She laughed. "Tell me that after they strike back."

She laughed harder at his expression.

"It's a good thing I love you so much," he grumbled, but she could feel his amusement. "Otherwise I might have to do something about your brothers."

"You wouldn't hurt them."

He stroked his hand down the curve of her waist to her hip.

"I'd never do anything to hurt you," he said softly.

"I know."

He kissed her again, hands skimming her body, driving the desire that always lingered into a conflagration.

"Now, Patrick." She scratched his back. "I can't wait."

She needed him inside her. Needed his possession, needed the connection between them. He kissed her neck before moving down to lick and tease her nipples.

"Not yet," he murmured. "You're not ready yet."

She was beyond ready. Her nails sharpened to claws and pricked his skin. He growled, but it was enjoyment—not protest—she heard in the sound.

"Behave," he ordered, and she felt teeth on the underside of her breast as he kept moving down.

"Come back up here and I will," she coaxed.

Teeth on her inner thigh this time. Pleasure and pain mingled, and then he swiped his tongue over her sex, lingering on her clit. She froze. She wasn't sure if she was reaching for orgasm or trying to hold it back. Not that he had any intention of letting her have that kind of control. He used his fingers, his tongue, his *teeth*. It was a maddening torment she hoped never ended. He stopped when the shudders began to wrack her body—so damned close she wanted to rail against the sudden loss. And then he filled her. Hot, hard, demanding.

"Look at me, foxy."

"What are you waiting for?"

"Look at me," he repeated, sounding one part amused and one part pure alpha.

She stared into eyes gone eagle hard. "Better," he said and then he moved. Strong, fast, just rough enough. "Touch yourself, baby. Come with me."

How could she refuse? Even so close to his animal side desire and love shone through. She couldn't deny him anything. She slid her hand between their bodies to her sex and strummed her clit. Nearly came as his cock stroked her G-spot. *Perfection*, she thought as she gave into the most intense orgasm of her life.

A long time later she sprawled across his chest, wrapped in his arms and worrying about the future. Somehow he knew.

"As long as we're together, baby, the world can fall apart as far as I'm concerned."

She knew he meant it and she knew neither of them would be satisfied ignoring the world, but that didn't matter. He'd retreat from everyone if that made her happy.

"I love you," she whispered.

A smile lit his eyes. Emotion wrapped around her. Warmth and love and belonging.

"I love you back."

Illicit Passions

Crystal Jordan

CHAPTER ONE

"I need a cigarette." Tori clutched the cup of coffee the waitress had just dropped off. She'd been feeding her caffeine habit to try to ignore her nicotine habit, but it just left her shaking, jittery and even more irritated. "Seriously, I'd give you my first-born child for just one puff right now."

"You don't have any children yet, and those cancer sticks will kill you, werekind or not. Have you tried the nicotine gum I recommended?" Lyra offered up her best concerned physician look and Tori wanted to lunge across the breakfast table at her.

Yes, she was feeling totally reasonable and rational today.

Of course, since she was a swan-shifter and Lyra was a wolf-shifter, Tori was pretty sure she'd get her ass handed to her if she tried it, concerned physician or no. But on the other hand, it might take her mind off the fact that she really, really needed a fucking cigarette. She eyed her closest friend. She'd taken on a predator shifter before and won. It could be worth it, just for the distraction factor.

Lyra smirked, flashing a bit of wolf canine in the process. "Don't take your violent urges out on me, birdie. No one's forcing you to quit if you don't want to."

"I know, I know," Tori moaned. "But it is bad for me and—"

"Is she still whining about the smokes?" asked a feminine voice behind her. Lyra's cousin, Celeste, sauntered up and parked herself across from Tori. Celeste was married to one of Tori's bosses, but somehow it had never felt awkward to be friends.

The waitress brought Celeste a cup of tea without asking, while Tori winced at the noise of people talking and silverware clinking. Everything seemed to scrape over her too-sensitive nerves these days.

They sat at a table in the restaurant at Refuge Resort—an exclusive getaway for shifters of all species—where Lyra ran the local werekind clinic. Her husband, Zander Leonidas, ran the resort. It was a rare patch of neutral territory in the often-contentious world of shifter clans. The resort also served as the headquarters for the Leonidas family businesses, which was where Tori worked. She'd spent the last five years as the administrative assistant to Jason and Adrian Leonidas, Zander's older brothers. The Leonidases also happened to be the rulers of the leopard shifter clan—and by extension, all feline shifter species in the US. Adrian handled the business end of things, Jason ruled the clan and Tori got to juggle their calendars and make sure their lives ran smoothly.

Lyra nodded to Celeste. "Yep, we might even get to witness a full-on meltdown from the beauty queen today."

Beauty queen. Tori hated that label. She owned a mirror, so she knew she was prettier than the average woman. Okay, gorgeous, stunning, knock-out. She'd been called all those things. She also had a body that made men drool. God help her if she ever dared to put on a bikini. Her platinum blonde hair and Miss-America-pageant-contestant looks made people assume she was all perky sweetness and light...and a bimbo too. Not that she wouldn't sleep with a guy on the first date if the chemistry was there, but she didn't indiscriminately drop her panties for anyone. Fuck the bullshit stereotypes. She bit back the urge to spit those words at her friend. The cigarette detox was making her overreact. Her fingers clenched around the ceramic of her cup and she told herself to chill out.

"Ooh, interesting. Maybe I'll get pictures and do an interview for a story on kicking the habit." Celeste's eyes gleamed with journalistic interest. She was a freelance reporter who wrote for both human and werekind publications. "Imagine the raging addict video on YouTube. We'd go viral in seconds."

"You guys are *hilarious.*" It took everything Tori had to hold back the swan-like hiss that threatened to erupt from her throat. She could feel her wings rippling just below the surface of her skin, and she wanted to shift into her bird form to fly far and fast from the craving that hounded her. Unfortunately, she couldn't escape herself. "I feel like utter shit. Like soggy, lukewarm, day-old shit."

"Wow, that's appetizing." Celeste put down the menu she'd just picked up.

Lyra waved her cousin away and addressed Tori. "Are you using the nicotine patch? It'll help."

"With what? Is it supposed to do anything other than feel weird and piss me off even more? At this point, I'm going to put some tobacco in it, roll it and smoke it." Tori took a sip of her coffee, but it didn't stop the desperate need clawing through her.

Her foot bounced against the floor, and she sat there amongst friends feeling like she wasn't even herself anymore. The smoking hadn't been a big deal, she'd thought, but suddenly it was all she could think about, all she could focus on. She'd been scattered at work since she'd been off the nicotine, had a sore throat and her skull hadn't stopped pounding in a headache for three—damn—*days*. She was also mood swinging like she'd slammed into full-blown menopause. At twenty-seven years old. Awesome. Why did she want to quit again? Oh yeah. Because it was *healthy.*

"Hey, did you guys see this?" Another friend, Cleo, strode up waving her tablet computer. "This has PR nightmare written all over it."

That didn't sound good. As the public relations officer for the resort, Cleo probably had a pretty good instinct for what might become a problem.

"What?" Lyra asked.

Cleo flipped her tablet around to show them the top headline on a newspaper website.

Scientists Claim Human-Animal Hybrids Exist, Fired From MIT

Tori felt her eyes bulge. Just what she needed today. Drama in the werekind world. "Oh, fuck me sideways with a hockey stick."

Snorting, Lyra cast a glance at her. "Well, that says it all, doesn't it?"

"Damn, he made the *Times*." Celeste sighed. "It's that human reporter again—Jeff Nichols—the one who won't let the shifter thing go. I've tried to bury him, but his articles keep getting better and better exposure. But the *Times*? Crap."

"Adrian believes Nichols has an inside source helping him. A shifter selling out other shifters." A growl rumbled up in Cleo's throat—the lioness within her showing through. She glanced at Celeste and Lyra. "What do your husbands think?"

With the exception of Tori, all the women at the table were married to a Leonidas brother. Cleo was a feline, so no one had questioned her mating, but the other two had had a rough time during their courtships. Celeste was a human, but she was the werewolf Alpha's stepdaughter. And wolves and leopards didn't mix. At all. It had been majorly controversial when Celeste had mated with the Leonidas heir, but it had blown people's minds when Lyra—an actual wolf-shifter—had married a leopard. Her father had disowned her for it.

Tori was just happy that, as a bird, she was neutral in all those disputes. Werebirds were ferocious in their neutrality. No one dragged them into clan wars. She'd take her eagle queen over these alpha males any day. Then again, the queen had married a Leonidas too. Nico—probably the scariest, most feral of the four brothers. Tori would *love* to see that particular cat caught in an eagle's nest, but she hadn't made it out to werebird territory in years.

Lyra's cup thumped loudly against the wooden tabletop, jolting Tori back to the unfortunate present. The she-wolf tossed her long black hair over her shoulder. "Zander agrees with Adrian. I think they've been talking about how to deal with this information leak."

"Jason's had a few phone calls with Nico about it too." Celeste leaned forward, dropping her voice. Not that anyone was close enough to overhear, but it paid to be cautious. "I'm recommending that we finally reach out to my family and see if the wolf clan has any intel on this. The Lykaioses have a different network of allies than the leopards or eagles."

"Uncle Michael has been saying for years that our exposure is inevitable," Lyra pointed out. "He's not going to help."

Celeste shook her head, stress pinching the corners of her mouth. "I'm not thinking the Alpha. I'm thinking we go with his second-in-command. My oldest brother is more reasonable than my dad."

"Bastian can also be a dogmatic, hardheaded pain in the ass." Lyra ran a finger around the rim of her mug, her forehead furrowed in thought. "We'd be asking him to go against his Alpha. I'm not sure he's ever done that before."

"I know he hasn't, even when he *really* should have." Old bitterness flashed in Celeste's gaze, but her mouth firmed into a stubborn line. "Still, it's worth a shot. Bastian is our best bet for help from the wolves. My husband, my nieces and nephews, *my whole family* is in danger if word gets out about the werekind, so I'm not standing around and doing nothing. I want to know who this inside source is, and I want him or her stopped."

Not just an inside source, but a powerful one if they were managing to bypass Celeste's efforts to discredit this guy. Tori's stomach churned for reasons that had nothing to do with nicotine withdrawal. The existence of shifters being revealed to the general population would be a majorly huge clusterfuck. She hated to think that anyone would be *helping* a human expose them, but the article claimed these scientists had blood and tissue samples. Where the hell would they get those, if not from a shifter?

This went way, way beyond a PR nightmare.

"I need a cigarette."

Scientists Claim Human-Animal Hybrids Exist, Fired From MIT
Bastian read the newspaper headline twice before the meaning sank in. His head began to throb. It wasn't the first time these quacks had made the papers, wasn't the first time this sleazy reporter had jumped on a story that might hint at the existence of shifters. It was a problem, mostly because the reporter and scientists weren't wrong. Shifters did exist—but no one outside of the werekind community was supposed to know that.

How the hell these humans had found out was a question Bastian would dearly like answered. So far, his sources—okay, his *spies*—hadn't been able to nail down anything concrete, but it was only a matter of time. Time he feared they might not have. His hands balled into fists and he sat back in his chair, a muscle ticking in his jaw. He felt his fangs press against his lower lip, the wolf within him rippling just beneath the surface. It wanted to hunt down whoever was trying to expose their species. Shifters might be stronger and more powerful, but by sheer numbers, the human population could overwhelm them easily. And if history had taught them anything, it was that mankind feared things that were different. Werekind fit pretty firmly in the *different* category, and that would make them targets.

He tossed the paper on his desk with a snarl.

"Ah, you saw the news." A gravelly voice spoke from his office doorway.

He smoothed his expression to one he hoped was noncommittal before the other man came around to look at him. It was wise to step cautiously around the werewolf Alpha. Even when that Alpha was your father.

Despite his age, Michael Lykaios was an imposing man who wore his authority like a cloak. He jutted his chin toward the discarded newssheet. "What do you think, Beta?"

Bastian straightened at being reminded of his place in the pack. Second-in-command, charged with protecting and defending his people, but still beneath the Alpha in rank.

"You know what I think, sir." And the two of them didn't agree.

His father grunted. "Remind me."

Doing his level best to keep any confrontation out of his tone, Bastian replied, "They know too much, have too many of the details right to be coincidence. Someone—a shifter—is spilling secrets. This is an inside job."

Some emotion flickered across Michael's expression, too fast for Bastian to tell what it was. His father cleared his throat. "It doesn't matter where the information is coming from. In the end, this was inevitable. Science and technology have come far enough that they can do tests and know what we are. This isn't ancient Greece anymore, son. Zeus isn't going to come sweeping in and save his favored children. We have to take care of ourselves."

Each shifter race had an ancient god or goddess who'd gifted mortal men with the ability to change into animal form. For wolves, it had been Zeus who'd turned King Lycoan into a shifter, and his children had inherited that gift. To reward Leonidas of Sparta's courage against the Persians, Artemis had granted all his descendants the ability to change into a leopard. The werebirds traced their lineage back to Marathon, the great messenger who'd been blessed by the god Hermes. Bears had their roots set in the Native American legend of Rhpisunt, a chief's daughter who married a bear and birthed halfling twin sons. Shifters originated from all over the world and had scattered to the winds over the centuries. Those who settled in America mostly answered to either the wolves or the leopards, with a few notable exceptions like the neutral birds.

Bastian snorted. "No one expects the gods to meddle in mortal affairs anymore. Shifters *have* been taking care of themselves—by staying out of the limelight and keeping our heads down."

"That's not going to cut it anymore." Michael scowled, slicing a hand through the air. "Science is going to win this one. We can't just pretend we're human."

It took everything Bastian had to hold back a growl. "We wouldn't have to worry about it if someone weren't offering up skin and blood samples to scientists and telling them what to look for. How long would it have taken them to figure it out on their own? Maybe fifty more years, a hundred, two hundred. DNA testing only matters if you have the samples to test." He stabbed a finger against his desk. "What I want to know is how these lab coats got those samples. Unlike you, I think it does matter who's putting us all in danger. *No one* has that right."

His father's mouth tightened, his tone turning condescending. "You're missing the point, boy. We need to be in control of this situation, make sure the only information humans have about us is what we want them to have. That's the only way to protect our people."

Bastian tensed at being referred to as *boy*, a word that hadn't applied to him for almost two decades. His father wanted him on the defensive. Why? He narrowed his gaze at the older man. "Secrecy has protected our people. Why are you so supportive of a traitor?"

His father flinched, and that was when Bastian saw it.

Guilt.

He felt like he'd taken a punch to the gut, and the air rushed out of his lungs. He was glad he was sitting down because his legs might not have held up under the shock. His father wasn't supporting a traitor—he *was* the traitor. There was nothing conclusive to tell Bastian he was right, and yet a lot of little inconsistencies in the last few years clicked into place and suddenly made sense.

Namely, the amount of time his father had been spending with their former enemy—the retired leader of the wereleopards, Hector Leonidas. Michael wasn't one to let go of a grudge that quickly, but those two had been as thick as thieves lately. Good, considering Michael's human stepdaughter had married Hector's oldest son, but to go from ready to rip a man's throat out to having a beer and hanging out with him on a Saturday night was a bit extreme.

Unless the two had been plotting to expose weres to the human world.

Michael crossed his arms, his nostrils flaring. "You're unable to be reasonable about this and can't see the truth when it's right in front of you. Our kind is going to have to go public. We either let it happen or we control it, and you want to stand back and let someone else run the show. That's not how a future Alpha should behave. You disappoint me, boy."

Bastian's assistant appeared in the doorway. "Beta, may I—"

"Leave us, Penelope." Bastian held up his hand. His tone was harsher than he'd intended and the woman cringed and scurried to obey.

His father sniffed, his gaze lingering on the closed door. "Your mother was hoping you'd want that one for more than just a secretary."

"No." There wasn't a single spark of attraction between them, for all that the woman was well-connected in the wolf pack.

"It's time you mated and started producing heirs."

A standard line, another area where Bastian disappointed. His jaw clenched and anger burned away some of his shock at realizing what his father was up to.

"I'll mate when I'm ready and not a moment before." Bastian's voice was every bit as implacable and arrogant as his father's, and he didn't give a damn if that pissed off the Alpha. Even a clan leader couldn't dictate a man's mating, and Bastian wasn't about to give ground on the issue. "Is there something else you wanted to discuss? I have a conference call."

Clearly disliking being dismissed, but not having anything else to say, Michael grunted and slammed out of the room.

Bastian stabbed the button on his intercom. "Penelope, can you get the New York office on the phone? And when you have a moment, grab a cup of coffee for me, please."

Her response was immediate. "Yes, sir. Right away."

It took all his control to remain focused during the call, and then he spent the rest of the day distracted. He *should* have been working on plans for acquiring real estate for a new apartment complex here in Chattanooga. Or any of the other ventures the Lykaios family or wolf clan was looking into. Instead, he spent the time turning facts over in his head.

The leaks had begun around the time Hector and his father had started getting chummy. It had been little things, initially. The sleazy reporter with an "inside source" but the stories had been published in a rag paper no one believed. At first. Then he started getting wider circulation in better news sources. The next thing they knew, there were photos of weres plastered across the internet. Then a big game hunter went after a female fox—a woman under wolf pack protection. Now, they had scientists with DNA proof.

It was too many things in too short a time frame to be coincidence. He'd known it had to be a shifter doing this, but until today, he'd been blind to the idea that it could be his *dad*, the fucking clan *Alpha*, behind it all.

Now what the hell was he supposed to do about it? Standing against the Alpha would be foolhardy, so he had to find a way to go around him. For all of their sakes. He refused to let anyone hurt his people, not even his own father.

"Bastian, I'm heading out for the day." One of his younger brothers, Tomas, poked his head in the door. "You want to grab some dinner?"

"No, I think home is calling my name." So was the bottle of scotch in his kitchen cabinet.

His brother propped his shoulder against the doorjamb, a lazy smile on his face. "Good, because I've got a sweet little she-wolf who wants to cook for me."

"Breakfast in bed?" Bastian arched a brow.

"If I'm lucky." Tomas's gaze dropped to the desk, his forehead furrowing as he caught sight of the newspaper. "The old man talk to you about that?"

Bastian snorted. "*Talking* isn't the term I'd use but, yes, words were exchanged."

"I don't agree with him on this one either." His brother straightened, his face falling into serious lines. He shook his head. "He's crazy if he thinks going public is the right move."

It was on the tip of Bastian's tongue to share his suspicions, but he bit back the words. Starting a family feud wasn't going to help anything. He needed more information. He needed proof. Frustration tightened the muscles in his shoulders, and he felt a headache begin to hammer at his temples again. Yep, this was definitely a night for a healthy dose of scotch. It wouldn't fix a thing, but if figuring out your father was trying to betray his entire species wasn't a day for a stiff drink, he didn't know when an appropriate time would be.

"I'll see you Monday. Have a good weekend. And enjoy your breakfast." Pushing to his feet, he tossed the paper into his briefcase.

Tomas shoved a hand through his hair and looked like he wanted to say more, but shook his head and turned away. "Later, Brother."

The drive home took Bastian through some of his favorite territory, and he felt a little of his tension unwind. Lush green hills and old-growth forest filled with birch, hickory, maple, hemlock and magnolia. The fog that gave the Smoky Mountains their name wound between the trees and curled up over the higher peaks in the distance. He loved it here. Clan land, *wolf* land. Someday his land to rule, his responsibility to safeguard. He'd understood that almost from the day he was born. Expectations had always been higher for him than for any of his younger siblings, but he'd had his father to show him how it was done, had never felt unprepared for the role he had to fill.

Until today.

He turned onto the private road that led to his house. His SUV bumped across the bridge that took him over a rushing creek. And there it was, a sprawling wooden house with lots of windows and a wide porch that wrapped all the way around. Home.

After parking out front, he grabbed his briefcase and dragged his ass inside. He'd never been so glad to see the place in his life. He poured himself a drink, pulled the newspaper out to read again and went out on the porch. A small round table sat between a pair of rocking chairs, and he set his drink down and sank into a seat. Even after picking through the article for any missed details, he didn't find anything that would conclusively link his father to the information leak, but his instincts told him he wasn't wrong.

They also told him that someone approached.

He lifted his face into the wind and inhaled. Wereeagle, diving in fast. He'd barely finished the thought when a flutter of wings brought the massive bird into sight.

"Patrick Aquinas." He raised his glass in a salute as the bird shifted midair and a large naked man landed no more than a foot away. "Been a while since you've made it out here for a visit."

"Wolf Beta." The eagle inclined his head formally, his expression a smooth, professional mask.

Ah, so this wasn't a social call. Which meant Patrick had been sent as a member of the elite werebird Messenger Corps. Birds were dogmatically impartial in all werekind disputes, which made them ideal go-betweens for official communiqués amongst warring factions. Or just for sending a missive you didn't want anyone to know about. Taking a sip of his scotch, Bastian arched his eyebrows. "You have a message for me?"

"Two."

"Let's hear it." He waved the wereeagle into the spare rocking chair. "And sit down. I don't need you waving your junk in my face. Save it for your mate."

That cracked the impassivity on the other man's face, and he smirked, but took a seat. "First, your stepsister Celeste and your cousin Lyra would like to invite you for a family visit."

Now that was interesting. They didn't trust the phones or email for this request. He sat back in his rocker, tapping the folded newspaper against his thigh. "And the second message?"

Patrick crossed his ankles, assuming a casual pose. "My queen would like to offer you…discreet transportation."

"Oh, really?"

He shrugged. "We do own the shifter airline."

Bastian tossed the paper on the table between them. "Who do you think is behind all this?"

The wereeagle hesitated for a moment too long, as if struggling with what he wanted—or didn't want—to say. "My queen has no desire to take sides in this. Birds have always been neutral and will remain so."

"Come on, Patrick." Bastian huffed. "We've known each other most of our lives. I'm not asking for the official royal decree on the matter—I'm asking for your personal opinion."

Another long pause before the wereeagle sighed. "I think Michael and Hector are up to their necks in this shit." His gaze sharpened. "And if I ever have proof they deliberately put my mate in danger, I will rip their throats out. That personal enough for you?"

Patrick had recently married the fox-shifter who'd been stalked by a big game hunter, and Bastian fought a wince at the reminder. His father had gotten himself, and the entire clan by association, into one hell of a tangled mess. Pissing off the eagle queen's closest advisor was not a way to keep relations friendly between their clans. Birds might not get involved in other clans' fights, but they were vicious when someone brought a fight to their doorstep. Not an enemy to take lightly.

"Yeah, that's personal enough." Bastian rubbed a hand over his forehead. "Thanks."

"No problem. I'll assume because you didn't threaten to murder me for accusing your father that you already suspected him too." Patrick nodded to the drink in Bastian's hand. "Got any more of that?"

"I do." He went to get the bottle and another snifter. After pouring a glass, he handed it over to the eagle and resumed his seat. They drank in silence for a while before Bastian spoke again. "If this gets out—I mean really gets out—your neutrality isn't going to mean dick. You'll be up to your necks like the rest of us squabbling, non-neutral species."

Patrick stared down into his scotch. "I know."

It might be a mistake, and the Alpha would most definitely suspect something was up, but the fact that Celeste and Lyra had sent the messenger meant it was serious. Whether or not they suspected Michael and Hector, Bastian didn't know, but there was one sure way to find out. And as much as it would have galled him to go to the leopards a few years back, the werekind world had changed, and he was willing to take the help anywhere he could get it.

He met Patrick's gaze. "I'll accept the ride."

The wereeagle nodded easily and finished his drink. He rose and stepped over to the top stair leading off the porch. "There's a private airstrip on the border between your land and ours. It's used just often enough that no one would notice an extra flight going out, but not so often that you'll need to worry about a lot of witnesses."

It was Friday now, so if Bastian was lucky, he'd be back before anyone noticed he was gone. "I know of the place."

"Be there at dawn. Good luck." The wereeagle shifted and winged away as silently as he'd arrived.

Bastian looked at the headline again and downed the rest of his scotch in one swallow. "Fuck."

CHAPTER TWO

Icy cold fingers ran down Barbara Powell's spine when she reread the headline in the *Times*. It was the eighty-sixth time she'd scoured the article. She'd been up all night, packing her office so she could leave before any of her colleagues came to watch her disgraced departure. She wouldn't give them the satisfaction. And every time she looked at the newspaper, it hit her again. There it was in black and white. Her humiliation was complete. The entire world knew her career was over and she was a laughingstock of the scientific community. Everything she'd worked for was gone in the blink of an eye. Nausea roiled in her gut and she wanted to bend over and howl in pain. But she wouldn't do that. That was what animals did.

And it was animals who'd brought her so low.

The ice inside her solidified to utter determination. She wasn't wrong, no matter what her colleagues said. Former colleagues. If she could prove it beyond a shadow of a doubt, they'd have to believe her.

She needed something conclusive. She needed a live specimen, not just tissue and blood samples.

Her research partner crept into her office, looking as if he was going to cry. "What are we going to do?"

"I should think it would be quite obvious." She arched an eyebrow. "We're going to find one of them and prove our theories are correct."

He swallowed, his prominent Adam's apple bobbing. "How will we do that? You can't just tell by looking."

"You're a scientist, Hastings. Act like one," she snapped, impatient with his stupidity, his weakness. "We'll find one by studying them."

It was well before dawn when Bastian pulled his SUV into the airstrip's small gravel parking lot. He didn't even bother heading into the corrugated metal building that served as the terminal. The scent on the air told him exactly where to go. He grabbed his bag off the backseat and headed for a small jet on the side of the runway.

"What are you doing here, Nico?" Even with his enhanced wolf sight, he hadn't seen the leopard yet, but he could smell him so he knew the other were was near.

"Going to Arizona for a family visit," Nico replied, appearing out of the darkness. He was tall and had an edge of the untamed about him that scared the shit out of most people. Bastian managed to keep his fangs retracted— barely—when confronted with another predator. He could hold his own in a fight, but he had no fight with this man, half-wild or not. Nico's gaze gleamed as if he knew he made other shifters battle their own instincts to attack. "And you, Lykaios? What brings you out this early in the morning?"

"I was invited for a family visit too." It was still a little earth-tilting that they were talking about the same people. Wolves and leopards in one family—who'd have thought they'd see the day?

Nico's presence certainly made this more interesting. It looked like one hell of a meeting was going to take place, with representatives from the wolf, eagle and leopard clans.

Such a thing was unheard of in their world, but this situation with the scientists had the potential to turn their world inside out and they needed to figure out how to deal with it.

The wereleopard arched an eyebrow. "We must be on the same flight. How convenient."

"Who's our pilot?" Bastian took a breath, but didn't get of whiff of anyone closer than the terminal.

"I am." Nico jerked his head to indicate Bastian should climb the short flight of steps to board the jet. Once they were in the front seats, Nico cast a glance at him. "When you have two fledgling eagles in the house, it's best to know a thing or two about flying."

"I see." Bastian looked over his shoulder at the many empty seats in the rear of the plane. "The wife and kids aren't coming?"

"Not this time." The leopard began flipping switches and doing readings for the pre-flight check.

"A shame."

It didn't take long until they were taxiing down the runway. Gravity shoved Bastian back in his seat and the ground rushed away. They turned west, a direction not normally safe for a wolf to go. The US was roughly divided along the Mississippi, wolves ruling the shifters in the east, leopards ruling the west. There were smaller territories carved into each of those halves. The decentralized bear clans were scattered here and there. Werebirds had their mountain sanctuary in the Smoky Mountains not far from wolf headquarters. And dolphins claimed most of the Gulf Coast.

The borderlands along the Mississippi River were wild, dangerous places for shifters. It was where most skirmishes between species broke out, where werekind clinics were most needed. His cousin Lyra had served in one of those border hospitals in New Orleans before she'd married into the leopard clan. He'd visited her there once, had done what he could to tone down the violence, but it still wasn't the safest area. It had gotten better since Hector Leonidas had retired and his sons had taken the reins of power. With two women directly connected to the wolf Alpha in the Leonidas family, the leopards were less interested in continuing the dispute. Hell, that dispute went all the way back to Zeus and Artemis wanting to make the better, more dominate shifter. A fight that should have been put to rest long ago. It was well past time that shifters stopped squabbling amongst themselves and started watching their collective backs.

Continuing to war with the leopards might put his sister and cousin in harm's way, and Bastian had no desire to do so. Whether they now belonged to another clan or not, they were still family, and that counted in his book. Other Alphas and Betas before him might have felt differently, that a person either belonged to the wolf clan or not, and those that didn't might as well be enemies. Bullshit, in Bastian's opinion. His clan and his family rated equally for him, regardless of whether family members mated outside of the wolf pack. Sometimes that meant he had to deal with conflicting priorities, but so be it.

No one promised life would be easy or simple.

His trip today was a case in point. He tried to keep the tension from showing, didn't want to let the other man see any weakness, but getting on this plane had meant turning his back on a lifetime of toeing the line with his father. Sure, he'd argued with his dad, but in the end the Alpha had always gotten his way. Bastian swallowed. If the Alpha got his way now, it could mean disaster for everyone. It came down to what mattered most, what made up the absolute core of Bastian's beliefs. Protecting his family and his clan would always come first. He'd disagreed with his father before, but this was the first time that disagreement was so fundamental that Bastian had to break with everything he'd ever known.

He was walking a high wire and there was no safety net. There was success or there was death. He made no excuses, offered himself no platitudes. If this meeting went the way he suspected it might, the Alpha would consider Bastian's actions treason. Michael could coerce the Wolf Council into putting Bastian to death. His best-case scenario was banishment from clan land. Forever.

If he lost.

If he won…hell, he didn't know what that might mean. Michael being forced to do the bidding of others for once? Michael retiring just as Hector had? Who knew? Bastian took a deep breath, steeling his nerves. This had to be done. To protect his people. He might fail, but he had to try. If he didn't, he wasn't a man worth having as a future Alpha anyway.

He glanced at Nico. "How much did Patrick tell you about our conversation?"

"Everything." A hard glint entered the man's green gaze. "The werebirds have suspected our fathers for a while now. Something needs to be done, so I'm coming to weigh in."

"Glad to have you," Bastian replied. Nico was an expert in security and had experience living within the cultures of two distinct clans. That made his input invaluable even if he was, occasionally, a half-feral pain in the ass.

The leopard's eyebrow arched as he gave Bastian's face an incisive glance. "You know, I think you mean that."

Bastian's lips twisted into a lopsided smile. "Welcome to the brave new world."

Tori glanced up as two tall men entered the lobby of the Leonidas headquarters. She had to blink a couple of times to clear her blurry vision. Four days with no smoking and she was on a killer jag of insomnia. Swan-shifter or not, her bosses were walking softly and watching her with wary gazes. Part of her was amused by that, but mostly she just wanted some sleep and the constant headache to go away. Or a cigarette. That would work too.

Sighing, she rose from her chair to greet the newcomers. One, she knew. Nico Leonidas. The other she hadn't met before, but she knew he was the wolf Beta. He was turned to the side to speak to Nico, so she could only see him in

145

profile, but she took a moment to look him over. Even from this distance, she could tell he was incredibly attractive. Broad shoulders that tapered down to a lean waist and sculpted ass. Long, muscular legs his pants did nothing to hide. He had the same inky black hair as Lyra, and while the cast of his features declared them family, his face was more angular. High cheekbones, square jaw. Mmm-hmm, he was a pretty piece of man-candy.

But when he turned and their eyes met, it was like a spark of electricity zinged over her nerve endings. Her breath seized in her lungs, and a shiver of pure sexual awareness caught her in its grip. Liquid heat sluiced through her body and settled in her sex. Some instinct she didn't understand roared to life and she *wanted* so badly it weakened her knees. His gray eyes burned to silver and he took a step toward her. A wicked, knowing smile curled his lips, as if he understood exactly what kind of affect he had on her. There was a touch of arrogance to his expression, as if he'd seen what he wanted and knew it would be his.

Get a grip, Tori. She shook herself, straightened her spine and stiffened her knees.

Yes, he was attractive and it was clear he knew it. Unfortunately, he also had that alpha male swagger that said he owned the world and had no problem telling people what to do. So not her type. All four of the Leonidases had that same attitude. Five, if she counted their father, Hector. Actually, Hector was the worst of the bunch and Tori hadn't particularly liked him the few times they'd met. She'd mostly wanted to put a boot up his domineering ass.

She was also fairly certain her intolerance of he-man bullshit was why Lyra had decided it would be good for Adrian and Jason to have Tori as an assistant. The thought made her grin.

Uh-oh. The wolf Beta's gaze sharpened on her the way men's did when they noticed she was more than simply pretty—she was drop-dead gorgeous. Her smile did that. Unlike most men, he didn't melt into a puddle of testosterone

146

at her feet. She liked that and wasn't sure she should. His grin turned easy and charming and it annoyed her that her belly did a quivery little flip.

"Hello," he said, the slow Southern drawl making the word sound like it was dipped in honey. "I'm Bastian Lykaios."

He held out his hand to shake and she hesitated while deciding if she really wanted to touch him. That would confirm a chemistry she wasn't sure she was in the mood to acknowledge. His eyes narrowed at her show of resistance, and a non-alpha male would have dropped his hand. Instead, he arched an eyebrow and waited her out.

It was the expression on his face, daring her to take his hand, that did her in. She'd never been one to back down from a challenge.

"Tori Haida." Thrusting her arm out, she wrapped her fingers around his broad palm. His grin spread and she got a flash of wolfish fangs. Oh, yeah. Chemistry out the wazoo. The slight calluses on his hand rasped against her skin, made a shudder pass through her. Her nipples tightened and her sex clenched. He tugged her closer, and his scent hit her. Hot male spiced with a light cologne. His thumb swept over the inside of her wrist, and her pulse leapt in response. His touch left sweet little tingles in its wake, and she had to yank her arm back before she did something really embarrassing. Like jump him. Or start panting.

Someone cleared their throat, and they jerked apart. She turned to see all four Leonidas brothers and three of their wives standing there staring at them. Jason coughed. "I see you've met our administrative assistant."

"Ah. Yes." Bastian shook himself, didn't even glance at her. "I'll take some coffee, Ms. Haida. Black."

Really? *That* was how he covered the overly intimate moment they'd just shared? By treating her like a servant? She resisted the urge to stomp her heel into his toes.

"Well, it's over there." She pointed to the fancy espresso machine on the credenza. "Help yourself."

He frowned. Oh, he didn't like it that she had no intention of waiting on him? Too damn bad. If she didn't do it for her bosses, she sure as hell wouldn't do it for him. She didn't care how fuckable he looked and felt, she wasn't going to roll over and play doormat for him.

Just to piss him off, she faced Nico and gave him a little curtsey. "Prince Consort. I'm honored by your presence."

He didn't crack a smile, but amusement glittered in his gaze. He inclined his torso ever so slightly in a bow. "Ms. Haida."

"May I get you anything? Coffee? Soda?" She widened her eyes as if eager to do his bidding. Luckily, he wasn't stupid enough to take her up on the offer.

"No, I'm good. Thanks."

Jason snorted, Adrian rolled his eyes and Bastian's frown turned into a scowl. He drew in a deep breath as if scenting the air. Then he asked, "What kind of bird-shifter are you?"

"Swan." The word shot out of her mouth like a bullet, and she waited for the smirk she often saw when men realized the too-pretty woman turned into an equally pretty bird.

Fortunately, the man had two brain cells to rub together and kept his face neutral. "I see."

An awkward beat of silence passed before Adrian spoke. "Uh, Tori…there was a conference call on my calendar—"

"Already handled. I rescheduled to Monday afternoon, with an apology." Tori slipped behind her desk and resumed her seat. She looked at Jason. "There's also a cougar-shifter who's been trying to get through to you for days—a border dispute between two groups of mountain lions—but I'm fending her off. You're welcome."

He nodded. "We'll probably have to do some mediating there, but not today."

"I'll pencil them in for late next week. You'll want to speak to both sides, of course." She tapped a few notes into her computer, ignoring everyone as they exchanged greetings and congregated around the espresso machine. There was a tension in the air that she pretended didn't exist. Important things could happen today, and that was one of the reasons she liked this job. She could help make a difference in the shifter world, but this wasn't what she planned on doing forever.

Maybe that was why she'd suddenly decided to give up the cigarettes. It wasn't as if she hadn't known they were bad for her before she'd ever touched one. Some instinct that demanded change had twitched to life within her a few weeks back. Even the healthy routine she'd started hadn't made that instinct quit nagging at the back of her mind. It had eased, but hadn't stopped. Something else needed to change. Maybe her career? She'd come to Refuge Resort on a vacation after she'd graduated college five years ago and had just...never left. She wasn't exactly using her degree in industrial design as a secretary. But other than working on her classic cars, she didn't have a particular direction she wanted to pursue. She didn't have a real passion for anything except hotrods. Probably not a good idea to make any sudden changes there, but she would look into her options. At the moment, anything could hit the chopping block until this instinct stopped prodding. It was beyond irritating and it just made the jonesing for cigarettes even worse.

"Tori?"

She looked up, meeting Lyra's gaze. "Yeah?"

The she-wolf set a hand on Tori's desk, leaning in a bit. "You okay? My cousin didn't—"

"He's fine." She picked up a pencil and twirled it between her fingers. "I'm having the resort's restaurant deliver lunch for you guys. Should be here shortly."

"You'll be having some too." It wasn't a question.

Tori grinned. "Of course. Though I think it's best I not actually join you. I'll eat at my desk." She got up and made shooing motions with her hands, herding them all into the conference room. "Go on, get some good politicking in."

The Leonidas family was used to both her managing them and generally displaying nothing like the submissive personality one would expect of a woman of her species and with her job title.

Everyone but Bastian went where she told them with a minimum of grumbling. He stared at her as if he had no idea what to make of her. Good. She hated fitting neatly into anyone's pigeonhole.

She arched an eyebrow. "You're going to miss your own meeting if you don't get a move on."

Something devilish flickered to life in his gray gaze, as if he wanted to call her on bossing people around, but he refrained from commenting. Anticipation shimmered within her, and she would have loved to hear whatever he was thinking. He sauntered slowly into the conference room. "I'll see you later, Ms. Haida."

The heavy promise in his voice made her insides clench with a need she couldn't decide if she wanted to ignore or pursue. Not that she was going to tell him she was considering tracking him down after work tonight. Arrogant alpha male or not, attraction like this could be explosively fun. For a night or two, anyway. He definitely wasn't the type she'd keep around long. And he was headed home soon, which made pursuing the attraction even more appealing. He couldn't expect more than she wanted to give if he was gone.

"Later? You wish." She grasped the handle to close the door in his face, noting the way his eyes narrowed. After there was a solid slab of oak between them, she let herself chuckle.

Tweaking that wolf's tail was the most fun she'd had since she quit smoking.

CHAPTER THREE

"Don't go, Uncle Bastian!" A little sprite of a girl came pelting across the living room to wrap herself around his leg. Adrian and Cleo's daughter, Daphne. She had the Leonidas green eyes, but looked like her golden lioness mother otherwise. She offered up a gamine grin. "One more spin?"

Even though he was only blood-related to Lyra and Zander's twin sons, Daphne had dubbed him *uncle* the moment he'd shown up for family dinner. She widened her eyes appealingly and he gave in. "Okay, one more."

"Yay!"

He grabbed her under the arms and did a slow series of spins so her legs flew out behind her.

Her gleeful squeals had everyone in the house chuckling. "Lookit me! I'm flying, Daddy!"

Adrian's tone was dry. "She's been wanting to fly since Ajax brought her girls for a visit and they demonstrated what eaglets could do."

After setting the little girl down, Bastian popped a kiss on the top of her head. "We can fly again tomorrow, sweet pea."

"Okay!" She ran off down the hall.

"Thanks for having me over." He shook hands with the men and hugged the women before he left and headed toward the Spanish-style bungalow he was staying in. It was usually reserved for resort guests, but the leopards had arranged for him to use it this weekend.

The dry desert wind filled his nostrils, the scent so different from his verdant Tennessee. His shoes crunched on the gravel path as he walked, and his brain replayed the details of the day. The meeting had revealed too much and not enough at the same time. Celeste and Lyra hadn't suspected Michael's involvement, but beyond their initial shock, neither had seemed particularly surprised. Celeste, especially, knew how adamant their father could be once he'd made a decision.

Shortly after Celeste had mated with Jason, Michael had demanded she return home. So she'd taken a flight to Tennessee, with Hector escorting her. They'd crashed, Hector had disappeared and been presumed dead, and Michael had told Jason that Celeste died. Once Celeste had recovered enough to leave the hospital, Michael let her think that Jason had abandoned her. No matter how much Bastian and his brothers had argued, Michael wouldn't be swayed. But he was the Alpha and they had to obey.

Even six years later, even knowing she was now happy and content in her life, Bastian regretted that he hadn't told his sister the truth sooner.

In the end, Hector had survived and hidden out in werebird territory. He'd suspected the crash had been no accident and he'd been right. It had been a conspiracy between an eagle-shifter who wanted to take the throne from his queen and a wolf who wanted to overthrow Michael. Dragging the leopards into it had been their way of putting up a smokescreen that destabilized the shifter world and made it easier to pull off their usurpation of power. It hadn't worked. Nico had defeated the eagle who threatened his mate and Jason had killed the wolf when he'd attacked Celeste.

Still, Bastian didn't think Celeste had ever fully forgiven the family for their actions. Or inaction. She loved them, but there was a slight distance there that hadn't existed before. Michael liked to put it down to her connection with the leopards and the fact that she lived two thousand miles away, but Bastian saw it differently. Maybe that should have been when he'd broken out from his father's stranglehold on power. Maybe things would be different now if he had, but he couldn't spend his life playing a game of what-if.

He had to deal with what was in front of him.

What made his task more difficult was that his father wasn't a bad man. He loved his family and people, did what he thought was best for them, but his love could sometimes be a smothering thing that didn't allow others to have an opinion of their own. The Alpha brooked no defiance from anyone. Ever.

Rock, meet hard place. And that was Bastian crushed in the middle.

The wolf within him bristled at the untenable position he was in. He needed to get away from everything, needed to leave the million layers of politics behind for a while. Time to go for a run. He'd barely reached the porch to his bungalow before he stripped down and shifted. His body twisted, reforming into a wolf. Fangs and claws erupted, a growl ripping from his throat.

After pivoting on his haunches, he tore through the desert brush and across the open expanse of endless sand and rock. No thoughts, no problems. Just animal instinct and adrenaline. It felt good. He didn't know how many miles he ran, but the wolf ruled the moment and he reveled in the wildness. Topping a rise, he threw back his head and bayed at the moon.

A scent on the wind caught his attention, and he looked down to see a pair of headlights sweeping along the highway from Tucson. Sweet, lush female.

Tori Haida.

There had been one of the few sweet spots in his day. Meeting her. The wolf growled in appreciation. Yes, both man and animal wanted her. Without thinking, he loped toward the road. She'd have to pass right by him on her way back to the resort.

He made it to the highway just before she reached him, and he stepped into the middle of the road, forcing her to stop her shiny red convertible.

She propped an elbow on the door ledge, arching her white-blonde eyebrows. "Is this your way of asking for a ride?"

Since he couldn't speak in wolf-form, she couldn't possibly expect an answer. Good thing, because watching the moonlight caress her features and turn her hair to silver-gilt would have rendered him speechless for a moment. She was, without a doubt, the most beautiful woman he'd ever seen, but it was her smart mouth that intrigued him the most. The swan had the personality of a warrior-trained eagle. Most non-predators learned to watch their step around people like him. Apex predator, powerful, deadly when necessary. He was at the top of the food chain in every possible way, and yet she hadn't flinched. How rare and refreshing.

It also didn't hurt that the moment her hand had slid into his, a lightning strike of awareness had shot up his arm. If it felt that good to touch her hand, what might it feel like to stroke more intimate parts of her anatomy? To have her fingers glide over his skin? A shudder shook him, his body reacting much the same way as it had this afternoon. He wanted her with a fierceness that he hadn't felt for a woman in…longer than he cared to remember. Maybe ever.

Damn inconvenient at a time like this, but then, if he'd read her reaction correctly—and he had, since there was no mistaking the smell of a woman's desire—she might be willing to prove a far better distraction than his whiskey had been the night before.

He shifted back into a human and slid into the passenger seat. "Nice car."

Apparently, that was the right thing to say because she beamed. Damn, she was lovely.

"A '65 Mustang." She patted the steering wheel fondly. "You should have seen the shape she was in when I bought her. I restored her myself."

The leather was plush under his bare ass and every inch of the vehicle looked pristine. "You do good work, Tori."

"Thanks." She put the car in gear and they sped toward the resort at breakneck speed. If it weren't for his enhanced hearing, the rush of the wind would have ripped her words away. "What brings you out here tonight, Bastian?"

"I wanted some quiet and solitude." He sighed, all the complications he'd managed to escape during his run coming back to haunt him. "I need a drink."

She opened her mouth to speak, but he held up a hand. "Yeah, yeah, I know. I can get it myself."

A tiny smile played around the corners of her mouth. "I was going to say we keep a nice stock of adult beverages in the guest houses. You should be able to quench whatever thirst you've got."

He grunted, but said nothing, just watched her. She handled the vehicle with the competence of a racecar driver, another facet of her that didn't fit the girly-girl mold. She fascinated him.

She fidgeted a bit. "I came out here so I could drive fast enough that I needed both hands on the wheel. Can't hold a cigarette that way."

"You're trying to quit?" Somehow, he could see her smoking just to prove to people that she wasn't too cute or too perfect. She seemed to like pushing people out of their comfort zones, and he hadn't missed her defensive tone when she'd admitted to being a swan.

"Yeah. Four days in and it blows. Hard." She wrinkled her nose. "I needed distracting tonight, but the more I try not to think about it, the more I end up thinking about it."

Sounded like his issues with his father. "I know what you mean."

"You need some distraction too?" A lilt entered her voice than made his muscles tighten. Her gaze slid over his body, the hunger he'd seen in her expression this afternoon firing to life again. His body reacted predictably to her interest, her nearness, her feminine scent. Arousal flavored the sweetness of her normal aroma, and his cock went rock hard in moments. He fisted his hands where they rested on his thighs to keep from reaching for her.

"Yes," he said. "Want me to distract you, Tori? I promise you won't think about anything but me for the rest of the night."

She licked her lips. "That's a tall order when someone is trying to kick an addiction."

He smiled wolfishly. "I can make good on it."

"I'll think about it." She looked him over again, her gaze lingering on his groin. He was naked, so there was no missing his erection. Other than raising her eyebrows and grinning, she ignored his physical response to her.

And that annoyed him. "Pull over."

She didn't slow down. "Why?"

"Because I *asked*."

A small humming noise came from her. "You actually didn't ask anything. I did, and you still haven't answered."

The woman was going to make his head explode. "Because I'd like to fuck you right here in the middle of the road. Is that distracting enough for you?"

"Oh, well, in that case." She hit the brakes and the car came to sliding halt. They bumped over onto the gravel shoulder and she shifted into park.

Mouth hanging open, he stared at her. *Really?*

"You were just kidding, huh?" Her tone turned mournful.

He'd been trying to shock her, but she'd turned the tables on him. However, he wasn't above taking advantage of the situation. He unsnapped her seatbelt, wrapped his fingers around her arm and hauled her into his lap. She gave a squeak of surprise, but then grinned.

He shook his head and grinned back. "Has anyone ever told you that you're a little bit crazy?"

Straddling him, she set her hands on his shoulders. Her eyes widened and she chortled. "Only a little bit?"

She was still laughing when he took her mouth. He shoved his fingers into her hair and dragged her down until he could plunder her soft lips. Everything about her was soft. Her hair, her skin, her lush body. He tightened his grip on her silky locks, pulling her head back so he could nip and suck his way down the swan's elegant neck. She struggled against his dominant hold, but he didn't let go, just bit the base of her throat. Her moan fired his blood. His heart pounded like a hammer against his ribs, and his senses expanded.

He scraped his fangs over the sensitive spot where her neck met her shoulder, and she gasped, her hips bucking. The fabric of her shorts rubbing over his cock sent a shudder through him. Wrapping his arms around her, he stilled her motions before she shredded his control.

"Bastian," she gasped. "I need to move. *Please*, Bastian!"

He liked the sound of his name on her lips, especially in that throaty, lust-filled tone. He slipped his hands under her shirt, feeling the warm resilience of her skin. She cupped her palms around his jaw, stroked her hands down his neck, his shoulders, his chest, petting him. It fulfilled a visceral need he'd never even known he had. The wolf within him writhed at the ecstasy of her touch.

Beast and man had never craved anything so much.

Well, the man knew how to distract a girl, that was for sure. He hadn't been lying. She wasn't even naked yet and she was more turned on than she'd ever been in her life.

Touching him was a tactile smorgasbord. Satin flesh stretched taut over steely musculature, crisp curls on his chest tickled her palms. She'd seen all of his goods before he'd gotten in her car, but having her hands on him made molten lava flow through her veins. She wanted, wanted, *wanted*. Her nipples were so tight they ached, her sex wept juices and she knew her panties were soaked. Every time he rocked his hips into her, it made the seam on her jean shorts rub her in just the right place to make her scream with frustration.

He took her lips again and his flavor filled her mouth. Coffee and sugar and something uniquely Bastian. It was a taste she could become addicted to. She shoved that thought out of her mind. There was no sense giving up one addiction just to take on another. His claws scraped against her back as he pushed her shirt up, and she shivered. God, yes. She wanted his hands on her skin.

Breaking the kiss, she grabbed the hem of her top, yanked it over her head and tossed it onto the driver's seat. Her bra followed quickly after, and the night breeze on her sensitized nipples was almost enough to make her sob.

A sub-vocal growl rumbled his chest. His mouth closed over the tip of one breast and she did sob then, it felt so fucking good. He sucked her hard, circled his tongue around her nipple. She felt the prick of his fangs and knotted her hands in his hair, wanting to hold him there.

She undulated against his lap, trying to communicate what she needed. Him, inside her. Right now. But God, the things his talented lips could do. He used his tongue to shove her nipple against the roof of his mouth. It sent a shockwave of delight roaring through her body. Her pussy fisted on emptiness, a precursor to orgasm just from what he was doing to her breasts.

She whimpered, her thighs clamping tight on his hips. "Bastian, Bastian, Bastian…"

His claws extended again and he shredded her shorts to rip them away. A quick tug and the elastic on her underwear snapped under his preternatural strength. Then she was bared for him and he dipped his fingers into her sex.

"Yes!" Her voice carried out over the desert, but she was too far gone to wonder if there might be anyone watching. Talons tipped her fingers and she dug them into his shoulders. "Inside me. Now. Inside me."

His laugh was a rusty sound. "I'd love to make you wait, sweetheart, but I don't think I have the willpower."

"Thank God for that. Hurry up and fuck me, Lykaios."

He groaned, his fingers biting into her hips hard enough to leave bruises. She felt the blunt probing of his cock and pushed her hips down to meet him halfway. The shock of penetration robbed her of breath. Damn, he was big. The stretch was pleasure and pain and so intense it made her cry out.

He froze beneath her, his hands holding her still. "Did I hurt you? Answer me, Tori."

"No," she gasped, shaking her head for emphasis. "Please don't stop."

If he stopped now, she just might die. Need drove her, forced her into motion. She rolled her hips as far as his grip would let her, nudging his dick back and forth within her. The sensation sent tingles skipping down her limbs, but it wasn't enough. She slipped her hands down his chest to rub her thumbs over his nipples. The flat discs beaded for her and a moan spilled out of him. But he still didn't move, didn't let her move. She was filled to the limit and yet there was no surcease in sight. It was maddening and erotic all at the same time.

"Please, Bastian. I need...I have to..." Her thoughts skittered out of coherency as her body throbbed. "Please, please, please."

Hell yes, she was willing to beg if that'd get her what she wanted. Pleasure had no shame. She ground his nipples between her fingers. A raw, feral noise ripped out of him and that was when she knew she'd won. He jerked her down tight to the base of his cock, driving deeper than he'd been before. She watched his face as his control stripped away and the true feral nature of the wolf flashed in his gray gaze. His fangs extended as he lifted and lowered her on his dick. She matched him stroke for stroke. Up, down. Faster and faster. Harder and harder.

The pace he set was punishing. Their skin slapped together as they moved, groans echoing across the desert. It was pure, animalistic lust and she reveled in it. The coarse hair at his groin stimulated her clit with each downward plunge. The head of his cock hit her in just the right spot every time, and goose bumps broke out across her flesh. The way the cool breeze caressed her skin only underscored the heat they generated together. Sweat beaded on her forehead, her breath rushed in little gasps and her muscles burned from the workout.

Her eyes drifted closed as he filled her again and again. Climax began to build so high and hot she thought she'd implode. A few more swift thrusts—that was all she needed to send her flying. And there was nothing a bird liked better than that.

"Look at me, Tori," he commanded. She did as he bid and their gazes locked. A satisfied rumble shook his chest. He reached between them, pressing his thumb against her clit. "I want to see your face when—"

Orgasm slammed into her, dragging her under in a riptide of ecstasy. Her inner muscles clenched and released on his cock in rhythmic waves that made her eyes roll back. He kept moving and it stretched her climax on forever. Every time he penetrated her, an aftershock of orgasm whipped through her. Her pussy clamped tight around his dick, milking the solid length of his shaft. Mewling little cries came from her throat and a tear leaked from the corner of her eye.

One, two, three more strokes and he tensed beneath her. The savage sound he made sent a shiver over her skin and he pumped his come deep within her. His chest worked like a bellow with every breath, lust flushing the angles of his face. His eyes burned to bright silver and the look he gave her was so reverent it made her feel powerful and humble all in one moment. "Tori."

"Bastian." She collapsed in his arms and he cradled her close. They stayed that way for long moments as their breathing slowed and their heart rates returned to normal.

Sheer lassitude sapped her will to do anything other than stay right where she was. *That* was what sex should be like every time. A smug, satisfied grin tugged at her lips.

"How do you feel?" He threaded his fingers through her hair. "Need a cigarette yet?"

A chuckle escaped her in a breathy rush. "Not yet."

"Good." His voice deepened. "Take me back to your place and I'll keep you in that frame of mind all night."

"All night, huh?" She pressed her palms to his chest and leaned back to meet his gaze. "I'm going to hold you to that."

There wasn't an ounce of cockiness in his smile, just the confidence of a man who knew *exactly* what he was doing. "You do that."

She intended to. Scooting over onto her side of the car, she sat on her discarded clothes. "You don't mind if I drive naked, do you?"

Fire hot enough to burn filled his gaze. "Not if you put the gas pedal on the floorboard, Haida. I don't want to wait."

"I like you so much." And then she gunned it, her laughter whipping away in the wind.

CHAPTER FOUR

The nature of shifters meant that most werekind didn't bother with modesty. When they changed forms, they couldn't take their clothes with them, so they learned at a young age that certain amounts of nudity in front of other shifters were normal.

Which meant Bastian had seen a whole lot of naked women in his life. Men too, but their bodies didn't interest him.

None of that had prepared him for watching Tori Haida stroll across her driveway in the buff. The woman was like poetry in motion. Moonlight turned her pale hair and skin to pure silver, but when she turned to grin and beckon him forward, his heart skipped a beat and his cock hardened in visceral reaction to her. The wolf inside him gave an appreciative growl, and man and animal had never been in greater accord than they were at that moment.

Nothing in the world mattered as much as joining with her.

He trailed her up the drive and into the small Spanish-style house that blended with the surrounding desert and matched the look of the rest of the resort. Inside, the furnishings were the same as those in his bungalow, but the decorative touches had Tori's distinct stamp. The living room was painted a muted blue, but several large metal sculptures were mounted on the walls. A smaller one sat in the middle of the coffee table. Each was in a different bright, primary color. It took a moment for him to realize what he was looking at, but then he grinned. "Cars."

She winked. "Yep. One of my brothers—Miles—is a metal sculptor. He made these for me out of classic car scraps."

"Nice."

"Thanks. I'd tell him the wolf Beta said so, but then he'd want to know what you were doing in my house. So not a conversation I want to have. Very protective, my brother." She sauntered into the kitchen. "Wait here."

Ignoring that, he followed her, unwilling to be denied the sight of her, even for a few minutes. "How many brothers do you have?"

She jerked a bit when he spoke, then glanced back at him. "I said to wait in there. You don't listen very well, do you?"

He shrugged unapologetically. When she said nothing, he prompted, "Brothers?"

Normally, he wasn't the type to pry into his lovers' lives. He preferred to keep personal separate from sexual. It was easier that way—it helped everyone maintain the proper perspective on the relationship. Fun, but not deep. Not permanent.

For some reason, Tori made him forget his own rules.

"Three. Orien, Miles and Krispin. Orien is the youngest and the tallest, which annoys Krispin, who's the oldest and the shortest. All very protective." She pulled two glasses and a bottle of gin out of the cabinet. "Don't worry, you'll never have to meet them. They don't live around here. I'm the only one who strayed very far from the nest."

He didn't bother to say anything about the chances a flock of swans had against a wolf, regardless of how protective they might be. Somehow, he had no doubt that they'd each have

163

as ferocious a personality as their sister. "You're the only girl, aren't you?"

"Yep." She tugged the stopper from the bottle. "Is it obvious?"

He leaned his shoulder against the wall, crossing his arms. "You have the same tough-as-the-boys attitude as Celeste. She's the only girl amongst brothers too."

"I know," she said simply.

"Right. You know her."

She poured them both a generous portion of alcohol. "That, and you're the Alpha's children. The werekind papers mention you occasionally."

"True." Though the media did tend to get their facts wrong every now and then, or ladle more sensation onto an event than the situation warranted. Plus, the Alpha's family learned to keep a low profile on truly private matters. Sometimes you won that particular chess match with paparazzi and sometimes you didn't. Still, she knew far more about him than he did about her. "I guess you have me at a bit of a loss then."

"I kind of like you that way."

He grunted. "I'll remember that for the future."

A little chortle came from her. "And take your revenge at the appropriate time when I'm least expecting it?"

"A dish best served cold, I've heard."

"It's true. Trust me. Though hot and fresh revenge is good too." She went to the fridge and got a few pieces of ice for the drinks.

An open sketchbook on the built-in desk to the left of the doorway drew his attention. He bent to get a closer look. Drawings of cars, but unlike anything he'd ever seen before. They were something out of a futuristic movie, so sleek were the lines, and yet something about them reminded him of old hotrods. There were a couple of designs tacked to the wall above the desk and a few more spread out on the wooden surface, each one as fascinating as the next.

"Hey, these are really good. Did you do them?"

"What?" A tiny note of alarm entered her voice. "Oh, it's just a hobby. Don't look at those."

She hurried over and plunked the glasses on the desk, quickly stuffing the sketches into drawers. To see her flustered for the first time was both amusing and endearing.

"Where did you learn to do that?" He snagged one drawing before she could stow it away. "Really, Tori, you're incredibly talented."

"I have a degree in industrial design." She held out her hand and gave him A Look until he gave her back the piece of paper. "Once upon a time I thought I'd like to design cars, but frankly I don't like the lame models they crank out now. All the cars look the same. I don't want to work for people who want me to conform to some standard. I don't do generic. It's not my style."

"So what do you call your style, then?"

"*Nouveau classique.*" She grinned. "Cuz everything sounds cooler in French."

"New classic, huh? Actually, that fits well with what I saw. Can I see more?"

"I have a better idea." She picked up the snifters and offered him one. Her gaze flicked over his body appreciatively. "I have another sculpture made from the chrome bumper of a '57 Chevy pickup mounted over my bed. Wanna see?"

He snorted and accepted a glass. "Having you use the word 'mount' in the same sentence with 'bed' is enough to make all the blood in my brain rush south."

Her gaze dropped to his cock, a grin blooming on her full lips. "I have no problem with that."

"Excellent." He clinked his tumbler against hers in a small toast. They drank in comfortable silence for a moment, but he could smell the rising scent of her arousal. It was the headiest aphrodisiac he'd ever known, and his dick grew stiffer. He finished his drink in two swallows and set the snifter aside. "Show me your etchings, Ms. Haida. Now."

"Since you asked so nicely." She chuckled, drained her glass and dropped it on the counter with a small *thunk*.

The sway of her hips lured him like a Lorelei as she headed down the hall. There was no way he could resist. Not that he tried. She flipped on the light and made a sweeping gesture. "My etchings. Sculpture. Whatever."

He barely spared it a glance. Shiny metal was not what he wanted to focus on in Tori's bedroom. He stepped up behind her, his hands cupping her luscious ass. She pressed back into his touch, her head falling forward. He nuzzled her nape, dragging in the hot, erotic scent of her. Sex and sweat and female desire. And Tori. Just Tori. It was the most arousing smell he'd ever experienced, like a hit of an incredibly potent drug. His cock throbbed and he ached to be buried inside her again.

Turning her head, she tipped her face up for a kiss. He took her mouth with a fierce hunger, and it was all lips and teeth and tongues. The coppery tang of blood hit his taste buds, and it made his wolf struggle for control of the moment. It wanted to take, to claim, to throw aside the veneer of civility and be the rutting, ferocious beast. His fangs extended, punching through his gums. He growled and spun her until her cheek pressed against the wall next to the door.

"Bastian." Her hands moved back to grasp the outsides of his thighs, her body arching into his. His fangs scored her shoulder, his tongue flicking against her flesh. A gasp spilled from her and her talons dug into his legs. The pain drove another shaft of lust through him, and he nudged his knee between her thighs, opening her for his possession.

Her hips tilted in invitation. "Fuck me hard, Bastian. I feel the need for some serious distraction."

"My pleasure." He thrust deep and hard, hilting himself in one swift motion.

She moaned. "And mine."

The tight clasp of her slick sheath was enough to make his skull explode. He shuddered and closed his eyes. Dear God, she felt so fucking good he had to hang onto his control with the tips of his wolf's claws. He didn't want to go so wild that he hurt her. Sweat beaded on his forehead and he clamped his hands around her waist to keep her from moving. She chuckled and squeezed her inner muscles around his shaft.

His eyes flared open, and his hips bucked in reaction. They both groaned. His restraint crumbled and he slammed deeper inside her. Again and again. No finesse, no gentleness. Her palms braced against the wall, her talons dug into the plaster and she pushed back into his thrusts. He set his hands over hers, holding her in place while he fucked her. His lungs burned as he worked his cock in her pussy. The feel of her smooth skin sliding against his was mind-blowing.

Nothing—*nothing*—had ever felt so amazing in his life.

They moved in perfect sync. Her back bowed every time he plunged in. The slap of their skin and the scent of sex filled the room, musky and earthy, driving his lust to new heights. A low hiss erupted from her, the swan coming to the fore. He could see the bird within flashing in her gaze, the flicker between her normal irises and those of the animal. He growled in appreciation of her struggle—his wolf fought to take over, to make this wild encounter even more so.

Needing the taste of her on this tongue, he opened his mouth over her shoulder. He groaned as her flavor flooded his taste buds. The wolf wanted to howl, and some instinct screamed to life within him, wrenching control away from the human as the wolf took over. He sank his fangs into her flesh, a sense of carnal possession and connection roaring through his body. She screamed and he felt her come around his cock, her inner muscles pulsing in rhythmic spasms. It only made him dig his fangs deeper. *Yes.* Wolf and man merged into one mind, one consciousness, one understanding. This woman belonged to him, every side of his nature claiming her. He threw back his head and snarled, and it took everything in him not to shift then and there.

Whipping her head to the side, she bit his wrist, just above where he had her hands pinned to the wall. Her teeth sank in, and he felt the claiming rip through him.

Mated.

He exploded into orgasm, pounding into her body, possessing and possessed. Come jetted from him, filling her as her sheath milked his dick. The orgasm went on forever, draining every ounce of energy out of him.

They sank to the floor in a boneless heap, not even bothering to try to make it to the bed. Blood rushed in his ears, and he could hear nothing over the pounding of his heart. He turned his head to look at her, saw her breasts heaving as she fought for breath. Her eyes were closed, but a little smile curled up the corners of her mouth.

God, she was beautiful.

And she was his *mate*.

A feeling of utter contentment suffused Tori. It was the foreignness of the sensation that woke her. Eyes still closed, she frowned. Birds chirped cheerily outside her window, and light filtered through her eyelids. It was morning, but the usual jangling of instincts and nagging headache were absent for the first time in days. She wasn't twitching with the need for nicotine or caffeine. Everything inside her was quiet, peaceful...serene.

A long, slow breath escaped her. She grinned and stretched against the mattress. Awesome. She felt awesome. The tips of her fingers encountered warm, resilient flesh.

Memories flooded in, the night before exploding through her mind. Her eyes flared wide, she bolted upright and her hand went to the back of her shoulder. A shudder passed through her, a lightning flash of sensation shooting straight to her pussy. Heart pounding, she sucked in a deep, calming lungful of air. His scent hit her, along with a hint of the sex they'd had. Repeatedly. All night long.

Oh, Jesus Christ. What had she done? Everything had felt natural and perfect the night before, but they'd *marked* each other. As mates. She was mated to the next wolf clan Alpha. Holy fucking shit. Pulling her knees up to her chest, she wrapped her arms around her legs. It was all she could do not to rock herself in a fetal position. There were no excuses she could give. She hadn't had enough booze to pardon this level of stupidity. She'd known what she was doing when she bit him—she just couldn't resist after he'd marked her.

Pinching her eyes closed, she shook her head. Panic threatened to blast through her control, and she tightened her arms around her legs, her nails digging into her skin.

He made a noise, shifting to resettle on the sheets. Turning her head, she looked at him. The intensity that usually seemed to radiate off Bastian had disappeared. Hair tumbling over his forehead, he was almost boyishly innocent in his sleep. A tiny smile curved his lips.

Something loosened deep inside her, something she didn't want to acknowledge at all. So she nudged him in the ribs, far less gently than she probably should have. There was no reason she should have to deal with this mess on her own—it was his problem too. "Hey. Wake up."

He grunted, a line forming between his brows. Silver eyes locked on her. "Good morning."

"Well, it's morning anyway." She squeezed her legs together, wishing she'd grabbed some clothes before she'd woken him. Normally, she didn't care about her state of dress, but somehow she felt more stripped naked than she'd ever been in her life. This man she'd only met yesterday was her mate. It was like a drunken Vegas wedding gone way the hell wrong.

Because she was now mated to the wolf Beta. Fuck. Fuck, fuck, *fuck*. Or maybe not, since fucking was what had gotten her into this in the first place. That, and her need to be distracted from the cigarettes. Which made her body suddenly remember that mating euphoria didn't cancel out addiction. A sudden headache bloomed at her temples.

Groaning, she scrubbed a palm down her face. "I really need a cigarette. No, I need to fucking chain smoke an entire carton."

"Wow, yeah." His voice was still rough with sleep, the huskiness far too sexy for her peace of mind. "That's exactly what a man wants to hear the morning after he's mated."

She snorted. "You know what I mean, Lykaios. What have we done? This...this..."

Reality hit her in a sudden rush, and this time there was no forcing down the panic. It felt like all the oxygen was sucked out of the room at once, and she couldn't breathe, couldn't think, couldn't speak. The room spun before her eyes in sickening circles, but then hard arms came around her, and she was cradled against a broad chest.

"Breathe, sweetheart. Just breathe. It's going to be okay."

The deep rumble of his voice was comforting on a level that scared her. She tried to push out of his embrace, but he tightened his grip and rocked her gently.

"It's all right, sweetheart," he crooned, stroking a hand down her hair. "Everything's going to be all right."

"How?" The hot sting of tears hit her eyes, and she clenched her fists to try to hang on to her composure. "How could it possibly be all right?"

His fingers buried in her curls. "I don't really know yet, but we'll figure it out."

While that was probably supposed to soothe her, make her feel like they were in this together, that thought alone was enough to freak her out. Her muscles tightened, and her mouth went dry, her heart rabbiting in her chest. Dread tangled and tripped over horror within her. She would swear her life flashed before her eyes. One night, one choice, and all her freedom just got wrenched away. Being the mate of a man like him meant never-ending expectations and politicking, meant her tinkering with cars and displaying funky artwork were out the window.

What had she done? That was the question that kept pounding in her head. What had she done? *What the hell had she done?*

Mating was something a shifter could never escape. There was no undoing it—there was nothing as civilized as a human divorce for her kind. It was too late to flee, because there was no way to out-fly herself. She felt like a cage snapped around her, locking her in, clipping her wings and keeping her grounded.

Forever.

CHAPTER FIVE

Bastian went back to his bungalow, showered and dressed for another day of meetings with the Leonidases. Tori and Bastian arrived at the office separately, didn't so much as look at each other and studiously ignored the pointed glances from the others. Tori was dragged into the meeting to take notes and, of course, the only chair available was the one next to him. No escaping the awareness that sparked between them.

He wasn't sure if the others could still smell her on him— he'd never been able to sense that a person was mated—but with him wearing long sleeves and her wearing a jacket over her blouse, he was certain they hadn't seen the new mate marks. But he *could* sense the intense curiosity of everyone in the room, so the secret was out. Or maybe it was just obvious Tori and he had slept together.

He didn't know, but he did know he hadn't slept much with the marathon sexfest, so he was short-tempered and irritable and covering it with the kind of excruciating politeness that made his sister and cousin wince. They knew him too well, which somehow added to his annoyance.

Even though he was ignoring Tori, it also pissed him off that Tori ignored him. It made no sense, and he wanted to kick his own ass for the stupidity. Clenching his jaw, he glanced across the table at Jason, the leopard leader.

No more skirting the subject, Bastian threw down the question no one had wanted to ask. "Well, if we all suspect our fathers, the question now becomes what are we going to do about it? What are our next steps?"

Jason tapped a thumb against the wooden tabletop. He looked at Celeste for a moment, then exchanged glances with each of his brothers. The silence stretched to a breaking point. He leaned back in his chair. "We need proof. There's no way to confront men with that much power and influence in our world without irrefutable evidence."

"They're too careful for that," Zander commented. "If it were that easy to get evidence, we'd have it by now."

"Maybe not," Nico and Bastian said at the same time. Bastian gestured to let the other man speak.

Nico nodded. "We've been digging for information, but have any of us gone to our contacts and said, 'these are the men we suspect. Look into them, specifically?' I know I haven't. I just wasn't sure enough."

"Exactly," Bastian agreed. "We have a preponderance of circumstantial evidence, hunches and gut instincts, but nothing conclusive. However, we haven't gone digging into our fathers' activities, not really. And how many of our informants would have the balls to go after a clan leader—retired or otherwise—without at least some subtle encouragement from us?"

"Mine wouldn't." Adrian shrugged. "Likely they suspect what we suspect, but have probably turned the same blind eye that we have. They didn't want to see it."

Zander snorted and scrubbed a hand over his hair. "Hell, I don't really want to see it. The old man has finally lost his ever-loving mind. Thinking you know best until you betray your own race? Shit."

"That hits the nail on the head," Tori said, speaking up for the first time. She hadn't written down a thing, despite her being ostensibly brought in for note taking. "We could all be screwed on this one." She glanced at her two bosses. "Okay, I have a few people I can ask discreetly, which is probably why you guys wanted me here today."

Jason nodded unapologetically. "As you said, all our asses are on the line right now. You always know everything almost before it happens." He cocked an eyebrow. "It's been an annoying habit for years, but it means you have contacts none of the rest of us do. Use them."

"Aye-aye, captain." She gave him a little salute, but stress lines formed around her mouth and eyes.

She seemed as tired and wrung-out as Bastian felt. It was the first time that day he'd really let himself *look* at her since they'd arrived this morning. Hours ago. She'd been obviously upset when she realized they'd marked each other, but he'd missed the fact that her anxiety level hadn't lowered at all. In fact, she appeared even more strung out than she had when she'd woken him. Not a good sign, especially with a woman as unpredictable as Tori.

The Leonidases and he made plans for getting in touch again after they'd had a chance to dig into their fathers' affairs and then broke for lunch. Nico and Bastian would be heading back home after the meal, and it hit Bastian that he'd have to leave Tori behind. Something close to panic gripped his gut. No. He couldn't leave without her. Everything inside him rebelled at the very thought. They were mated, thus they belonged together. She'd just have to get used to it. And she was unlikely to do so from thousands of miles away.

He tossed his sandwich on the table and rose to go search for his mate. She'd disappeared with an excuse that she needed to use the restroom, but that was fifteen minutes ago. Drawing in a breath, he followed the sweet smell of her until he reached a room filled with filing cabinets. She was bent over an open drawer, and he had to admire the way her skirt pulled tight across her backside.

He'd been watching for only a few moments when her muscles tensed and her head made a little jerky half-turn. The movement was very bird-like, and very much the action of prey who'd sensed they were being hunted.

"Yes, Bastian?" She didn't even look at him, but he liked that she automatically knew it was him. He had no idea how sensitive a swan's nose or ears were, if her senses told her it was him or if it was something else. Did she also have that *awareness* that told him whenever she was near?

"Come with me to Tennessee." It was not quite an order, but the tone wasn't one that invited discussion on the matter. It was a tone he'd learned from his father.

Still, in the rational part of his mind, the human part that wasn't reacting to animal instinct, he had to ask himself what the fuck he was doing. This was the worst possible time to try to establish a relationship, to get mated. But sometimes the wolf's instinct ruled, and the animal within had declared the time here and now and the woman to be a shifter not of his species. An infuriatingly independent, stubborn, smart, beautiful woman. A *swan*.

This was insane. Clearly, he'd lost his damn mind.

And yet, what came out of his mouth just continued the madness. "I have to go home, and I want you to come with me, Tori."

She finished tucking a file into the drawer, bumped it closed with her hip, and turned around. She folded her arms. "I live here. I work here."

"And?" He kept his pose casual, his voice reasonable. "They don't give you vacation? I'm just talking about a visit to see if we can sort out this mating business."

Her eyes narrowed, as if she didn't quite trust what he was saying. Smart woman. He definitely wasn't as reasonable as he sounded, but he'd say whatever he had to say to get her home with him. The wolf in him would not leave her. He'd rather not tie her up and toss her on the plane, but it might come to that.

Her lips pursed. "Uh-huh. And when I want to leave at the end of the visit and you don't want me to?"

It was all he could do to hold in a growl. He didn't quite manage to maintain a laidback attitude, but at least he didn't throw her over his shoulder he-man style. But, damn, he wanted to. "We're mated. It's a done deal."

Oozing nonchalance, she shrugged. "Mate in haste, repent at leisure."

His brow lowered, and a muscle began ticking in his jaw. "So, you don't accept our mating?"

Anger flashed in her gaze, along with something almost…scared. "I don't accept that it means you own me and tell me where to go and when. *I* still make the decisions about *my* life."

Tori…scared? He tried to see beyond the aggressive tone. The fastest way to defeat an opponent was to put himself in their shoes, then use their weaknesses against them. Not that he wanted to take advantage of his mate's weaknesses, but from her point of view, he could see how terrifying this situation could be. In the end, because of his position in the wolf clan, his life was less flexible. He had to live on pack land; his career wasn't exactly optional. He was born to the job. Which meant it was her life that would be uprooted and changed completely if they were going to live together as mated couples should. She had every right to be upset, worried, scared.

Even knowing all that, the wolf clawed inside him, demanding its mate accept what they were to each other. "Last time I checked, slavery was illegal in this country. I never claimed to own anyone, least of all you. I haven't taken your choices away. *You* decided to mark me too, Haida." He leaned against the doorjamb. "It wasn't all me, it was you too. Plus, my instincts demanded it. And I'm guessing yours did as well."

A reluctant grin tugged at her lips. "Yeah, like I'd confess to anything like that."

He winked. "It would certainly play into my nefarious plot if you did."

"Very nefarious." She tossed her hair over her shoulder. "Fine, you want me to come to Tennessee? Then I want your word—as the wolf Beta *and* as a man—that if I come to visit you and then I want to leave, you will let me go."

Damn, she'd maneuvered that well. She had him over a barrel and she knew it. He had to admire that, even while he was annoyed by it. He already knew he'd give her what she wanted, because as much as he might fantasize about tying her to his bed and keeping her there forever, that wasn't realistic. She had to be willing. Still, he stared her down for a full thirty seconds before she jammed her fists down on her hips and hissed at him swan-style.

"Your word, Bastian, or you can hop your canine ass on that plane and leave. Without me. I'm sure it'll be a fun trip with Nico for company."

He bit back a grin, enjoying ruffling her feathers as much she had no doubt enjoyed harassing him the day before. "You have my word."

Her pert chin firmed. "Your word that…"

Really? She felt it was necessary to have him spell it out? That was insulting. He ran his tongue down a long fang. "You have my word that if you come to visit me and then you want to leave, I will let you go."

"And you won't encourage or allow anyone else in your clan to stop me?"

And that was where his temper snapped. "I'm not a fucking kidnapper, Tori! I don't have to hold a woman hostage to keep her around. If I say I'll let you go, then I will. Give me some credit."

She winced, glancing away. "You're right. That was over the line. I'm sorry."

He jabbed a finger at her, noting it was tipped with a deadly talon. "I didn't force any of this on you, so don't act like I did."

She blew out a breath, the sound rife with frustration. "I'm not, but you are making assumptions about what this means. Marking you does not automatically mean that I have to give

177

up my job, my house, *my life*. And don't act like you aren't thinking that, because I know you are."

He was wise enough to keep his mouth shut.

Now it was her turn to stab a finger at him, also talon-tipped. "You may be all that and a bag of chips in the shifter world, but here in this room, we are equal. You're not in charge of me and I don't answer to you." She waved that hand around. "My life is just as important to me as your life is to you."

He sighed, knowing she had a point, but seeing no way around it. Unsolvable problems—the story of his life lately. "How do we make this work, then?"

Her head fell back against the file cabinet. "I don't know."

Stepping forward, he curved his hands around her shoulders, feeling the delicacy of her joints. Possessiveness and tenderness welled within him, emotions he didn't usually associate with his lovers. But she wasn't just his lover, was she? She was his mate. "I don't want to give you up, and I don't want to give up the life I lead."

She met his gaze, her lips twisting. "Neither do I. On all counts. Though admitting it probably plays into that nefarious plot of yours."

A chuckle rumbled in his chest and he shook his head. "Just…come for a visit. Because neither of us wants to be apart right now. If I could take this slow and easy, I would, but I can't. I have to go back and deal with my father. I have to try and stop this information leak." He stroked a lock of her silky hair back. "But I want you with me. I want you the way I have never wanted anyone or anything in my entire life. Say you'll come, Tori."

She closed her eyes, and he watched the struggle on her expression. He'd felt the same struggle himself, so he waited her out. If this mating thing was working on her the way it was working on him, there was no way she could resist. She groaned. "Let me talk to Adrian and Jason about taking time off."

"Okay."

She speared him with a glare. "This doesn't mean—"

He cut her off with a swift kiss. "I know."

He'd gotten what he wanted—there was no need to argue further. It wouldn't help. The decision was made. The decision had been made the moment they'd marked each other. Maybe even the moment they'd met.

Thankfully, her bosses had given her the impromptu time off with no questions asked. Tori had a bad feeling that they'd already figured out why she was leaving…and that they didn't expect her to come back. That last part annoyed the shit out of her, but since she didn't really want to talk about it, she couldn't very well argue against people's assumptions. Frustrating.

That was a perfect description for the whole situation: damned frustrating.

She crashed out on the plane ride east. Not shocking considering she'd probably gotten all of forty-five minutes of sleep total the night before. The slumber also gave her the opportunity to escape what could only have been an awkward conversation between scary-as-hell Nico, her new mate, and her. No thanks. Sleep beckoned and Tori took the easy way out. Sue her.

When she woke, she found herself cradled in a set of familiar arms. "Bastian."

"Shh." He brushed his lips over her brow, and the scent of him was comforting. "Go back to sleep, sweetheart."

She sighed and let herself drift back into dreamland.

A rough bump jolted her awake and she bolted upright. A moment of mind-bending confusion gripped her. She was in a car and it was nighttime. What the hell? "This isn't the plane."

Bastian's deep voice filtered through the darkened vehicle. "No, this is the road to my house. We just turned off the highway."

She blinked owlishly and licked her lips. "Oh."

He chuckled. "Not a morning person, huh?"

"Not a wake-up-bouncy person, no matter what time of day I'm snoozing." She rubbed the sleep from her eyes, but it didn't clear the grogginess from her brain. "Give me caffeine and no one gets hurt."

He made a little humming noise that was both sympathetic and amused. "I have beans I can grind and a coffee maker at the house. In the pantry there might even be a French press my mom bought me."

Caffeine, yay. She glanced at his shadowy outline and smiled. "That sounds promising."

"I'm glad. We'll be there in a few minutes."

Trees surrounded them, towering above the SUV. It reminded her a little of where she grew up in the Rocky Mountains, though the trees were different. Nothing like the desert she'd been living in for the last few years. A break in the forest brought them to a clearing, and she could make out the darkened bulk of a house with a few outbuildings in the distance. One looked like some kind of barn or maybe a massive garage. Something to explore later, since she'd be here for two weeks.

Bastian pulled up in front of the house. "Forgot to leave a porch light on."

As he shut down the vehicle, she popped open the door and slid to the ground. She had pretty decent night vision as a bird-shifter, so she easily navigated the uneven gravel drive to the back of the SUV to get her bag. Slinging it over her shoulder, she followed Bastian up the porch steps.

He flipped on the lights as he stepped inside, then waved her in while he punched in a code on his security system. She blinked as her eyes adjusted to the glare and took in the living room. Big, cushy leather sofa and chairs, gleaming wood everywhere—floors, built-in cabinets, fireplace mantel, even the ceiling fan. She set her bag aside and wandered around, poking her head in doors as she went. An office lined with bookshelves, a dining room that appeared mostly unused and a guest bedroom that looked even less used. A flight of stairs went up to a second floor, and she slid her finger over the polished newel post as she walked by.

Bastian trailed after her, but said nothing. It wasn't until she glanced back at him that she realized he was nervous. Bastian? Nervous? The man hadn't flinched when he found out his one-night stand had turned into his mate, which had sent her straight into a tailspin. *Now* he was uncertain?

He straightened to soldierly attention as she turned to face him. Then it hit her. He was worried she wouldn't like his house. The wolf Beta actually wanted her approval. Something painful and sweet squeezed inside her when that realization hit home.

Holding back the onslaught of tender emotion that threatened to swamp her, she offered up a grin. "Nice place you have here, Lykaios, but where's the television? There's a NASCAR race I was hoping to watch this week."

"Inside the cabinet. I also have one in my bedroom." He gave her a small grin in return, his stance easing a little. "If that interests you."

She'd have to be half dead for that not to interest her. *Bastian. Bed. Mmm-hmm.* Yeah, she should probably hold out on him so he didn't think he had this whole mating thing sewn up, but if she had the willpower to resist, she'd have stayed in Arizona.

Biting her lip, she gave him a flirtatious wink. Heat began smoldering in his gaze and it was all she could do not to jump him then and there. After spinning away, she scuttled down a short hall past the stairs. "Kitchen's this way?"

"Yes. Bathroom's on your left, if you need it."

Now that he mentioned it... "I do, actually."

"Me too. It was a long flight, and I've never quite been able to make myself turn my back on Nico."

"Aw, he's a cute cuddly kitten."

One dark eyebrow rose. "Really?"

"No, he's a terrifying motherfucker, but he's perfect for our queen, so I like him for that alone. Plus, they have the cutest eaglets and it amuses the shit out of me that *that* leopard's got a flock of birds to contend with." She gave him her most guileless smile. "He deserves it, don't you think?"

Bastian's laughter rolled out, mellow and sexy. "Absolutely. I couldn't agree more."

They shared a conspiratorial grin.

He gestured toward the bathroom door. "Ladies first."

"Don't mind if I do." Southern gentleman, how nice. Her mom would say they were overrated, but since Tori's dad and brothers were big, burly, grumpy types, her mom's opinion wasn't shocking. Tori kind of liked it though. Not that she'd admit it aloud, but still. Nice.

A few minutes later, she found Bastian banging around in the kitchen. He had two plates and two bowls on the counter. Something sizzled on the stove and he stepped over to flip what looked like a couple of cheese sandwiches. The scent of food floated in the air, and her stomach gave a grinding gurgle to remind her that she'd slept through dinner.

"Come watch these and slide them onto the plates when they're done, would you?" He handed over the spatula and scooted past her to make a run for the restroom.

"Mmm." The tops of the sandwiches were a perfect golden brown and cheese oozed from the sides. They looked divine. Of course, leather boots might look tasty right about now, she was so hungry. After lifting one corner to take a peek at the bottom, she quickly transferred the grilled goodness to the waiting plates.

The microwave mounted over the oven beeped and she pushed the button to open the door, finding a plastic tub filled with chicken noodle soup. "Oh, awesome."

Rifling around in drawers revealed a ladle for the soup and she divided it between the two bowls. The combined scents were making her stomach do backflips of anticipatory joy.

"I figured grilled cheese and chicken noodle were pretty universal in their appeal, so I doubted you'd object." Bastian shot an amused glanced at her noisy midsection as he returned.

She patted her belly. "No objections, just mild starvation."

"Also?" He reached out a long arm and snagged a full pot off the coffeemaker. "Liquid caffeine, as requested."

"You're a god among men, Lykaios," she said, *sotto voce.*

He shook his head, his gray gaze gleaming with mirth. "I've always dreamed of a woman saying that to me. Of course, in my dreams, we were in bed together, but I'll take what I can get."

Tori laughed in his face, and he waggled his eyebrows before handing over a heavy ceramic mug filled with dark-roasted deliciousness.

They dove into the food without further comment, and Tori almost licked the bowl, the soup was so amazing. "This can't have come from a store. It's too good."

"My great-aunt, Hattie Jane, has a secret recipe that she guards with her life. My aunt—Lyra's mom—is terrified the old lady is gonna die before she hands it over."

Tori widened her eyes theatrically. "A completely legitimate fear. This secret *cannot* die with her."

"She gives me tubs of it every time I visit her, which I make a point to do on a regular basis. I freeze what she gives me for those days when I want something awesome, but don't want to cook it myself."

She cast him a dubious glance. "You cook?"

His expression turned mildly offended. "That sandwich didn't make itself."

Seriously? This was what he called cooking? She just took a bite of the grilled cheese and tried to keep the amusement off her face.

"Wow, you really bought that, huh?" He chortled.

"So, you can't cook?"

"Yes, I can." He paused while he polished off the last of his dinner. "My best work is done outside on the grill though. I make some killer barbeque sauce for my pulled pork, brisket, ribs. Real Southern style. None of that shit they just *call* Southern elsewhere. It's not the same, trust me."

Even after that fabulous meal, she had to admit her mouth watered a little. She loved good barbeque. "Well, you'll just have to prove it to me."

"I will."

They looked at each other for a long moment, that tiny sizzle of attraction humming like a live wire between them. Warmth pulsed through her and she swallowed, trying to contain the feeling. With him, there didn't seem to be any control, and that worried her. She grabbed her dishes and went to the sink to wash them.

Bastian came up behind her, wrapping his arms around her in order to deposit his dishes. "I could have done that, sweetheart. You're a guest here."

"It's no problem." Her voice came out low and breathy. The heat of him surrounding her made her brain turn to mush. He nuzzled the back of her neck, and desire bloomed deep in her belly. Wetness slicked her sex, a reaction that had never been so intense with any other man. A dangerous thought, but she couldn't deny the truth of it.

When he rubbed his lips over her shirt, brushing across the mate mark on the back of her shoulder, an electric shock zapped through her. Her shifter nature meant it had already healed completely, but the mark was so sensitive it had become an excruciatingly erogenous zone. Utensils dropped from her nerveless fingers, and she bit her lip to hold in a moan.

"I can smell how wet you are for me, Tori." He reached out and shut off the faucet, then turned her to face him. "God, I want you."

She grabbed his ears and hauled him down to kiss him. There was nothing tentative or gentle about this—it was rough claiming that only made her burn hotter. They fought for control of the contact, nipping and sucking at each other's mouths. She threaded her fingers in the satin of his hair, holding him close. He ran his palms over every inch of her he could reach, leaving fire licking over her flesh everywhere he touched. So good, so amazingly good. When he squeezed her breast and zeroed in on her nipple, she bucked against him. Her sex clenched on emptiness, and she wanted his hard cock thrusting inside her.

The ridge of his erection dug into her stomach and she couldn't resist the temptation. She drifted her hands down his shoulders, his chest, his abs and then unfastened his zipper to dip her fingers inside. He was perfect, long and thick. Moisture beaded at the tip of his dick and she smeared it across the bulbous head. He jerked and shuddered, pressing into her touch.

She broke her mouth away from the kiss, letting her head fall back as she fondled him. He slid his tongue down her neck until he could bite the base of her throat. Lust fisted within her and she rolled her hips into his to communicate her need. "Bastian, I…"

"Yes?" His teeth scraped over the sensitive tendon that connected neck to shoulder.

"Um…I think I want to watch TV now."

He paused for a moment, his ragged breath rushing over the damp skin he'd just kissed. "The one in my bedroom?"

Nodding, she ran her fingertip around the crown of his dick. "Right now."

She felt his lips curve against her throat, and then he snapped his arms around her and she was airborne. A squeak escaped her as she landed ass-up over his broad shoulder. All the blood rushed to her head, and the world spun in a dizzying circle when he turned to head for the staircase.

Laughing, she swatted his firm backside. "Lykaios, put me down!"

"Nope." He hurried up the stairs, holding her legs against his chest to secure her in place.

"You don't listen very well." She shoved her hand down the back of his open pants, slipping in to tease the cleft of his buttocks.

They reached the top of the stairs, and he moved down a hallway. He froze in a doorway when she pressed in to tease his anus. His legs were braced apart to hold her weight, which made it easier to push her fingertip into his ass.

He groaned and clutched at the doorjamb. "Wh-what are you doing?"

A stupid question she didn't bother to answer. Instead, she added another finger, sliding deeper into him. He shuddered and she grinned.

"I like ass play," she purred. "It looks like you do too. Isn't that nice?"

"Jesus."

She heard him swallow, and then he moved with that lightning speed of his. He strode forward and flipped her so she bounced against the bed. She saw a flash of straight white teeth before he turned away. "I'll be right back."

Propping herself on her elbows, she watched him walk toward what she thought might be a bathroom or a closet. He stripped as he went, and she got a very nice view of the bunching muscles in his backside. Mmm-hmm. The man was built like a Greek god. A light flipped on and he disappeared through the door. Definitely a bathroom.

While he was gone, she sat up and slowly undressed while looking around at his room. Heavy oak headboard framed by simple rounded bedposts, matching nightstands and dresser. She tossed her clothes over the side of the mattress. The walls were painted a medium blue similar to her living room in Arizona, which was unsettling for reasons she couldn't quite name, and the comforter on the bed was a deep navy blue with piping the same shade as the walls. The sheets and pillows also matched the blue paint.

"Your room is color-coordinated," she called. "Are you sure you're single?"

"My mom helped me pick everything out when I bought the place. She told me she was afraid it'd look like a frat house otherwise, but I think it just gave her an excuse to shop." He stepped out of the bathroom carrying a small bottle. "And, no, I'm not single. I'm recently mated."

The shock of that statement made the breath wheeze out of her lungs, and her heart tripped against her ribs. But she didn't have time to freak out because he held the bottle up for her to see. Lube. Oh God. She could guess what he wanted to use that for. A spear of need went straight to her core. He twisted the top off the bottle and pulled away a protective seal.

"Roll over." He squirted some of the clear liquid onto his finger. "And we'll see exactly how much you like ass play."

A lot. She liked it a whole lot. Heat flooded her, and air rasped into her lungs. She got on her hands and knees, and the mattress dipped as he crawled onto the bed behind her. His palm stroked up her thigh and his fingers slipped inward to toy with her pussy. He traced her slick lips, teasing more moisture from her core. She arched her back, pushing into his touch. *More.* She wanted more of this, more of him.

His other hand moved so that his lubed fingers pressed to her anus. He circled the tight bud, working one thick digit and then another into her rear passage. She forced herself to relax while he stretched her, though excitement whipped through her with every passing moment. His hands were driving her to sweet madness, so when he pulled away the one teasing her pussy, she cried out a protest.

"Shh. We just need a bit more of this," he rumbled. Cool fluid hit the cleft of her buttocks and she shuddered at the contrasting sensations. He pushed his fingers deeper, adding a third finger to her anus. He pumped them in and out of her. "I'm going to fuck you here."

"Yes." She wanted that. "*Now*, Bastian. I'm so ready."

That elicited a small groan from him. His hand moved away from her backside and then she felt the slide of his cock as he rubbed the head against her anus. He pressed forward, and the pressure of his thick shaft inside her was pleasure and pain all at once. With her eyes pinched closed, her mouth opened in a silent scream. She dropped her torso down until her cheek pressed to the bed. The angle made the penetration both better and more intense all at the same time.

He rocked against her, nudging farther and farther into her ass until he was seated to the hilt. She whimpered at how good it felt, her hands bunching in the bedspread.

Cupping a palm over her hip, he asked, "Are you okay?"

"Uh huh." She nodded and her hair rustled against the blankets. "Keep going."

Easing backwards, he slipped almost free of her before plunging in again. Tingles skipped down her limbs and her toes curled every time he sank inside her. She arched her body into his thrusts when he picked up speed, moving with him as easily as breathing. The sound of their flesh slapping together, the creak of the bed beneath them only underscored the eroticism of the encounter. Sweat dewed her skin, moans spilling from her lips as ecstasy whipped higher and higher.

He reached around her to play with her clit, his thumb rubbing back and forth across the sensitive bundle of nerves until she sobbed. Ripples of climax began to build inside her, pushing her closer to the edge of utter completion.

"Bastian, I need to…I'm going to…"

The words were barely coherent, but he seemed to understand exactly what she wanted because he pressed down directly on her clit, shoved his cock deep into her ass and ground his pelvis against her.

Orgasm slammed into her with the force of a tsunami, dragging her under. Her pussy flexed, a cry wrenching from her throat. Talons slid from her fingertips and shredded the bedspread. He continued to pound into her ass and flick his thumb over her clit, sending her tumbling into climax once more. Tears leaked from the corners of her eyes as pleasure overwhelmed her. Goosebumps broke down her skin every time he entered her, and shivers quaked her body.

"*Tori,*" he gasped. Burying his cock in her one last time, he filled her with fluid, a low groan breaking from his throat.

She collapsed to the bed, boneless, and closed her eyes. There was no way she'd find the will to move until morning. Maybe not even then. "Oh my God, you killed me."

"Fucked you to death, huh?" He patted her thigh as he flopped onto the mattress beside her. "I guess I don't need to ask if it was good for you too."

She grunted. "I will spank you for that smug tone. Later."

"Looking forward to it." He chuckled.

Sighing, she drifted in and out of consciousness. Not quite asleep, but content to stay right where she was. It could have been minutes or hours later, but she felt her body being lifted and stirred herself to ask, "Where are we going?"

"Shower. And then I'm going to fuck your pussy until you scream my name."

That perked up her interest. She gave him a wink. "Looking forward to it."

The languid heat filtering through her turned to something much hotter, greedier. She swirled a fingertip around the flat disc of his nipple, making it bead for her. Very nice. She pinched the small nub, twisting. "Hurry it up, Lykaios. It's time to get to the screaming part."

His serious face lightened as he laughed and picked up his pace. "Anything you want, sweetheart."

She wanted him. She wasn't sure about anything beyond that, so she blocked out all thoughts about the future and the complications and problems that might be coming their way. Enjoying the moment was her best bet, and Bastian seemed more than willing to keep her mind off anything except him.

He really would be easy to become addicted to.

It was the last rational thought she had for a long, long time.

The reporter was the logical option. Jeff Nichols had identified specific shape-shifters—a male and a female. The female was a fox, but the male was less clear. Barbara needed to know where to find the fox or any other shifter. A female would probably be easier to manage, especially if she shifted into a smaller animal species. The concern was being able to tell just by observing. If a petite woman became a massive animal, that could be a problem. Or perhaps the size of the person dictated the size of animal.

Scientific understanding of these hybrids was so thin. They still had so much to learn—they *needed* to have a live specimen, needed to observe her or him closely.

An educated guess told Barbara the reporter had to suspect more than he'd written so far, which meant he had notes or files somewhere. He was a freelance reporter, so he didn't have an office, and he was staying in a hotel outside of Atlanta, which limited his security. That was to her advantage.

It was funny how the reporter who followed people around never suspected someone might be following him, watching him. Learning his habits, when he came and went. He went to lunch at a café near city hall every day, usually meeting with people there, which gave Barbara the opportunity she needed.

And just to be sure, she had Hastings watching the restaurant. He'd call her if the reporter so much as twitched.

The maid left her open Pepsi on her cart, and it was laughably easy to slip something into it that would knock the young woman out for an hour—maybe a bit less, so Barbara needed to hurry. With any luck, the maid would think she'd fallen asleep on the job. The drug was subtle enough for that. Getting the card key was a simple matter, and then she was in the reporter's room. Pity she couldn't get whatever notes he might be carrying with him, but she was taking whatever he might have at the hotel. She'd noted that he never had the maids come to his room, which meant there was a reason he didn't want people in there.

He had information stored here and she wanted it.

He'd actually left his laptop behind, which made her giggle with a dark, spiteful glee that was entirely unlike her normally staid self. She clamped a hand over her mouth and rocked back on her heels. *Pull yourself together, Dr. Powell.*

After plugging in her external hard drive, she copied everything on the laptop. Such an unexpected bonus. He usually had the computer with him. One sloppy move on his part was a huge boon for her. The files were probably encrypted, but one of Hastings's many degrees was in computer science. The man might actually prove to be useful for once.

Every piece of paper she came across, she took a picture of. From what little she read as she worked, she found that Nichols suspected he had the same anonymous source for his shifter information as she did. He even had some ideas about who that person might be. Keen interest burned inside her, but she didn't have time to consider all the ramifications. The maid would be waking soon, and Barbara wanted to be long gone by then.

As she exited the room, she took the "Do Not Disturb" sign off the doorknob and dropped it so it drifted to the floor a bit down the hall. It would look like it got knocked off accidentally, and by the time Nichols was done with lunch, there'd be nothing to suggest anyone but the maid had been there.

Excellent.

CHAPTER SIX

The first day, Bastian knew Tori had explored his house, the barn he used as a garage and all his other outbuildings. He'd gone in to work and managed to have a private meeting with his brothers about what had happened over the weekend, but he could smell Tori everywhere when he got home. With anyone else, he would have bristled at the invasion of his privacy, but not with her. He liked that she was curious enough about his home—about *him*—to want to know more. The feeling was unsettling, it was so unfamiliar.

By the second day, he sensed she was getting restless, bored, and that unsettled him even more. A small kernel of panic lodged in his chest, knowing she could fly away any time she wanted and he might never see her again. He needed something to distract her, since there was no way he could take time away from the clan right now.

Then it hit him, the perfect thing to keep her at his place and to keep her entertained while he was out of the house.

He called her cell phone from his office. "Hey, I want you to check something out. Do you have your laptop turned on?"

"Oh Jesus," she said. "Is it another article from that fuckwit reporter? Because so far my sources have come up with squat on the dads."

"No article, thankfully. It's better than that."

He heard rustling through the phone before she spoke again. "Okay, I'm online."

"Go to this website." He rattled off the URL. "Tell me if you find anything you think has potential. I'm in the market."

A pause and then the sound of typing.

"Classic cars," she cooed.

He grinned at the sound of her pleasure. "It's a local site that specializes in what's available in the area."

"I have to go. I like to car porn in private."

The line clicked as she hung up on him. He laughed and tucked his phone into his jacket pocket.

"You are sounding far too cheerful in a shitty world, big brother." Paul stuck his head in Bastian's door. The two were the closest in age, but since Paul was his human stepbrother, there hadn't been the kind of jockeying for power that often went on amongst siblings in leading families. It had been a relief for Bastian not to deal with that. His father was more than enough to handle on any given day.

"Someone's cheerful?" Dominic, their youngest brother, pushed his way past Paul.

"You haven't met Tori Haida?" Tomas joined them, rounding out the brotherly lineup. "If she were my mate, I'd be whistling Dixie all day long, even if the apocalypse were coming down on my head."

Eyebrows arching, Dominic grinned. "Oh, really? I may have to come out for a visit. Welcome her to the family. It'd be polite."

"No gawking," Bastian snapped. "Because we both know y'all couldn't be polite unless Mom had a gun to your head."

Dominic made an offended noise, but then sniffed the air. "Yes, I can see why you wouldn't want company. You've got a bit of lingering sex about you along with…lube? My, my, an adventurous lady you have there."

The youngest Lykaios brother's nose was legendary. He could scent and track from miles away—an ability he'd used to endlessly annoy his older siblings when growing up.

Bastian rolled his eyes. "And I repeat, you wouldn't know how to be polite company unless threatened with murder, which is what would happen if you said something like that to my mate." Though somehow he doubted Tori would be shocked—she might actually cold-cock his baby brother. Then again, that might be fun to watch. "Did you want something? Other than to harass me, that is." And he wondered how long it might take him to get rid of them so he could go home to his mate. The thought almost made him smile again.

"Yeah." Paul reached out and shut the door. "I found evidence that Dad's been talking to that reporter."

Instantly sobering, Bastian sat up straight, his attention riveted on his brother. "Tell me."

He could only be relieved that his brothers had taken the news he'd broken about the weekend meeting well. It turned out they'd all privately started to suspect Michael and Hector, but hadn't wanted to say anything. Or hadn't known how to say anything. Even having this conversation could be seen as treason. It was a very thin tightrope they walked, but the brothers were united in their belief that werekind should remain hidden. There were very few times in their lives that the Lykaios brothers had been in complete agreement. Now, it united them against their father. There was a sad twist of fate.

"Dad keeps a couple of burner phones at the house." Paul lifted his hand when Bastian opened his mouth. "Yeah, you know that already, but you haven't checked the call log on those phones, have you?"

Bastian shook his head. Of course he hadn't. Something so blatant would have gotten his ass kicked by the Alpha. "Among other reasons, I assumed they were password protected."

"They were." Paul snorted. "Child's play."

"Says the resident hacker-boy," Tomas interjected.

"I am an IT professional. Who do you think keeps the network and computers running around here? It ain't you, MBA-boy." As he turned back to Bastian, Paul's gaze glittered with triumph, the way it did whenever he pulled the wool over a wolf's eyes. "Dom kept a lookout and I bootlegged a copy of everything on Dad's phones into a file on my phone. Then I could take my time scrolling through the numbers he's been calling."

Tomas snorted. "He's gonna smell you all over those phones."

"Yep, me *and* Mom. She asked me to bring her cell to her and I brought those." Paul widened his eyes innocently. "I wasn't sure which one was hers and I'm not a wolf, so I can't smell people's scents on things."

"You're going to hell for lying to your mother," Tomas drawled.

"You're welcome," Paul returned casually.

Bastian sighed and stepped in to referee. "I assume one of the numbers Dad called belongs to the reporter?"

"Yep." Paul nodded. "There were multiple calls to that number. On the other burner phone, there was another number he'd called several times. It had a 617 area code. Cambridge, Massachusetts. The number is unlisted, but I hacked into the local phone company's records—it belongs to Barbara Powell. She's one of the MIT scientists that got canned for discovering shifter DNA."

Bastian sat back in his chair and steepled his fingers together. "It's proof, yes, but proof he can easily discard and deny. Also, he can pretend they aren't his phones. That's what burners are for."

"I know." Paul shrugged. "I said I had proof, I didn't say I could blow this wide open."

"No, but it gives us more than speculation, which is all we had before." Bastian leveled his gaze at his human stepbrother. "Though it could get you in deep shit if Dad suspects anything."

"We had to know," Paul replied matter-of-factly. "It's my family's safety on the line here. Mom and Celeste are human like me, but that won't make us safe if the Wolf Council turns on the Lykaioses. Dad needed to clear it with the Council before he went and did something like reveal werekind to the world. They could put us *all* to death if they felt like it. Old feuds notwithstanding, I'm thanking God Celeste mated with that leopard. He can give her some additional protection."

Dominic looked to Bastian. "What are we going to do? How do we fix this?"

Bastian felt the weight of his responsibilities settle on his shoulders. This was how it would be if he ever became Alpha—everyone looking to him for leadership the way his brothers were now. Somehow that possibility seemed to be drifting away. It was all about damage control at the moment. Becoming Alpha had never been his priority—protecting his people had been.

A small voice in the back of his mind asked if *not* being the Alpha would be such a bad thing. He knew part of Tori's resistance to their mating was that he was from a leading family, that expectations would fall on her. That she'd be caged by her mating to him. But what if that wasn't the case? What if he wasn't the Alpha? What if the Lykaioses just picked up and left? They could hide what Michael had done, secure the family's safety, and Bastian could keep Tori happy.

And then he felt like an asshole for seeing any benefit for himself out of his family's tragedy. It wasn't as if it would be that simple anyway, not unless Michael suddenly got a lobotomy and started doing as he was told.

Shaking his head, Bastian answered his brother's question. "I'm not sure there is a way to fix this, not completely. What we need to do is contain and eliminate the problem to the best of our ability." He met each of their gazes in turn. "Dad fucked up, there's no getting around that. We do what we can to protect him from the consequences, but we have to stop this before it goes any farther."

"Agreed," Tomas said.

Paul and Dom nodded.

"Were there any other numbers he'd called, Paul?" Bastian smoothed his tie against his chest.

"Yeah. Several."

"Okay, why don't you see what you can uncover about them? We need to find out if this info is being leaked to more than just one reporter and a couple of scientists." He sighed and rose from his seat.

"Should we dig farther?" Tomas asked. "At what point do we confront Dad and Hector?"

"Let me talk to the Leonidases, then we'll make some firmer decisions. I'd like to keep this in the family, if possible. With Hector involved, his sons have a vested interested in smothering this quickly and quietly too." Bastian powered down his computer and grabbed his briefcase, waving his brothers out the door. "Now, I need to get home."

Dom made a few kissing noises and Bastian smacked him upside the head as he walked by.

Rubbing his no doubt stinging ear, Dom grinned unabashedly. "Dad knows you were out of town too. Mom mentioned that he asked if she knew where you'd gone. A little too casually, which made her suspicious, so now she wants to know what's going on. Don't be surprised if she drops in on you."

The thought of Miranda Lykaios suspicious and digging into anything was enough to give any man pause. She might be human, but she was as tenacious as a pit bull with lockjaw when she wanted to be. "Thanks for the warning."

"You deserved it."

The drive home was a blur of conflicting thoughts and feelings. Rolling down the window, he drove at breakneck speed and let the wind rip through his hair and plaster his clothes against his skin. He could feel his life tilting on its axis, where everything he thought was right no longer was and everything he thought he wanted might not be perfect after all. Then there was the nerve-racking uncertainty of who was going to try to kill him first—the Alpha or the Wolf Council.

He turned off the highway onto his road and Tori's scent hit his nostrils. *Mate.* Something unwound inside of him, calming his roiling emotions. Knowing she was there waiting for him changed nothing. The world was every bit as fucked up as it had been two minutes ago, but he felt better. That alone should have freaked him out, but he was too damn tired and stressed to care. If anything made this situation more bearable, he'd take it.

A few minutes later he was tugging off his tie as he walked in the front door. He found her sprawled out on her stomach on his couch. She didn't even look up at him, her gaze pinned to the computer screen in front of her.

"Oooooh," she moaned.

The deep ecstasy of the sound made his insides tighten with automatic lust, and a dart of heat went straight to his groin. "The only person who should be getting that noise from you is me. Who do I have to kill?"

"Not a person, a *car.*" She rolled to her side and pointed at the screen. "Look at this."

"Did you find something for me?"

"No." She huffed. "For *me.*"

"I thought I asked you to look for me because I was in the market for a new car." Sitting next to her, he checked out the vehicle. *Whoa.* He tried to think of something flattering to say, but all he could come up with was, "It's a wreck."

A happy little hum of agreement came from her. "I want it. 1969 Chevy Impala convertible. I've never had one before."

He eyed the car's matte coat of gray primer marred by rust spots. "You haven't even seen it in person yet."

Propping herself on an elbow, she gave him a huge, beatific smile. "Want to go for a drive?"

He arched an eyebrow, fighting the urge to grin back. Her appeal was all but irresistible. "You already called the owner and scheduled an appointment, didn't you?"

Pushing herself to her knees, she bit her lower lip. "I can just take your SUV if you want to stay here."

The utter lack of apology made him chuckle. "No, come on. Get in the car."

"You're so awesome." She grabbed his face and popped a kiss on his mouth.

"Thank you. You still owe me for this." Wrapping his arm around her waist, he hauled her flush against him and deepened the kiss. Her lips parted willingly and he delved into her mouth, his tongue twining with hers. Slipping her fingers into his hair, she arched her breasts into him. A growl rumbled up from his chest, and he felt his claws extend. His cock pulsed against his fly and he fought the need to shred her clothes, mount her and ride her hard.

Her head fell back and he nipped and sucked his way down the long, elegant column of her throat. He scraped his fangs softly over her collarbone. She moaned, her hands fisting in his hair. "Okay, I owe you. I'll pay up."

"I'll make sure of it." He eased away from her. Standing up was a painful proposition, but he managed. "I'm going to go change out of the suit and then we can be off."

She rolled to her feet. "I'll put on my shoes and grab my purse. Oh, and I'll call the guy and confirm we're coming right now."

They were pulling away from the house in short order, headed out to the main road. Tori slipped a can of Dr. Pepper into the cup holder, rooted around in her handbag and then slapped a sticky note to the dash. "Address and directions. I hope you can follow this because there's a part about turning off at the small white church right after the big bridge and making sure we keep the river on the left."

"You've never been given Southern directions before, huh?" He thickened his drawl until it was molasses slow.

She laughed. "Weird directions, yes, but usually they have *some* street names."

"Nah. That would make it too easy for outsiders to find their way around." He shot her a lopsided grin.

"You ain't from around these here parts." She exaggerated the worst drawl he'd ever heard, and he winced. She half turned on the seat to face him. "So, local boy, do you actually know where we're going?"

"Of course." He shrugged. "There's a great barbeque place near there. Actually, it's more like a dilapidated shack with a huge porch attached, but the food is fantastic and the view of the river is amazing. Dinner?"

"I'm game. I've never eaten in a shack before."

They headed away from Chattanooga and out into the middle of nowhere, so few cars passed them. He felt her gaze move over him as he guided the vehicle along the road. "What?"

She reached across the seat and ran her fingernail down the side seam in his khaki shorts. His muscles tensed and he glanced at her to see she wore the kind of grin that could make a man's blood rush south. She tilted her head. "What did you have in mind as payment for coming with me?"

A variety of ideas flashed through his brain, but then he realized it would be a hell of a lot more fun to let her surprise him. She was good at that. He liked that about her. Not many people managed to shock the shit out of him. "I'll allow you to be creative."

Unclipping her seatbelt, she slid along the bench seat. "I'm thinking maybe a down payment is in order. For you being so accommodating."

Her nimble fingers shifted his seatbelt and unzipped his shorts. She tugged his cock free of his boxers and stroked the shaft in unhurried sweeps. "Keep the car on the road, Lykaios. We have an appointment we don't want to miss, but crashing would be bad."

He sucked in a ragged breath as his dick went diamond hard in under three seconds. "You. Are. Insane."

"And you like it."

God, yes, he did. It occurred to him that he was a little too sane, too grounded. A good thing in many situations, but there were times when he could use some madness in his life.

No wonder he'd picked her as a mate. She was perfect for him.

Then her mouth closed over his cock and all philosophical life-choice thoughts fled his mind. It was all he could do to keep the car in his lane. If not for his wolf reflexes, they might have been in real trouble.

Her tongue swirled around the head of his dick, and he clenched his teeth as hot, wicked pleasure danced like fire over his skin. *Ah, God.* After letting one hand drop from the wheel, he threaded his fingers through her hair. He meant to pull her away, to stop the craziness. They shouldn't be doing this. It was stupid and irresponsible, but she sucked him hard and he didn't give a shit about right or wrong. He just *needed.* "Fuck."

"*Mmmm.*" She hummed and the sound vibrated down the length of his erection. His eyes damn near rolled back in his head, it felt so amazing. He had to struggle to stay focused on the road. The sharp dichotomy between concentration and incipient release made him shudder.

"Tori," he gritted out.

She cupped his balls, rolling them between her slim fingers, and he groaned. Her teeth scraped gently at his shaft and he almost came then and there, but he wanted to hang on to this feeling for as long as possible. The erotic and forbidden all rolled into one. He'd had plenty of sexual encounters in his life, but he'd never had a woman give him a blowjob in a moving vehicle.

Slipping her hand upward, she began to stroke in the same rhythm with which her mouth sucked him. His breathing sped, his heart hammering in his chest. He tightened his grip on her hair, pushing down so she took him deep. Squeezing him in the ring of her fingers, she moved faster, her tongue working down the underside of his shaft.

Sensation boiled up and he knew he wasn't going to last much longer. "Jesus. Fuck. Tori, I'm going to come. If you don't want—"

She sank down, taking him deeper than she had before, and he felt the back of her throat contract around his cock. Choking, he exploded into her mouth, his hips arching off the seat. Come jetted from him in hot waves and shudders racked his body. She kept sucking him until the sensation became almost too intense. He pulled her gently away. "Enough, sweetheart. Too much actually."

She let him slide from between her lips. "So you fucked me to death and I sucked you to death?"

A laugh straggled out of him. "Yup."

His ragged breathing took a long moment to settle into some semblance of normalcy. He licked his lips, watching as she sat up, scooted over and strapped herself back into her seat. Blinking, he realized they were at their exit and hit the brakes, whipping into a quick turn. They both surged against their seatbelts and Tori clutched the grip handle, a grin on her face.

"That was fun." She winked.

He shook his head. "That was crazy. All of that."

She grabbed her soda and took a swig. "True, but wasn't it just a little bit hotter because we *really* shouldn't have been doing it?"

"Oh yeah." He snorted, unable to deny the truth. "I really like you, you know."

"Likewise." She chuckled and drew one knee up to her chest. "Are we there yet?"

"Very close." He coasted down the bumpy road, keeping an eye out for the turnoff that would take them to the right house. He almost missed it—the weeds grew so high around the mailbox. It looked about as well-kept as the car had in the pictures. He kept that thought to himself.

The house was a rundown old homestead with multiple cars in various states of rust parked in the yard. Though, to be fair, there were also a couple mint condition vintage models tucked under a large carport.

"There it is." Tori was out of the SUV the moment he pulled to a stop. She trotted over to the particular rust-bucket she wanted as an older man in a John Deere cap and a wifebeater stepped from the house.

Bastian flagged the man down and exchanged greetings, but the moment the old guy got a look at Tori, it was as if Bastian didn't exist.

She was all over the car. She crawled beneath it, dove under its hood, flipped every lever, pushed every button. Then she took it for a test drive. Bastian sat in the passenger seat, and the owner parked himself in the back, his elbows resting on the front seat. Clearly, he was loving the fact that a hot babe like Tori knew so much about cars. For a motorhead like him, Tori had to be a walking wet dream. Hell, who was Bastian kidding? She was a walking wet dream for any heterosexual man. And gay woman, probably.

But it was Bastian she turned to with a luminous, heart-stopping smile. "I want."

His entire body reacted with visceral need. Goddamn, he hoped she still got to him this quickly fifty years from now. "Whatever you want, sweetheart."

If anything, her smile got brighter. "Right answer."

He tugged on a lock of her silky hair. "Not always going to be my answer."

She wrinkled her nose at him, then glanced back at their audience. "I'll give you two-thirds of your asking price. It's *running*, sure, but it's gonna need a lot of work to get it purring." She gave the man a hard, don't-bullshit-me look in the rearview mirror. "There's more wrong than you said in your ad. Do you want me to give you a list?"

He pulled off his ball cap and slapped it against the seat. "Two-thirds works for me. I haven't had time to fix her up the way I wanted. I'm glad she'll be going to someone who'll take care of her."

Tori nodded her approval. "Good man."

Bastian propped his arm on the door of the car. "Happy?"

"Very." Her eyes twinkled, her fingers tapping a cheerful beat against the steering wheel.

"Good." He wanted her happy. And he wanted her here with him. With the exception of family members, there'd never been anyone in his life whose contentment was as important to him as hers was. Even then, it was an entirely different beast with his mate. It was mind-bending and gut-wrenching that he could feel this way after only a few days of knowing her, but he wouldn't change it for anything.

He just hoped he could change her mind about wanting to go back to Arizona.

CHAPTER SEVEN

The next afternoon, Tori had just finished giving the Impala a tune up when her cell phone blared out a ring. Since she was still covered in grease, she gave her phone voice commands. "Answer call. Speakerphone."

The cell beeped an acknowledgement and then the line opened. "Hello?"

"Hey, it's Ajax."

She blinked in surprise, then grinned. "Your Majesty, it's a delight to hear from you. I just saw your yummy hubby the other day."

A dry snort came through the phone. "Shut your beak and fly over for a visit, Haida."

While she'd really wanted to do that for the last couple of days, a few minor concerns had kept her grounded. First, since she'd gone and marked the wolf Beta, there would be those in the shifter world who assumed that she was automatically under the wolf clan's rule. While she hadn't officially taken a loyalty oath to the Alpha—nor did she particularly want to—that would be a mere technicality to some. Which meant it became kind of political for her to visit bird lands, even though she was a fricking *bird*. Stupid and frustrating, but making waves about it might draw attention to this mating thing that she just didn't want, so she hadn't brought it up with Bastian.

However, with a personal invitation from the bird queen, that should make it all kosher. Hopefully. Who knew with the wolves? She was more in tune with the dynamics of the leopards, so maybe the wolves would get bitchier about crossing into other shifters' territory. Or maybe it would be cool. She wasn't going to stop and ask. It was easier to ask for forgiveness than permission.

On the other hand, if she didn't actually go to bird territory…

"I have a better idea." She grabbed a rag and wiped away some of the grease on her hands. "Why don't I take you for a ride in the fabulous classic car I just bought? It's a barely running hunk of junk, but you've got to see the before so after I fix it up, you'll be blown away."

"You and your cars." Tori could all but hear Ajax rolling her eyes. "You need to design planes or something. It's more befitting of a bird."

A fair point. "Maybe I'll invent a flying car someday."

"Now that'd be cool."

"You gonna come see my new ride or not?" Tori's voice became cajoling. "There might be coffee in it for you."

"Sure. The girls and I will fly down and meet you in the parking lot."

Meaning the spot where all the bird-shifters parked their cars before soaring up into the tree houses they lived in. It was also the head of a nature trail for hikers, backpackers and stream fishermen, which meant the mass of cars didn't seem weird if any human authorities came across it.

"Great. I'll call you when I'm almost there, so you guys know when to start flying."

"See you soon. I can't wait to hear all about your trip to Tennessee." Ajax's tone was drier than leaves in winter.

"Let the grilling begin." Tori hung up the phone before the bird queen could respond. There were going to be questions anyway, so why not start at the top?

Besides, Tori would get to drive her new baby. And there would be coffee.

She set Bastian's tools on his workbench and dropped the car's hood back in place, then hustled for the house and the shower she pretty desperately needed by now. She hosed off, hopped out, slapped on some clothes, left a note for Bastian in case he came home early or she got back late and then slung her purse over her shoulder on her way out the door. Luckily, Bastian had given her a code for his security system and shown her how to make the system lock and unlock the doors.

House handled, she raced for the garage. The deep rumble of the Impala's engine made her grin as she fired up the car. It already sounded better than it had yesterday, but she was going to need some new parts. Plus, it needed a lot of bodywork.

A new project. Her favorite thing in the world. She cruised down the road with the convertible's top down, radio blaring while she hummed along. Maybe she'd stop off at an auto store in town on the way home.

Home. She cringed at the thought. She should not be referring to Bastian's place as *home*, even in her own mind. It was his home, not hers. She lived in Arizona, though she wouldn't really call that home. Maybe the closest thing she had to home was still her parents' house in Colorado. Which wasn't really home anymore, was it? She was an adult now, and while she could go back, it would never be quite the same as it was when she was a child. So where the hell did she belong? She had a feeling Bastian wouldn't hesitate with the answer to that question, but she wasn't quite as ready to commit.

Shoving those thoughts away, she made the turn off the highway toward the werebird parking lot. She grabbed her cell and pushed the button to call Ajax, who picked up on the first ring. "Should we fly down?"

"Yep."

"See you in a few."

The line clicked and Tori dropped her phone back in her purse. Glancing in her rearview, she saw that a couple of other cars had followed her off the main road. Weird time of day for the place to be so popular, but it was as likely to be human outdoorsmen as it was to be shifters in those vehicles.

She swung into a parking space and let the engine idle. Tapping her fingers on the wheel, she tried to ignore the nagging need for a smoke. It was easier to ignore now, especially if she kept busy. Maybe the need was fading so quickly because she was a shifter, but the human literature said this intense craving could have gone on for weeks or months. She was hovering right around a week and the need only hit her occasionally. Sometimes having an awesome immune system, advanced senses and a kickass metabolism had serious benefits.

An eagle's cry brought her focus skyward and she watched Ajax and her eaglets circle in before they landed in a designated spot in the woods where they could shift back to human form and don some clothes before stepping out into the more public lot.

The wind ruffled through Tori's hair and she sighed. The Smoky Mountains really were a great place to fly. She'd always loved it when she'd visited her mom's family as a kid. It reminded her a bit of the Rockies, but that wasn't surprising after five years in the flat desert of Arizona. She hadn't realized how much she'd missed the mountains until she'd come here with Bastian. There was something visceral that called to her when she stepped out onto the porch every morning and saw those peaks soaring in the distance. It felt right. But that was just because she was back in the mountains, *not* for any other reason.

And that excuse was starting to sound thin and pathetic even in her own head.

A little girl came pelting out of the forest. "Sarah Beth!"

Sarah Beth? Arching her eyebrows, Tori looked around. Another woman hopped out of one of the cars that had followed her off the highway. She scooped the girl in her arms and twirled around. "Alex!"

Ajax stepped from behind a tree carrying a younger girl on her hip. She waved to Tori, who wiggled her fingers back. Both women and girls converged on the Impala. There was something vaguely familiar about the woman who held Alex, but Tori couldn't put her finger on what it was.

Sarah Beth said, "Hey, where are you headed?"

"For a joyride in Tori's new lemon. She's buying coffee." A subtle grin played around the queen's mouth. "Sarah Beth Aquinas, Tori Haida. Make nice."

Tori stuck her arm over the door for a handshake. "Good to meet you. Want to come along?"

"Actually, yeah." Sarah Beth smiled. "I like a classic jalopy as much as the next Southern girl. When did you buy it?"

"Yesterday." Tori hopped out and gave an elegant bow as she held the back door open.

Sarah Beth chuckled and set Alex on the seat, then climbed in when the girl scooted over. "Nice."

"Bouncy seats!" Alex pumped her legs and made the springs squeak underneath her.

Ajax plopped her youngest in Tori's arms. "Okay, let me grab the car seats out of the Suburban. It's hard to keep eaglets strapped in, but the law says we have to try."

The kid giggled and wrapped her fingers around the strap of Tori's tank top. Tori jiggled her. "So you're Ayla, right?"

"Uh-huh." The girl nodded so vigorously she almost head-butted Tori.

"Whoa, Princess. Adjust your flight path."

"Crashes happen sometimes," Alex offered sagely. She'd crawled from the back to hang out the driver's window. "But fledglings don't always fly good. So you hafta practice. Mama says so."

"Your mom's a very smart lady." Tori arched an eyebrow at the child. "And you're in my seat."

"Daddy lets me sit on his lap and steer." Her eyes went huge and winsome.

"When your mom's in the car?"

She giggled. "No."

"Then it's the backseat for you, munchkin." Tori winked. "Maybe next time, though."

Excitement lit Alex's gaze. "Cool!"

"Coo'!" her little sister echoed.

Tori met Sarah Beth's eyes and said, "They are just all kinds of adorable."

"I know," the other woman replied. "Patrick and I are hoping for one of our own soon."

Bam, it clicked. Tori suddenly knew where she'd seen this woman before. They'd never met, but Sarah Beth's picture had been plastered across the papers by that obnoxious human reporter. He'd outed her as a fox-shifter. Then a big game hunter had gone after her, hoping to bag the biggest game ever. Sounded like one scary-ass nightmare to Tori.

Something must have shown in her face because Sarah Beth winced and raised her chin. "I survived."

"Good. I hope no one else has to deal with anything like that again." But even as Tori said it, she worried that it was a false hope. If what Bastian and the Leonidases suspected was true, they might all be exposed, hunted down like animals. She prayed that possibility never became reality. If anyone could stop it, she'd put her money on those guys.

Ajax reappeared, a booster seat carried under each arm. She handed one to Sarah Beth and then went around the car to strap the other booster in. "Sarah Beth, I can sit in the back with my girls. You ride shotgun."

"With the roof down, there's not a bad seat in the house." Tori slipped back in and revved the engine. It was a sad sound, but it would be much cooler once she'd really gotten her hands on this baby.

"Do you know where you're going, Haida?" Ajax leaned forward and arched her eyebrows.

"Nope, but there's no use being late." Tori eased out of the parking spot and took off down the road. "But, seriously, Chattanooga has to have a Starbucks or twelve."

"We're not that backwoods here in Tennessee," Sarah Beth quipped. "We need caffeine like everyone else."

"Well, the girls need hot cocoa, not coffee."

The rush of wind would have made it impossible to have a conversation if they weren't shifters, but their extraordinary senses meant they could speak without shouting and still be heard. Tori glanced in the rearview mirror to meet Ajax's gaze. "Whipped cream with that cocoa?"

"Naturally," Ajax murmured while her girls squealed their agreement.

Tori flipped on her blinker to merge back onto the highway. "I'm sure arrangements can be made. As a kid, I preferred those tiny marshmallows, myself."

"Of course you did." Ajax's mock-condescending tone didn't manage to mask her mirth. Then she reached over the seat and tugged the strap of Tori's tank top aside. "So…it is true. You really are mated to Bastian Lykaios. I almost accused my consort of lying through his fangs."

Tori shrugged away from her touch, feeling exposed. For once, her glib tongue failed her. No matter how much she'd considered her predicament, she still didn't know what to say, how to explain. If he were anyone but a clan heir, it would be so much easier.

Sarah Beth gave her a sympathetic glance before swiveling to speak to Ajax. "Well, it's no more shocking than when you mated to Nicodemus Leonidas."

The queen snorted. "Yeah, well, I totally called you mating with Patrick."

Sarah Beth propped her arm on the top of her door. "Really? Because it shocked the heck out of me."

The banter continued all the way into town, and Tori's car made the journey there and back with no problems. It was a great day. Good conversation, reconnecting with an old friend, making a new one and being amused by the antics of the little princesses.

She could picture this as her life far too easily. Going out for coffee with Ajax and Sarah Beth and some of the other birds she knew. Working on her cars, maybe as more than just a hobby.

Having Bastian come home to her every night.

God, that sounded good. Amazing. Perfect.

Except it wouldn't be that simple, would it? Who'd ever heard of an Alpha's mate who was a grease monkey for a living? She sure as hell wouldn't be his secretary. He might start thinking he could boss her around then. Nope, nope, nope.

After coffee, she took the others back and went for a quick flight with the queen and her girls—being careful not to venture into bird territory—and she loved those sweet moments of freedom where there was nothing but the wind flowing over her wings. That high up in the air, it was easier to ignore the problems down in the rest of the world, but that didn't make them go away.

Sooner or later, she had a feeling she was going to crash.

Barbara had started with the woman identified as a fox in Nichols's article. His notes told her exactly where the fox and her family could be found: Chattanooga, Tennessee. So here she was in this backwater little city, trying to capture a live specimen. Hastings was working to set up a lab space for them, one that was discreet and isolated. If the "clans," as Nichols called the shifter groups, were as tight knit as he suspected, it would be difficult have a missing hybrid go unnoticed.

With Hastings busy, Barbara had to follow the fox as she came and went from town. Every day, she ended up in this parking lot. There were usually a lot of cars around, and people came and went at times that indicated they were going to and from work rather than going for a hike in the mountains.

Barbara surmised they lived here, which meant there was a significant colony of hybrids in these woods. That caused a stir of intellectual excitement within her. *So many potential specimens!*

She tried not to make her presence too obvious, since animals had senses that humans couldn't match, and their studies hadn't yet shown the extent of the sensory crossover there might be between animals and animal-human hybrids. They might have the ability to smell or hear the way any dog or cat would.

Sitting up straight, she took note of the fox interacting with two other women and children. The little girls had arrived with a fierce-looking woman with spiked blonde hair. Barbara had seen the fierce woman once before but something about her made Barbara wary. Perhaps this one was an animal that was more dangerous than the others. A fox wouldn't be too difficult to manage, and the other woman was almost angelic-looking. She might be even easier to deal with than the fox, depending on her species. When the group piled into an ugly, beat-up old car and drove off, Barbara slowly tailed them.

The children gave her pause. Barbara hadn't yet considered them as an option for experimentation. But then, she also had no idea if a child hybrid had the same abilities as a full-grown adult. At what age did their animal side manifest?

The group went to a coffee shop in town, laughing as if they hadn't a care in the world, as if no one had ever taken everything from them, as if their lives had never imploded on them. Their joy made something dark squeeze and writhe within Barbara, but she ignored it. Emotions were for weaklings like Hastings. She needed to stay focused.

The women disappeared into the woods and a few minutes later a series of loud birdcalls made Barbara look up. A group of birds flew overhead. A massive bald eagle, a swan and two smaller bald eagles. But the eagles weren't attacking the swan—they were just flying together, swooping around in dizzying circles. That wasn't natural behavior for animals. Birds of prey didn't cavort with *swans*.

213

These were hybrids. It was the only logical explanation. The bald eagle was the fierce woman and the smaller eagles were her young. That meant the angelic woman was a swan. Barbara's mouth twisted in a smile. Yes, a swan would be even simpler to handle than a fox. Predator versus prey...she'd pick the prey as a first specimen.

When the angelic woman returned alone to the parking lot, Barbara tailed her until she turned into a private driveway.

If she didn't live in the colony with the others, maybe she'd be easier to isolate and take alive. This warranted further investigation.

CHAPTER EIGHT

Bastian's father had to go out of town for a couple of days to deal with a squabble between two factions of red wolves in North Carolina. A relief, really. It made it easier to avoid the Alpha. There were questions and accusations in the older man's eyes that Bastian couldn't face. It became harder and harder to hide his anger as more damning evidence came in from the bird and leopard clans.

He strode into his house in a pisser of a mood, ready to snarl at anything that moved. Probably not the best way to come home to his mate, the one woman he hoped would stick around. But the wolf within him could feel the threat closing in around it, and its hackles rose.

Tori sat on the couch, her back resting against one arm of the sofa, totally absorbed in whatever she was doing. There was something serene in her expression that was so un-Tori-like that it gave him just enough pause not to snap upon greeting.

He shoved a hand through his hair. "I spoke to Celeste today."

"Shit!" She startled, her head whipping around to look at him. "Scare me to fucking death, why don't you?"

The first smile of the day creased his face. That was the Tori he knew and loved. Something squeezed tight within him and he staggered. *Loved.* God, yes. He loved her. The rightness of the emotion hit him with the subtlety of a punch to the gut. In under two weeks, the woman had wormed her way into his heart and taken up residence. Maybe it shouldn't be so stunning—his instincts had demanded he claim her that first night—but he stood there staring at her like a simpleton for several moments.

"You look dumfounded." The corners of her eyes crinkled. "What's up? What did Celeste say?"

He shook himself out of his reverie, pushing the shock of his revelation away. "Uh… She had to do a lot of digging with her journalist contacts, but there are other reporters Michael and Hector have been talking to. Except Nichols, most laughed it off. But some of them are starting to sniff around the story after those scientists claimed to have DNA proof. This could become an even bigger clusterfuck."

She dropped her chin to her chest. "I have bad news too. My ring of informants is admittedly small, but they found something."

"Fuck." Bastian jerked off his tie and tossed it and his messenger bag on the table beside the door. "Tell me."

Rubbing a finger between her eyebrows, she sighed. "There was another set of scientists who were contacted by an anonymous man and offered hybrid samples."

The ground tilted under his feet and he leaned back against the front door to keep from falling on his ass. "Did they take the samples?"

"No, they passed, thank God." She flashed him a look. "But still. What if there are more? Those are just the ones we know about."

"Fuck," he said again, with feeling. "Did you tell anyone about this?"

She shook her head. "I'm not sure how secure your office is, whether your admin assistant can overhear things, where her loyalties might lie, so I figured I'd wait and tell you in person."

Which meant she also hadn't called the leopards or birds about it either. The statement was telling. Her loyalties were shifting to him, whether she realized it yet or not. He almost smiled at that thought, but managed to refrain.

Her gaze leveled on him. "When are we calling the dads out on this?"

"My brothers and I spoke to the Leonidases today. Adrian, Jason and Celeste are going to fly in at the end of the week to visit Nico. My dad should be back in town by then. So that's when we'll do it—together."

"Staging an intervention." She shook her head. "That's one way of uniting the clans."

"Yeah."

Neither of them mentioned that the Leonidases' visit would make a great time for her to go back to Arizona. She could just hop on the return flight with the leopard contingent. Easy. Over and done.

No. The wolf inside him reared up and snarled, and Bastian felt his fangs emerge to scrape his lower lip. He clenched his jaw and shoved the wolf down.

After pushing away from the door, he approached the couch to kiss the top of Tori's head. He breathed in the scent of her and a band of emotion tightened around his chest. God, he didn't want to lose her. But they'd carefully skirted talking about her remaining in Tennessee, and he couldn't force himself to bring it up now.

His gaze dropped to her lap and he saw what she'd been so focused on when he arrived. A sketch of a new car. It was as amazing as all the others he'd seen—and he'd cajoled her into letting him see the whole sketchpad days ago. She was so talented, and that talent was wasted working as a secretary.

"I want you to design a car for me," he said suddenly, and even he wasn't sure where the words had come from, but as soon as they were out of his mouth, he knew they were absolutely true.

She ran her fingers over the notepad's pages, making them whiz passed like a child's flipbook. "You don't want one of these?"

"These are sports cars." He bent down to rest his chin on her shoulder. "I'm six-three, honey. As much as I like fast cars, they aren't fun to squeeze into for the daily commute."

She tapped the end of her pencil against the paper for long moments. "Why?"

"Because I'm going to have it made." Or have her make it for him, but that might be pushing too far. For the moment.

After twisting at the waist, she gave him an incredulous look. "Do you know how much that would cost?"

"Don't care." He dipped one shoulder in a shrug. "I have money—why not spend it on what I really want?"

She bit her lower lip, something vulnerable and uncertain in her gaze. "I'll think about it."

"You do that. In the meantime…" He caught her mouth with his and slid his hand into the neckline of her shirt to cradle her breast. A sexy little whimper broke from her as she arched into his palm. He plunged his tongue into her mouth, the kiss as possessive as he felt. Sweeping his thumb across her nipple over and over again had her writhing for him, and the scent of her building desire was a heady aphrodisiac as it hit his nostrils. His cock was so hard he ached, but he liked tormenting her too much to do something about his own needs just yet.

She tugged on the front of his shirt. "Come down here with me."

He grabbed her hands and pulled them over her head, forcing her to slide down the couch while he pinned her in place. The position lit a wicked longing deep within him. He grinned and let her go. For now. "I have a better idea."

Jerking upright when he stepped back, Tori snapped, "For the record, walking away is *not* a better idea."

He strode toward the laundry room. "I'll be back and then you'll thank me."

"Unlikely!" she shouted, sounding seriously put out.

He whistled a cheerful little tune to annoy her further. Probably not the smartest thing he'd ever done, but he did enjoy riling her. About as much as she seemed to enjoy riling him. When he got to the laundry room, he rifled through a few cupboards until he came up with the spare clothesline he'd recently purchased. It was a soft cord that would work well for his purposes.

Ripping off the plastic packaging as he went, he walked back into the living room. She'd tossed her sketch onto the coffee table and sat there with her arms folded. "Teasing and leaving are *not* okay unless it's a life-or-death situation. Serious bloodshed doesn't even make the cut. Imminent death only."

"Noted." He wadded up the plastic and lobbed it toward her sketchbook. Then he let the rope uncoil while her eyes widened.

Tongue darting out, she licked her lips. "Lykaios…"

"Ever tried being tied up before, Haida?"

Her nipples tightened until he could see the clear outline of them through her shirt. She pressed her thighs together. "I could get free if I really tried. Even swans have enough strength to snap rope. Or I could shift."

"True." He walked over to the end of the sofa and bent to fasten one end of the clothesline to the thick wooden leg. "But that assumes you *want* to get free."

Her breathing sped up, and he could see her pulse hammering at the base of her throat. Her heady scent wafted on the air.

"Want to play, sweetheart?" He put just enough challenge into his tone that he knew she'd never be able to back down.

Her gaze narrowed on his face. "Fine."

She jerked to her feet, stripping off her clothes. The smooth paleness of her curves came into view and his dick throbbed, chafing against his fly. Her beaded nipples all but begged to be sucked, and he licked his lips.

"Come on, slowpoke." She snapped her bra in his direction, and it hit him in the face. "Keeping a lady waiting is just bad manners. Didn't your mother ever tell you that?"

"Yes, and that's the last I want to say about my mother while I have a woody." He stepped out of his shoes and shucked his clothes. "Lay down on the sofa."

She did as he ordered, but her gaze was glued to his thick erection. "I want you."

A groan escaped him. She was killing him. It took a matter of seconds to have her arms drawn over her head and secured by the clothesline. Ah, yeah. That was a view that would stay with him for the rest of his life—his mate, naked and bound, waiting for him to fuck her.

"Let me suck you," she demanded, tugging at her bonds.

"Nope." He dropped onto the couch between her thighs, forcing them wide. Then he let himself take in the incredible view. She was flushed with desire, her breasts quivering with each quick breath. His gaze dropped to her sex. Slick with cream, the lips were swollen and gaping wide. Perfect. He drew in a lungful of air spiced with her musky smell.

Flicking his tongue out to tease her clit, he felt her body bow against the cushions. A mewling sound spilled from her as he settled in to feast. The flavor of her wetness was like a mellow liqueur that went straight to his head, and he drank deep. Her hips bucked, but he held her down, driving his tongue in and out of her pussy. She twisted like living flame in his arms, but he continued to fuck her with his mouth. He caught her clitoris between his teeth, tugging gently. A sharp cry broke from her, and he felt her shiver with her first orgasm. He loved how responsive she was, loved how he could make her incoherent with want.

He glanced up at her face as he pressed three fingers into her pussy, a swift stroke designed to shock her system. Her eyes flared wide, and her breath stopped. "Bastian, please!"

"Don't I please you, sweetheart?" He withdrew his fingers until he circled the outer edges of her slit. Extending his claws, he used the very tips to toy with her flesh.

"*Yes*. You please me. Don't stop!" She spread her legs wider, rocking her hips up.

After retracting his talons, he slammed his digits back in, filling her. "Never."

Watching her squirm made fire boil through his veins. He nipped at her inner thigh, and she squeaked. Her wetness increased and she pulled on the ties that lashed her down. She was the sexiest thing he'd ever seen. But he wanted to feel her come against his mouth again. He licked her clit while he worked her with his hands.

"Oh. Oh God. That feels so fucking good." Her words rushed out as she undulated on the sofa. "Don't stop, don't stop, *don't stop.*"

Her thighs closed over his ears, muffling his hearing, but that sharpened his other senses. The feel of her silky skin, the scent of sex, the exquisite taste of her cream. Her need fed his own, and he rocked his hips into the leather cushions. The friction was a lesson in control, but he couldn't stop himself from moving. Forming his lips around her clit, he sucked hard, then batted his tongue against the little nub. Her heels dug into his back, and he felt another orgasm roll through her. The tiny spasms of her inner muscles rippled around his thrusting fingers.

He came up for air, his cock so stiff and aching he thought he might explode before he ever got the chance to be inside her. She lay limp against the couch, the rope digging grooves into her wrists from where she'd pulled on them. Her breasts rose and fell in rapid pants, and he reached up to tweak one pert nipple.

"Thank you," she gasped.

Blinking, he startled into a laugh. "What?"

She spoke between ragged breaths. "You said...I'd thank you...when you got back."

Well, then. A chuckle bubbled out of him. He didn't think he'd laughed so often in a long time. She was good for him. He dropped a kiss to her belly.

Her toes flexed against his shoulders and she sighed. "That was *definitely* worthy of giving thanks, Lykaios."

"I love you," he stated quietly. He didn't know why he felt this was the right time to say it, but he did.

She sucked in a sharp breath, her mouth forming a perfect O of shock. "*Bastian.*"

Rubbing his chin over the lower slope of her stomach, he pushed his case. "I know you're thinking about leaving, and I wanted you to know that if you go, you'll take my heart and soul with you."

Tears filled her eyes, her lips quivering as she spoke. "That's not fair."

"I never promised to play fair." Then he lunged up and buried his cock inside her.

"Bastian!"

He heard the rope creak and knew she'd snap it soon. So he twined his fingers with hers and pinned her down. She arched into him, her legs tight around his waist. He plunged into her hard, and she was so wet the glide was smooth perfection. His heart raced, and his lungs worked like bellows as he moved as fast as his wolf speed would allow. She met him thrust for thrust, their movements in sync. It was too good, and he was so hot he was shaking.

"I love you, Tori."

"Oh God." Her sex clenched around him, her legs cinching tighter. He saw tears quiver on her eyelashes, but then she glanced away and rocked her hips into his. "Please, Bastian."

No way was he making it that easy for her. He stopped moving, even though his body screamed in protest. "Tori, look at me."

Her eyes focused on him. Conflicting emotion flashed wildly in her gaze, and he watched self-preservation war with something much more tender.

"I love you." He thrust into her. Once. Slow, but hard.

"You can't—"

"I love you," he repeated. And he plunged in again. He wouldn't let her deny this or run away from it. If he did, she might never stop running. "I love you, my mate. My Tori. I love you."

He kept up that rhythm. One full thrust, one declaration of love. Her gaze never left his and he saw her resistance begin to crumble, saw how his words affected her. A tear tracked down her smooth cheek, but she met each of his movements, silently urging him on. He began to pick up speed, and they shuddered and gasped together. Her sex fisted around his cock every time he entered her. She quivered on the edge of climax and he knew it. Need stretched taut between them, almost to a breaking point.

"Tell me," he demanded.

"I love you too," she sobbed, and shattered in his arms. Her body stiffened, then quaked with orgasm. The sensation of her inner muscles milking his dick sent him careening over the edge after her.

He spurted into her in hot jets, the climax so intense stars burst behind his eyes. Pinpricks raced over his skin, and he fucked her until he began to soften inside her. A quick yank and he snapped the cord binding her, then he sank down on top of her, shaking in the aftermath.

A long time later, she sighed. "It doesn't change anything. You're still the Beta, and I'd still have to give up everything in order to be with you."

"You're assuming the life you'd have with me would be worse than the life you'd have on your own." *Or with someone else,* but he couldn't bring himself to say that.

"Not worse, just not of my choosing," she corrected quietly. "I can't just be your mate, I have to be the Beta's mate too. I'd choose you in a hot second, Bastian. Don't think I wouldn't. But a clan leader's mate?" She shook her head. "Loving you doesn't suddenly change me into a good candidate for a ruler's mate. I'm blunt and outspoken, I swear a lot, I have a bullshit tolerance in the negative numbers, and *none* of those are good qualities for the political lifestyle."

"I don't want you to change." Never. He loved her exactly as she was.

"Thank you, but you can't speak for your whole clan on this one, can you?" Her gaze was serious, but something pained lurked in her expression. "Tell me you honestly think your clan would welcome me with open arms just as I am. Hell, tell me the Alpha alone would."

He couldn't. They both knew it. His father would never tolerate the kind of insolence Tori dished out. And there were those on the Wolf Council who were positively archaic in their views on women. But there was no way in hell Bastian would give her up if she *wanted* to stay with him.

"We'll find a way." He put as much confidence as he could muster into the words.

Her gaze was doubtful. "I wish I could believe that."

"I love you, Tori." His tone brooked no argument. "We will find a way to make this work."

"I love you too." A small smile curved her lips. It was sweet and sad at the same time. "But I could use some distracting right now, my mate."

So could he. Covering her mouth with his, he gave them what they both wanted. It solved nothing, but he craved the connection and he sensed she did too. He could only hope he was right. That they'd find some compromise, or he feared he'd spend the rest of his days regretting that love just wasn't enough.

Four days left. Two weeks had slipped down to one, and now Tori was counting down the days and hours. The Alpha would return today, the leopard leaders would be here the day after and then...she had to make the hardest choice of her life. She tried not think about it, tried to make the most of every second.

Creativity poured out of her, and she worked on the design for Bastian's car with more focus than she'd ever had in her life. Because it was for him or because this was the first time it would actually become something *real?* She wasn't sure, but she knew she needed to get the ideas in her head onto paper.

Her life had fallen into a kind of rhythm over the last few days, where she tried not to dwell on how quickly her two weeks of vacation were slipping away. How she'd have to leave Bastian. While he worked on family business or clan affairs, she worked on the sketches or on the Impala. She went into town every other day to pick up parts she needed and when she was there, she'd meet up with a few old bird friends or members of her mom's family.

Today, she was having lunch with Sarah Beth. They'd only just met, but Tori already knew she liked the fox-shifter. Tori strode into the little Italian place Bastian had introduced her to the night before. It had been stellar enough that she wanted to try everything on the menu, so a repeat visit was more than welcome.

"Hey, Tori." Sarah Beth waved from a booth in the corner.

Bypassing the seating hostess, Tori joined the fox. "How's it going?"

"I'm working on a new house with my brothers. The testosterone was getting pretty thick, so I was glad when you called."

She chuckled. "Happy to give you an escape route."

"I love the chicken parmesan here." Sarah Beth set down her menu. "Have you tried it?"

"Last night was my first time and I had the three-cheese lasagna. Amazing. Chicken parmesan sounds good though." Tori slapped a hand over her grumbling stomach. "And I'm ready to order if you are."

"Bastian's showing you all the good places, huh?"

Indeed. They'd spend most of dinner making out at one of the café tables outside. The man had the most amazingly talented mouth she'd ever had the pleasure of kissing. What they'd done in the backseat of the SUV on the way home was enough to make her blush. Damn, but he got to her in the naughtiest possible way. And it seemed to get better every time. She squirmed a bit and made herself tune back in to her lunch companion, who was still talking.

"There's supposed to be a new Greek place opening next month. We should check it out. Ajax likes Greek food."

Next month? She was supposed to be leaving at the end of this *week*. A dart of pain shot through her chest at the thought. She didn't want to leave, but she wasn't sure she should stay. Her dismay must have shown on her expression because the fox-shifter gave her a knowing glance.

"You haven't decided if you're going to stay yet," Sarah Beth said quietly.

"No."

"It took me a while to accept my mating too." She grinned unrepentantly. "I drove Patrick a little crazy."

"He was a little crazy anyway." Tori waved that away. She'd met Patrick Aquinas when she was a teen. He was incredibly hot and as overbearingly alpha male as they came. "Tell him I said hi, will you?"

"Will do." Sarah Beth's expression sobered. "Do your parents know yet? Your mom's got quite a reputation among the birds. I've heard she can be—"

"She can be. And my dad can be worse." So could her brothers. Hell, so could Tori. She wasn't an easy woman. She had attitude out the wazoo and wasn't afraid to call a spade a spade. People either loved her or hated her, and that went double for the rest of her family. She cleared her throat. "I haven't told them yet. I'm not ready. Not until I know what I'm going to do."

She'd talked to them on the phone, but she didn't get really specific about why she'd decided to vacation in Tennessee. To relax, to reconnect with her mom's flock of swans—never the whole truth. She never mentioned Bastian at all, and she felt awful lying to them, even by omission. Her family was usually brutal in its frankness, but now she was being everything except frank.

"That has to be hard." Sarah Beth made a face. "My mom would kill me if I kept that big a secret."

Tori snorted. "Yup. Just call me deep-fried."

They both laughed. The waitress showed up to take their orders and the conversation turned to less controversial topics. Tori had a good time, but she was living in the moment. Not able to make plans too far in the future, not knowing where she'd be.

After picking up a few car parts she needed, she headed back to Bastian's. Her mind wouldn't let the mating problem rest. But that problem had to be weighed against the benefits of keeping Bastian. They *loved* each other. But it didn't make their lifestyles any more compatible. Her heart and her logic were locked in an argument that didn't quit.

She had to admit that working on cars more was incredibly fulfilling, and having Bastian fulfilled her in other ways. If he were anyone other than the Beta, she honestly didn't think she'd hesitate. However, clan leader was a lifetime commitment. Shifters weren't elected like humans. It was who he was, and she didn't want to change him. So where did that leave her?

On the other hand, she'd loved her time in Tennessee. The jangling instinct within her that cried for change had dimmed to almost nothing. Sometimes it was surreal, sliding so easily into a life that had never been hers. Like it had just been waiting for her to show up and start living it. But if she did that, would she still be the Tori she'd always been? The simple existence she'd fallen into the past week and a half hadn't yet sucked her into any of the bullshit of clan politics. She hadn't been lying to Bastian—her tolerance for bullshit was somewhere between low and nonexistent. With the Leonidases, she'd had some emotional distance. It was just a job she could walk away from any time she wanted. Involved, but not really invested. That would no longer be an option if she stayed with Bastian. She'd be all in. Was she willing to deal with that? Because it was harder and harder to imagine walking away from Bastian.

The thoughts nagged at her as she drove back to Bastian's place. And found that the wolf clan had descended.

Her political reprieve was over.

Shit.

Bastian's SUV sat in front of the house, but so did two other trucks. This did not bode well. Bastian was far too careful to let people show up unexpectedly when he was keeping something—or someone—secreted at his house. Which meant whoever was here outranked him in the clan. Or was family. Probably both.

Double shit.

She eased her foot off the brake and drove her car around to park in the garage. After this, she was probably going to want to bury herself under the hood and not come out for a while. Pulling up the convertible's top allowed her to stall for a few more minutes, but then she had to face the music.

Squaring her shoulders, she strode toward the porch steps. A vicious little twist of nerves within her had her wishing she could light up a cigarette and inhale deeply. Nice time for her body to decide that she hadn't quite kicked the habit.

She followed voices through the house to the living room. Bastian sat with two other men and a woman. Pausing in the doorway, she took in the scene. Bastian saw her first and something pained flashed in his gaze. His mouth opened to speak, but all conversation stopped as his family rose and turned as a unit to stare at her. Refusing to feel like a pinned bug under a microscope, Tori gazed back just as boldly and lifted a single eyebrow. "Hello."

The men looked so much like Bastian, there was no doubt of the relation. One was Michael Lykaios—she'd seen photos of him in the werekind papers. The woman was an older version of Celeste, which meant she was Michael's human wife, Miranda. Meet the parents time. *Greeeat.*

"It's nice to finally meet you." A sinfully charming smile curved the lips of the last man. "My older brothers have all had the pleasure before, but I clearly don't visit my big sister often enough."

"By process of elimination, you must be Dominic." Tori stepped forward and shook his hand, unsure if she should smile back because the glint in his gaze told her he was being so effusive to needle Bastian.

Dominic waggled his eyebrows. "For a woman as pretty as you, I'd be anyone you wanted."

"Really, Dom," Miranda admonished. "And, Bastian, you haven't introduced us yet. Mind your manners."

Again, that almost-pain flickered deep in Bastian's gaze, but the smile that touched his mouth looked genuine enough. "Mom, Dad, this is Victoria Haida. She's the administrative assistant to Jason and Adrian Leonidas. Tori, these are my parents, Michael and Miranda Lykaios. He's the Alpha, as you know," he finished drily.

After stepping forward, Miranda squeezed Tori in a tight hug. "We're happy to have you join the family."

That sent a hot shock through her system. They knew about the mating. And they thought she was joining their family. Oh God. She couldn't breathe. It wasn't as if Bastian and she were *married*. But they'd marked each other as mates, and in the shifter world, that was even more important. Still, she had no idea what to say to these people any more than she'd known what to say to Ajax. She was only just getting comfortable using the "mate" word around Bastian.

"Oh, I—"

Michael cut Tori off. "I came out to formally acknowledge your union. The clan will be pleased that Bastian's finally taken a mate. We're all looking forward to new wolf cubs."

What? He already had her barefoot and pregnant? Hell. Cocking her head, she gave him an incredulous look. "You're assuming we'd have wolves and not swans."

He gave her a mildly condescending glance in return. "The dominant predator in a pairing always dictates the offspring. Surely you know that."

No, I don't know that's always *true, but fuck you very much for trying to educate me on the matter.* She was an example of how that wasn't always true. Her father was a grizzly bear, an apex predator. Her mother was a swan. According to conventional wisdom, *all* of their children should have been born bears.

Tori's brothers were, but Tori was demonstrably not a grizzly. She kept her mouth shut though. Her parents had never advertised to the shifter community that they were a predator/non-predator pairing who'd borne a non-predator child. For all Tori knew, she might be the only one, but her parents were ferocious about their private family life remaining private. Tori had no desire to discuss this with the wolf Alpha. He gave her the same overbearing vibe as Hector Leonidas, and it ruffled her feathers. The swan within her wanted to hiss in reaction.

Instead, she just smiled at him. "I don't count my eggs before they're hatched, Alpha."

He snorted, but his eyes narrowed as if he wasn't sure if she was being funny or impertinent. She doubted he was the type to brook impertinence.

Just the kind of guy every sarcastic wench like her wanted for a father-in-law.

What she'd like to know is how the Lykaioses knew about the mating because if that was really why the Alpha had come, then he'd known before he got here. Bastian hadn't been forced by an unexpected familial drop-in to explain her presence. She was going to kick his ass.

Feigning a pleasant tone, she asked, "Can I get you guys something to drink? Maybe a snack?"

"A beer for me," Dominic jumped in before his parents could politely refuse, which they looked like they were going to do.

Blessing him, Tori offered him a smile. She glanced at the parental units. "Michael? Miranda?"

Miranda said, "Some sweet tea, if you have it."

"For me too," rumbled the Alpha.

"Great. Bastian, can you help me carry all the glasses?" Latching on to her mate's arm, she dug her nails in and pulled.

"Sure." The resignation in his expression made her want to punch him.

"Mind if we watch the game?" Dom didn't bother waiting for an answer. He grabbed the remote, turned on ESPN and cranked up the volume.

The sound would cover her conversation with Bastian, so she was going to kiss his brother later. The moment they entered the kitchen, she rounded on her wolf. "What. The. Hell. I know the Leonidases aren't the types to run off at the mouth, so how the hell do they know about us marking each other?"

Bastian thrust a hand through his hair, his silver gaze sparking ire. "He confronted me about my trip to Arizona—I had to tell him something."

"So you threw me under the bus?" She was going to have an aneurysm, right there on the spot. Boom. Head exploded.

"You're being melodramatic." He sighed, looking annoyed that she dared question him, which just made her want to staple things to his forehead. He shrugged. "Distracting my father with the mating seemed like a better idea than opening the door to what that meeting was about. Or what's coming tomorrow."

Just as she'd suspected, what she needed took a backseat to diplomatic intrigue. Frustration crawled through her, tightening her muscles until she wanted to cry. Or scream. She understood that he was under a lot of pressure, that the stakes were high, but his "just come for a visit" line had now turned into a big fat lie. People weren't supposed to sacrifice their *mates* for the sake of convenience. Her father would never, ever have done this to her mother.

"They're hugging me and welcoming me to the family, saying how they can't wait for me to pop out your wolf cubs." She flung out her arms. "What happened to not pressuring me?"

He had the grace to wince. "Tori, I—"

"Don't." She held up her hand. "Just don't."

Her purse was beside the door and she grabbed it, automatically reaching for the cigarettes she usually smoked

231

when she was stressed. Only they weren't there anymore. Shit.

"What are you doing?"

"I need some air." She hitched the strap of her bag over her shoulder. "I'm sure you can make excuses to your parents. There has to be someone else you can throw under the bus next."

He glowered at her, and the subvocal growl of the wolf made every animal instinct she had screech to life. Her inner bird wanted to spread its wings and launch skyward, escaping the predator's threat. The human side of her knew Bastian would never harm her, so she suppressed her instincts. Instead, she dug out her keys and slammed through the backdoor, heading straight for her car.

She had to get out of here. She needed a moment to get her head on straight, because it looked like it was time to make some permanent decisions. Ready or not, the wolves had come.

Resisting the urge to peel rubber down the driveway, flinging gravel behind her in her haste to escape, she kept the car to a sedate speed.

Thank God the highway was curved enough to make her concentrate. It gave her something to focus on, something that wasn't Bastian Lykaios. A wonderful man who came with so many strings attached. But if she wanted the man, she'd have to take those strings too.

She loved him, and it was tearing her apart inside. A tear slid down her cheek and she swiped at it roughly.

Another car roared up behind her, riding her bumper. Normally, she'd leave the jerk in her dust, but she wasn't in the mood for racing today and she wasn't that confident in the Impala's abilities. The other car feinted a few times, nearly clipping her fender before the driver sped up to pass her. Her heart rate bumped up at the close call.

"Road raging assclown," she grumbled, slowing to let the maniac go by. "Where the hell is a cop when you need one? Never around, that's for damn sure."

Just as the car drew even with her, she glanced over and saw a middle-aged couple inside. Neither of them looked at her. No, they were busy arguing with each other. The driver's face was flushed as he shouted. The woman in the passenger seat reached over and slapped him. Hard. Then she dove for the steering wheel.

Tori slammed on the brakes and jerked the Impala toward the side of the road, but not fast enough to keep from getting sideswiped. Head whipping unnaturally to the side as metal crunched on metal, she felt muscles and tendons scream in protest from the abuse. Fighting to control the car as it began to spin, she managed to get the Impala onto the shoulder while the other car kept right on going, still swerving across lanes.

Breathing hard, sweat dripping down her face, she tried to control the shaking in her limbs. Her knuckles showed white where they gripped the wheel, but she couldn't seem to make herself let go. "Fucking cunterrific douchenozzle pissant motherbitches. Irresponsible asshat drivers are gonna get people killed. You're goddamn lucky *I'm* a good driver or you might have gotten us *all* killed."

She kept muttering as she unbuckled her seat belt, which took an embarrassing amount of concentration because her fingers still quaked. Getting out the normal way proved impossible because the other vehicle had hit just in front of the driver's side door, wedging the door shut. It had probably warped the frame too, which pissed her off because of all the things that had been wrong when she bought the Impala, the frame had been nice and straight.

"Bastards." Finally, she twisted and squirmed until she could haul herself out of the window to check the extent of damage.

Yep, bent frame, dented door, scrapes, dings and other problems, but nothing she couldn't fix. The engine was okay and they hadn't hit the wheel well. So…it could have been worse. Then there was her physical damage. Her neck tinged and ached, and even with her shifter healing abilities, it was going to take at least a day for the whiplash to subside.

The rumble of an engine approached and she glanced up to see the idiots returning. "Oh, they just now noticed they maybe hit someone, huh? Fuckwits."

Shifting around to face them as they did a U-turn and pulled in behind her, she propped her hands on her hips.

The woman hopped out first. "Oh, my goodness. Are you all right?"

She had a distinctly nasal New England accent, which meant she wasn't from around here. Their car looked like a rental, so Tori guessed they were tourists. She tried not to roll her eyes. "Yeah, I'm fine. My car, however…"

The older woman cast a dubious glance at the Impala. "How can you tell?"

Oh, really? Run her off the road and then insult her new baby? No way in hell. Tori crossed her arms and glared. "I'm going to need your insurance information. Now."

"I have it." The gangly driver approached, looking nervous and sweaty, his Adam's apple bobbing. Something about him was…off. Tori didn't know why she thought so, but something about him had her wanting to back away. He looked *too* twitchy. Drugs, maybe? It didn't help that the woman—his wife?—pinned him with a murderous glare that could have peeled flesh off bones. She suddenly didn't look so harmless. What was up with these people?

"We'll need your information, so we can report this." The woman gave her a sickly smile, and Tori edged away. The whole situation felt weird and she wanted to escape as quickly as possible.

"Fine." Tori hustled around to her passenger side, reaching through the window to open the glove box and grab her paperwork. Her neck locked in protest at the quick movements and she gritted her teeth. She heard the crunch of gravel underfoot as the couple followed her, which made her hurry. She didn't like having to turn her back on them, mere humans or not.

Then she felt a sharp, stabbing pain in her thigh. After jerking upright, she spun around to see the woman smiling with deranged glee as she lowered a strange-looking gun. Tori looked down where her flesh stung. A needle protruded from her leg and the sharp pain turned to burning fire in her muscles. "What the f—"

And the world went black.

The sun had long set and Bastian sat on the porch, waiting for Tori. She wasn't answering her cell phone, but these mountains didn't get the best reception. So maybe she wasn't ignoring him. Maybe.

Some deep, agonized part of him suspected she might have decided to keep on driving until she reached Arizona. She'd said she'd leave whenever she wanted, and he'd sworn not to stop her. Uneasiness scraped at his nerves, and it took every last ounce of his control to keep from tracking her down and…what? Wrestle her into coming home with him? Force her into staying? That wasn't how mating worked. Plus, a bird-shifter could fly away any time she wanted unless he intended to lock her in a cage forever. She had to *want* to stay.

Restlessness ate at him, and he jerked to his feet to pace his way around the porch in endless circles. The knowledge that something was wrong nagged at him until his sanity was in tatters. Of course something was wrong. His mate had left him.

His mate had left him.

The pain of that thought was staggering, and the wolf inside him howled, clawing for release. But primitive beast couldn't win this one—the human love game was far more complex than wolf mating. He bent over and grabbed his knees, sucking in a deep breath. God, how would he convince her to come back? How could he make her want to stay? Today was just a taste of what his family would offer. Entanglements, demands, always in each other's lives and business. He loved that about them, but for a woman who lived nowhere near her family, maybe that was a little too much togetherness. Then there was the future-Alpha thing. Sure, Bastian had power and connections, which so many women had wanted in the past, but a handful of days with Tori had shown how little that impressed her. What did he have to offer a woman like her? Not enough, apparently. Or maybe too much. More than she was willing to put up with.

He didn't know. He just knew he ached like he'd been sucker punched. Watching her walk away had been the hardest thing he'd ever done. He hadn't even been able to think clearly enough to come up with excuses for his family. They'd tried to stay and fuss over him, but after a couple of hours he'd ejected them from his house. He needed to lick his wounds in private.

His phone's screen lit and Tori's ringtone sounded. The cell almost vibrated itself off the porch railing while he lunged to grab it. She was calling. What did that mean? Had she decided not to leave after all? God, he fucking hoped so.

"Hey, did you get lost?" He forced his tone to casual, bottling up the frustrated fear that ate at his soul.

A long, crackly pause came over the line, and he worried she might be losing cell reception. Then a cold, terrifyingly calm voice answered him.

"We have Victoria Haida."

CHAPTER NINE

After they'd gotten the swan installed in their lab, Barbara
meticulously sorted through the blonde's purse for any
further clues to her identity. Her driver's license listed her as
Victoria Ann Haida of Tucson, Arizona, which meant she
didn't live in the house they'd followed her from. So who did
live there? More hybrids? Another colony, perhaps? Or just
the man they'd seen her in a lip-lock with at an Italian
restaurant in Chattanooga the night before?

Barbara had combed through all of Nichols's article notes
and he believed many of these werekind lived in groups—
clans—scattered around the country. He'd been in Georgia
because he believed the town's mayor might be a shifter and
wanted to expose the man. But that was his problem, not
hers. Picking up the swan's cell phone, Barbara scrolled
through the contact list and call log, wondering how many of
them were also hybrids. There were several missed calls from
someone named Bastian Lykaios. The picture that popped up
on the screen for him was certainly the man they'd seen the
swan kissing.

Lykaios. The name jolted through her like electricity.

Nichols thought a man named Michael Lykaios was his anonymous informant. Which made him *Barbara's* informant too. Her chest burned, and her hands trembled for a moment. How closely was this Bastian related? She swiveled her desk chair to face her computer and went searching through all of Nichols's many notes. It took a while, but she found the connection. The fox-shifter's family was close to the Lykaios family. Nichols thought that Michael Lykaios might be their clan's leader. Nichols had dug through public records to find what he could about the family, and Michael's eldest son was named Bastian. And Bastian owned a home with the same address where they'd tracked Victoria Haida.

Lykaios had cost her everything, and hate flooded her, bitter as bile. Her breath rushed out and her hands balled into fists, but a smile spread across her face. She wondered what Michael or his son might do to get Victoria back. There might be some leverage in that for Barbara to get what she wanted—recognition. And vengeance.

"I never agreed to kidnap anyone," Hastings bleated, pulling her attention to where he slumped against the wall like a petulant child.

She gave an incredulous snort. "What did you think we were going to do when we followed her? Ask her to tea?"

His mouth worked, and then a pugnacious expression stamped his features. "You could have killed her when you rammed her car. Then where would we be? Observing a dead body?"

"Don't be ridiculous. We barely tapped that junk heap she was driving," she retorted with exaggerated patience. Didn't he realize how important their science would be to the world? They would be *legends*. They would have their revenge on those who'd scorned them. They'd have their revenge on those who'd gotten them into this mess in the first place— hybrids. Michael Lykaios, more specifically.

Barbara Powell would have the last laugh. She'd go down in history.

But that didn't mean she had to take this weak-willed milquetoast sop with her into academic renown. She folded her arms. "So what do you want to do, Hastings? What's your grand idea?"

"I don't know." He ran his hands through his already disheveled hair. He gestured to the room around them, a defunct medical clinic out in the sticks. It worked well for their needs. "I set up the lab. You were supposed to find us a specimen."

"And I have."

"A willing specimen!"

She arched an eyebrow. "You thought we'd set up an illegal lab that doesn't follow any of the normal human subject testing rules and then we'd get willing subjects?" Then again, these hybrids weren't exactly *human* subjects, were they? The normal rules didn't apply. What they were doing was really no different than performing tests on rabbits or monkeys. Of course, they weren't following approved protocol for that either, so why bother splitting hairs?

"I just want our work recognized. I never…I never planned to…" He flapped a weak hand toward the unconscious blonde strapped to a gurney.

Barbara stared at him. He was an idiot, unfit to do the work they needed to do, but she might be able to turn the situation to her advantage. "Fine, then we'll give her back."

"We will?" Shock made his jaw sag.

"Yes." She turned her laptop in his direction. "She's a friend—possibly girlfriend—of a clan leader's eldest son. Perhaps they might publicly acknowledge the validity of our findings in order to get her back."

Of course, that didn't mean Barbara couldn't experiment in the meantime. Unholy excitement went through her at the idea. Perhaps she wouldn't give the woman back regardless. But going through the motions would shut Hastings up until she could find a way to get rid of him. Unfortunately, he'd become a liability.

His lips twitched as he considered. "That's blackmail."

Really, the man was pathetic. All he did was complain, when they were on the verge of greatness. Barbara ground her teeth, reaching for her usual detached calm. It had been harder and harder to come by lately. "Is it really worse than kidnapping? Everyone will get what they want, won't they?"

"Okay." He nodded, looking the picture of misery.

Grabbing the swan's phone, Barbara took a deep breath. Then she made the call. "We have Victoria Haida."

There was a pause. This Bastian didn't ask who she was, didn't demand if this was a sick joke, didn't plead. None of the things she might expect. Instead, a deep voice that was as cold and dangerous as black ice came through the phone and a chill went down Barbara's spine.

"If you hurt my mate, I will hunt you down and tear you limb from limb."

His *mate*. So not just a lover or girlfriend. That gave them an even bigger advantage here, but a low growl came through the phone and the hair on Barbara's nape stood on end. Swallowing, she rallied. "Your mate is safe, for the moment. What you do now will determine her fate."

"I want proof of life before I do a damn thing."

"You'll get it." But on *her* terms.

The kidnappers had agreed to allow Bastian a videoconference with Tori under two conditions. The first was that no law enforcement was involved and the second was that his father was also there to witness it. Which meant her abduction had something to do with the Alpha. Someone trying to overthrow him? The clan had been fairly stable for years, but this wouldn't be the first time someone had attempted to stage a coup.

He didn't know, but he called his father while driving like a bat out of hell to get to his parents' place. Terror was a living, breathing thing inside him. Consuming him until he wanted to howl. When he arrived, Paul had already fired up the computer and tested to make sure they'd have no technical issues on their end.

Tomas and Dominic collided with each other as they rushed into their father's den. Tomas's voice was a staccato demand. "Any news?"

Bastian shook his head. The room fell silent for a few minutes, the tension thick as everyone waited. The waiting was what killed him. Was she hurt? Scared? He refused to think she was already dead. He just…his mind wouldn't go there. They'd taken her for a reason and contacting him meant they wanted something. So they had a reason to keep her alive. For now.

"Have they asked for money?" Hector Leonidas asked from where he sat in one corner.

"No," Bastian replied shortly. "They haven't made any demands yet."

The leopard-shifter had been there when Bastian showed up, but had decided to stick around for the show. As if Tori's kidnapping were just some entertaining TV program. Bastian wanted to kick the cat's ass. It was all he could do not to put his fist through the nearest wall. Anything to make the fear ease for a single moment. The sick dread that had settled like lead in his gut from the moment he'd taken that call got heavier and heavier by the minute. The wolf in him wanted to hunt down and tear apart anyone who dared touch its mate, but the man maintained ruthless control. Now was the time to think, not react.

Tori's life depended on it.

"We'll get through this, son." Michael clapped his hand on Bastian's shoulder, squeezing in support.

He swallowed hard, grateful for the bulwark of strength his family offered. If he needed them, they came. No questions asked, no hesitation.

"They wanted you here to witness this." He met his father's gaze. "Do you think someone's staging a coup? Do we have any enemies I don't know about?"

Unlikely, but he had to ask. It wouldn't be the first secret his father had kept.

The Alpha shook his head. "The last problem we had was back when Derek conspired with that bird-shifter to ruin us and kill Celeste. But he's long dead and he had no family left."

Bastian pinched the bridge of his nose, fighting to remain calm. Who had taken his mate and why? But more importantly... "Why Tori?"

"Maybe she was a target of opportunity," Dominic suggested. "Maybe anyone close to the Alpha would do. She did leave the house when Mom and Dad were there."

Michael shook his head. "How did they know she had any kind of relationship with me? We haven't made any big announcements about Bastian being mated."

"I don't know," said Dom.

"We're just chasing our tails with this," Bastian growled. "We need more information. I'm not getting the cops involved, but we have our own contacts that can track these bastards down. I want her found. I want *every* resource we have thrown at this. Is that clear?"

Everyone nodded silently, even the Alpha, who wasn't used to taking orders from anybody. It would have been funny if it weren't so fucking tragic.

The computer trilled and Paul nodded. "You're on, Brother. I have some software running that should be able to trace their IP address. Depends on how good they are at covering their digital tracks."

"Here's hoping they don't have a computer expert." After grabbing his father's arm, Bastian escorted the older man over to the monitor, so they'd both be clearly visible over the video. He tapped the button to answer. "Where's Tori?"

"Here." Her voice was clear and then the camera turned on and her face appeared. Behind her was a blank white wall and he could only see her from the waist up, but she was wearing the same clothes she'd had on earlier in the day. She looked pale but healthy. And pissed.

The anger on her face did more to relieve him than anything else. If she'd been scared, it would have been so much worse. But it was bad enough.

"I'm okay," she said. "They drugged me, but otherwise…"

"Good. That's good." He nodded, keeping his voice as calm as possible. "What do they want?"

She glanced to the side at something or someone beyond the range of the camera. Then she refocused on Bastian. "These are the scientists fired from MIT when they reported discovering human-animal hybrid DNA." Her throat worked and rage tightened her features. "They've told me that if you don't immediately confirm their scientific findings to the press, then they will kill me. Dr. Powell says that she'll perform a recorded vivisection of me and release the video to the media."

A choking sound was Bastian's answer to that. They were going to cut his mate open like a frog in science class *while she was still alive*. Bile pooled in his mouth and every sense of rational calm he had drained into a puddle of panic in his belly.

"We'll do what they say," Michael said smoothly.

Tori shook her head, locks of hair slapping her cheeks. Determination mixed with the anger in her expression. "*No*. I can get myself free. Don't do what they say. Bastian, don't—"

A needle slammed into her arm and she collapsed out of view.

Bastian felt that needle as if it hit his flesh, and the breath exploded out of him. The noise that wheezed from his throat was that of a wounded animal. The wolf within him raged, barely leashed, and Bastian quivered with the need to hunt down and kill those that hurt his mate.

An older woman stood in front of the camera. The slicing and dicing Dr. Powell, no doubt. "You have two hours, and I had better see it on CNN. Local news simply won't cut it. My findings are correct and I will prove them any way I have to. Even if it means ending Ms. Haida's life. For the advancement of science, of course."

She had a detached coolness to her expression, but a terrible triumph flashed in her gaze. He had a feeling if he stood in the same room with her, the air would reek of madness. This woman would do exactly as she said—she would kill his mate without a qualm. For the advancement of science, of course.

Her gaze went to one side of the screen, to the Alpha. "Jeff Nichols and I are both of the belief that you, Michael Lykaios, are responsible for the information we've been given about hybrids. By not coming forward and confirming my results—results you clearly wanted me to find—you made a laughingstock of me and my research partner." A small smile twitched at the corner of her mouth. "When you play with people's lives, *animal*, this is what you get."

Then the screen went black.

A red haze filled Bastian's vision, his hands curled into fists, and his talons pierced his palms. He turned to look at his father, who'd gone pale and tight around the mouth.

"She's not wrong, is she, Dad? You are the one leaking information about werekind." To hell with the intervention they'd planned. He wanted this out in the open here and now.

Arrogance flashed across the Alpha's face and his chin lifted. "What does it matter now who—"

Restraint snapping, Bastian had one fist balled in his father's shirtfront and the other hand wrapped around his throat in the blink of an eye. He slammed the Alpha back against a bookshelf, a roar breaking free. "*Admit it!* I want to hear it from your mouth. You and Hector Leonidas have been leaking information about the werekind."

Fangs bared, his father snarled. "Yes. We've been *controlling* the release of information that would have inevitably gotten out anyway." He wrapped a hand around Bastian's wrist, but couldn't break his grip. "Now get your hands off me, boy."

Bastian's fingers tightened until his father gurgled. Exclamations from his family were shocked and scared, but he kept his gaze locked on his father. The words that came from his mouth were far calmer than he felt, the kind of terrifying calm that came at the eye of a storm. "You're a traitor. When this is all over—no matter what the outcome—you will retire as Alpha."

Michael's eyes narrowed. "You can't—"

"If you don't retire willingly, I will challenge you for leadership. Do you honestly think you can beat me in hand-to-hand combat?"

A flicker of doubt crossed the older man's features.

Bastian continued, relentless, anguished. "Because of you, these scientists got our DNA in the first place. Because of you, they had to prove their results *at any cost*. Because of you, my mate has been kidnapped and her life is in danger. If she dies…" His voice trailed off in a growl. He couldn't even finish that sentence. If Tori died, he didn't know what he'd do. It gutted him to even think of her jeopardy. That it was his father's fault ripped his loyalties in half. Everything he'd ever believed, ever known about his world, was crumbling to dust around him. In his world, the Alpha never put his people in danger. In his world, his father was never wrong.

His world had come to an end. Now he just had to pick up the pieces.

It took every scrap of discipline he could muster to ease his grip on his father's throat and step back. A collective breath went out from behind him. He turned and saw varying degrees of wariness and fear on his family members' faces. Hector looked blandly uninterested.

Michael tugged at the bottom of his shirt to straighten it. "I'm giving the news conference."

"Yes, you are." Bastian stabbed a finger at both Michael and Hector in kind. "You will be demonstrating how people shift into animals, and you'd better make it a damn good show."

Hector rose from his chair, eyes narrowed. "A clan leader isn't a circus sideshow performance."

Eyebrow arched, Bastian snorted. "You made this mess and you will take responsibility for it. Publicly. You wanted the truth to come out and so it shall. All of it."

A husky feminine voice came from the doorway. "I agree with you. But I'll do it if he won't."

Miranda spoke for the first time, her eyes red-rimmed. "Who are you?"

"Phaedra Leonidas."

There was a slight hesitation on the surname, but Bastian could see the sharp resemblance to her sons. The green eyes were the exact same shade and shape, and though her inky black hair had a few threads of gray, its color reminded him distinctly of Jason's. Bastian wondered if she might also be a melanistic leopard like her eldest son.

"What are you doing here, Phaedra?" Hector asked, his voice sounding like gravel in a blender. He took a stumbling step toward her, looking as pale and shaken as if he'd seen a ghost.

She arched an eyebrow. "I told you I'd only come back when you weren't the clan leader anymore."

"I stepped down several years ago," he said gruffly. "I assumed the boys would tell you. I know you've emailed them."

"I've been out of contact for several years. My work takes me away from civilization, you know."

"I know." There was a resignation with just a hint of old bitterness to the simple statement. "Studying wild leopards in their natural habitats."

Her head tilted in acknowledgement, but her green gaze pinned him in place. "You've made a mess, Hector. I always told you arrogance would be your downfall."

"I'm so overjoyed you're here to witness it, then," he replied drily.

Her lips twitched up in a smile.

Ignoring the older couple, Dominic turned to his brothers. "I hate to be the one to point this out, but haven't we been fighting to keep this kind of exposure from happening? Isn't that why Jason and Adrian are coming tomorrow? To help stop these two traitors?"

There was an awful silence in answer to that, and Bastian drew in an unsteady breath. He swallowed hard. "You're right."

When he spoke, Michael's tone cracked like booming thunder. "What have you—"

"Stop talking." Bastian didn't raise his voice, didn't so much as meet his father's eyes, but the Alpha's teeth clacked together as he shut his mouth.

"I'm sorry, Bas." Dominic faced him squarely, a muscle twitching in his cheek. "Someone had to say it."

"I know." Hell lived inside of Bastian. He could all but hear the ties that bound his family beginning to shred and snap. But all the wolf within could focus on was the fact that Tori's life was on the line. The minutes she had left were slipping away, and the wolf cared nothing for politics. Animal instinct said his mate won out over all other considerations. He met each of his brother's gazes in turn. "My objectivity is shot. We all know it. I'm not going to stand in the way of the news conference. I can't. Don't ask it of me."

"We won't," Tomas replied.

Dom's face twisted in protest and Bastian lifted his hand. "I won't stop you if you try to prevent it. But I could never forgive myself if it's what would have bought the time needed to save her life."

"They're going to kill her anyway," Dominic fired back. "The moment you've given them what they want, they have no reason to keep her alive."

Paul punched his youngest brother's shoulder. "What the fuck, Dom? It's *his mate* you're talking about."

"You're all thinking it too!" Dom threw out his arms. "You don't know we can't track them down first. You haven't even tried anything else yet."

Tomas sighed. "You also don't seem to realize that what we've found this week means the information leak is far bigger than we suspected. We're using Dixie cups to bail out a sinking barge."

The younger man rounded on him. "So now *you* think this is inevitable too? You're on their side?" He jabbed a finger toward Michael and Hector.

This was normally the time Bastian would step in to break it up, but his brain was spongy with panic. He didn't know what was the right thing to do, didn't know which brother to back. He was used to the occasional divided loyalty, between family needs and clan needs, but this was the first time his personal needs demanded precedence. But at what cost?

"It wasn't inevitable until those two made it so. A self-fulfilling prophecy." Tomas scrubbed a hand down his face. "If this has to happen, I'd rather do it in the name of saving a woman's life than in the name of catering to Dad's whims. If this buys us more time to track them down before they try to kill her, I'm in favor of that."

"I agree," Paul put in.

"No. No, no, *no*." Dominic jammed his fists down on his hips, but then his cell phone trilled, and he fished it out of his pocket. "Shit. I need to take this."

He stepped away, but didn't leave the room. There was a brief conversation before he hung up and turned to Bastian. "The shifter we have in the police department says they've found Tori's car abandoned off of northbound I-75. They're starting a search for her, but our guy has met her before on vacation at Refuge Resort. He knew she was werekind and he could smell you'd been in the car recently, so he called me."

Northbound. No wonder Bastian hadn't seen the Impala on his way here. He'd gone south. Meeting Dominic's eyes, he asked, "Can you join the search? You're the best tracker in the clan. If anyone can find her…"

Dom tapped his phone against his thigh, his brow furrowed. "Aurelia Rossi and Cyrus Vallas are also damn good. I want them on the search too."

Speaking up, Michael pinned a look on his youngest son. "Does that mean you're not going to try to stop the news conference? Call in the birds for reinforcements to silence me?"

248

"No, I'm going to fucking track these bastards down."
Dom's jaw firmed. "If you really do go through with this
media blitz, don't expect me to throw myself in front of the
bullets when other clans send assassins after your ass. And
they will. Maybe the Wolf Council too. Did you stop and
think about that, Dad? *Did you?* Did you think about what
would happen to Mom and Paul? They can't smell an assassin
coming. Or did you honestly think everyone was going to go
along with you peacefully, because you're the Alpha?"

"I did this to protect you!" Michael exploded, red-faced.
"By deciding what information the humans—"

"I'm sure Bastian feels your actions have really protected
his mate," Dominic drawled sarcastically.

Michael paled, swaying on his feet.

"That's enough, Dominic," Miranda whispered.

He met her gaze. "I wish that were true, Mom."

Bastian set a hand on Dominic's shoulder. "You have an
hour and forty-five minutes. Seconds counts, Dom."

"I'll find her," he swore. He jerked his chin toward
Michael and Hector. "If you're not going to stop them, you
better make sure they don't fuck this up. You're good at
handling people."

A ghost of a smile crossed Bastian's lips. "Thanks, I
think."

The bottom line was, he was emotionally compromised.
He was so desperate to find Tori, he was liable to make a
mistake that tripped up the search. Other wolves would
expect leadership from the Beta, and he couldn't give that,
not with any sort of rational objectivity. Which meant he
shouldn't be involved in the hunt. It was the hardest truth
he'd ever had to face. It made him feel like less of a man, a
pathetic excuse for a wolf, and a terrible mate.

His baby brother tore out of the house like his tail was on
fire, and Bastian said a silent prayer that Dom succeeded.

Dragging in a shaky breath, Bastian turned to Tomas. "Set
up the news conference. Make sure you get CNN."

"Consider it done." The younger wolf pulled out his phone and followed Dom outside.

"Tori said she could get herself free," Miranda pointed out softly.

Yeah, and Bastian had rejected that idea out of hand. Tori hadn't even made it to the end of the videoconference still conscious. She wasn't a predator species—she didn't have the natural defenses wolves had. "There's no time to wait and see if she's right. I can't take the risk that she might be wrong."

Paul had parked himself at the computer and was typing frantically. "I've traced the scientists' credit cards to Atlanta and then Chattanooga, where they emptied their bank accounts and went to ground. They did have to use ID to rent cars."

Frowning, Bastian considered options. "They have to have taken her somewhere nearby, and unless they're using kitchen knives, they have to have gotten their hands on medical supplies—scalpels, syringes, sedatives."

"I'll see what I can find." The human swiveled back to his keyboard.

Tomas returned to the room. "Alpha, I need your opinion."

"What?" Michael looked up from his chair next to Hector.

But Tomas wasn't looking at his father. He was looking at Bastian, speaking as if Michael had already retired.

Just like that the world took another turn into unreality.

CHAPTER TEN

"I thought you were giving them two hours! They have thirty minutes left. You haven't even waited to see if they do what you want."

Hastings's whine grated on Barbara's nerves. They had the swan on the operating table, the video camera was running, ready to record the vivisection and Hastings stood there with a syringe full of anesthesia to put the blonde under. Instead of administering the dose, he wanted to argue about the procedure.

"No, your problem is you haven't thought anything through since we left Massachusetts. It doesn't matter what I said to those animals. I don't trust them anyway. Why would I? They've left us hanging before." Observation and samples weren't going to be enough. She needed more. She needed to get inside and see how this species ticked. X-rays showed the organs were of a similar size and location as those of a *homo sapien*, but there had to be other indications besides blood work that showed these weren't normal humans. Barbara was going to find it before she ran out of time.

"I never agreed to murdering anyone." Hastings shook his head wildly, his fingers trembling so hard they made the needle wobble maniacally. He wouldn't be able to give the swan the shot. He was useless, just as Barbara had suspected all along. Weak. Stupid. A liability.

She jerked her chin toward the door. "Leave then. See how long it takes the cops to pick you up. You won't even get to make history first."

"You're insane," Hastings breathed.

"What did you just say?" The corner of her eye twitched. Those were the words her department chair had used before he'd fired her. Something in the back of her mind snapped, and she lunged for him. "*What did you just say?*"

Tori woke to the sound of an argument. Her mind swam for a moment, her head pounding. Bright light shone down on her so she didn't want to open her eyes and be blinded. Bastian's face flashed through her mind, but she pushed the image away. She had to focus now or she'd never manage to see him again. Swallowing hard, she made herself listen. And heard what she didn't want to. They were deciding whether or not to gut her like a fish right then and there. Great. She could feel the tight grip of restraints around her wrists. Wriggling them showed no give. She didn't think she could muster the strength to break free. There was no way out.

Not in her human form anyway.

Her shift would have to be swift, so they didn't have time to react. She took a few deep breaths, steeling her nerves. Her heart rate sped, her muscles tensing. The arguing grew louder, angrier. When she heard the crash of metal and the sound of struggling, she turned her head and opened her eyes. They fought over a needle, grappling to get the upper hand while Tori lay on a cold metal table.

Now was the time, if she was going to make her escape.

Freeing the animal within her, she let the shift take her. Feathers erupted from her skin, her body reshaping itself in the space between breaths. She wriggled free of her clothes. Wings spreading, she surged upward into flight. The low ceilings hampered her liftoff, but at least she could move.

The scientists stopped fighting, shouting and scurrying to find some way to cage her.

"Get her!" Dr. Powell waved her arms in the air as if she might reach Tori. "Hastings, get her!"

"I'm trying, Barbara!" Hastings came at Tori with a broom, jumping and swatting while Tori careened into the top of a tall cabinet, knocking things off it and into the man's path. She jump-flew to the operating table to do the same with all their sharp, pointy surgical tools.

"Ha!" Barbara slashed with a scalpel, ripping open the skin beneath Tori's left wing.

Screeching, she flapped her wings and pecked at the woman. Barbara scrabbled back, colliding with her partner and they both fell on their asses. Launching upward, Tori wheeled around, trying to find an exit.

There wasn't one. Not that she could open without hands and human body weight.

Fuck.

She had to get one of them to open the door. Hissing loudly, she dived at the man on the floor, striking at him with her beak, clawing at him with her feet. He pedaled back, his shoes squeaking on the linoleum. His arms covered his face as he screamed.

Whirling up again, Tori tried to avoid the slash of Barbara's scalpel. Spittle flew from the woman's mouth. "I'll kill you, you fucking animal. I'm going to cut you open and pull out your insides for the whole world to see. You're not human—you'll never be human. You're no better than a lab rat!"

That was it. Until that very moment, Tori had been focused on escaping, but now her powerlessness and rage coalesced into something far more dangerous. They all thought she was helpless because she wasn't a predator. Fuck. That. She'd been drugged, kidnapped, terrorized, and this woman was going to pay for her crimes. Right now.

Circling, Tori waited for an opening and dove again, driving her beak into the woman's eye. Blood and gore exploded from the ruined socket and the sound that issued from Barbara's throat was one that would haunt Tori for the rest of her days.

Pain exploded through her as Barbara swung blindly and jabbed her scalpel into Tori's side. Bellowing, the scientist tried to wrap her hands around Tori's long neck, but she used her claws to rip through the skin of arms and wrists. Flapping her wings at the woman's face, Tori flopped backwards and scrambled away. The scalpel slipped free as Tori lifted off, but the wound was deep. This was not good. She was airborne, but in agony. Still, she wouldn't die, and she had both her eyes. Unlike Barbara Powell.

She'd call that a win. Mostly.

Hastings screamed when Tori turned on him. Shielding his eyes, he ran. He shoved open a door and Tori was after him like a shot, diving hard to make it before the door swung closed.

And…she…was…*out!*

The door tried to rip out a few of her tail feathers, but she squeaked through. A shriek of rage came from behind her, and she heard Barbara slamming open the door again, but Tori was up, up, up and beyond the mad scientist's reach. Free, but not yet safe. There wasn't much in the way of towns or even homes below her—no lights, no chimney smoke. Even if she found someone, she didn't know how friendly they'd be with a naked, bleeding woman showing up on their doorstep. Maybe friendlier than she wanted and then she'd be in real trouble.

But she'd flown these mountains before, and she got her bearings after a few minutes. A flick of her wing and she turned toward shifter land. The birds were closer than the wolves, and Ajax would help her contact Bastian.

She just hoped she made it there in time to stop him from making the biggest mistake of all time.

Hurry—that was all she could think. She flapped her wings as fast as she could. Her muscles burned and lungs strained as she pushed for speed, but she was hampered by her wounds and weakened from the repeated druggings. *Hurry, hurry, hurry.*

"We are here today to confirm that human-animal hybrids exist. We want to confirm the reports of Jeff Nichols." Michael spoke at the press podium and nodded to the reporter who lurked off to the side of a crowd of news crews. "And to acknowledge the validity of Dr. Powell's and Dr. Hastings's DNA research."

A ripple of reaction went through the crowd, a few coughs of smothered laughter that made Michael flush. In anger? In embarrassment? Bastian wasn't sure, but he knew his father had been Alpha long enough that he was *not* used to being mocked or disbelieved when he spoke. The older man shifted his weight and glowered until people settled again.

"We'll be demonstrating for you," he continued in a tone barely above a growl. His gesture took in Hector, who stood next to him, and himself. Bastian, Paul and Tomas sat in the front row along with Miranda and Phaedra.

Bastian's gut churned with anxiety. They'd managed to pull off this news conference within the allotted time, but every moment of it had been agony. The seconds ticking by on the clock felt like years. Was Tori unharmed? Was the most vibrant, beautiful, amazing woman he'd ever known still breathing or had her connection to him gotten her killed? The very thought made him want to vomit.

Moving so they stood on either side of the podium, Hector and Michael faced the dozen cameras aimed at them. Then they began to shift. Fangs punched through their gums and claws sprouted from their fingertips. Hair covered their skin, then their bodies began to twist, their clothing tore to shreds as they stooped and transformed into their animal forms.

The crowd gasped, everyone surging to their feet and scrambling back. A few shouts rang out, and the female reporter sitting beside Bastian fell out of her chair, hand covering her mouth with horror. Shit. They hadn't considered the reaction to having a full-grown wolf and leopard unleashed on a pack of humans. These were animals they feared, animals that could kill them. They should have had a non-predator species here, but they didn't.

Michael quickly shifted back to human form, while Hector remained a leopard.

"Do you all believe me now?" Michael demanded. "Shape-shifters are real."

Bastian glanced around and saw trepidation flash across the faces of the reporters. His father's massive physique and gruff demeanor said strength and power in the wolf clan, but these people saw those same qualities as something to fear.

His father wasn't handling this well. Another knock to the invincibility of the Alpha. Bastian should be too old to be so disillusioned by this, but that was the month he was having. He needed to save this, fast. Whether they knew it or not, every shifter in the world was counting on this introduction to human society going well.

Grabbing the robe his mother held, Bastian hopped up on the stage and shoved it into his father's hands. "Here, put this on, will you? Your junk is on national TV."

A few giggles and snorts of laughter followed that remark, and Bastian turned to the microphone. He smiled, the easiest, most charming grin in his repertoire. "Ladies and gentlemen, I know this is a surprise to all of you. If you read Mr. Nichols's articles or heard about Dr. Powell's and Dr. Hastings's research, you probably laughed it off. But I'm telling you here and now that shifters have been among you for millennia. You know us already. We can be your neighbors, your coworkers, your politicians, your favorite actors—"

A man in the back shouted, "Which politicians and movie stars are shifters?"

Bastian tsked and wagged a playful finger. "Nice try. I'll let them out themselves when they're ready."

The reporter shrugged. "I had to try. That'd be some juicy news."

And this wasn't? Bastian kept that thought to himself and continued his campaign to make these people like him. "What I'm trying to say is that we are regular people. You can't tell who we are just by looking. Most of us go to work every day and try to make a living, just like you. We try to do the best we can to keep our families safe and happy. The reason we've been reluctant to come forward before now is *our* fear of *you*."

"Us?" asked the female reporter in the front row.

"Yes, you." Bastian nodded. "There are all kinds of myths and hysteria about werewolves that could make people think shifters are dangerous or a threat to people, when nothing could be further from the truth."

The woman tipped her head to the side. "So, a werewolf doesn't bite people during full moon and make them werewolves too?"

He gave her a wolfish grin. "Is that an offer? Because I only bite in bed."

She blushed and tittered. "Are you single?"

Celebrity sex symbols were better than lab rats, so he smiled slowly. "No, but my brothers are. Stand up, guys."

He shot them a look. Who cared if Paul was human or not? These people didn't know that. He was good-looking and ladies flocked to him. That was all that was required at the moment. Both brothers rose, faced the cameras and reporters, and each of them smiled easily at the women in the crowd, who sighed audibly.

"But seriously," Bastian continued, "being a shifter is genetic, like hair and eye color. We don't drink blood or bite to change humans into werekind. We're just people."

"People who turn into animals," someone muttered.

"Yes, we do change into animals." He shrugged and set his hands on the podium, leaning forward earnestly. "But it's an ability we're born with. We can't help it any more than we can help being born brunette or blond. It's important that the world realize that. We don't do anything wrong to become this way. There's no devil worshipping or witchcraft or hocus pocus involved. This is a genetic condition we inherit from our parents." He let out a breath, sensing the emotions in the room had shifted more to curiosity than hostility, especially among the females. "I'm sure you all have a lot of questions, so—"

About twenty hands went up at once, a few people yelling out questions without being called on.

"One at a time, please." Bastian lifted a palm and the room quieted. He pointed to Nichols. "Jeff, I think you deserve first shot at a question, considering you've been on this story for a while now. Annoying the crap out of us too."

Several reporters chuckled at that, and Nichols wore a grin as he stepped forward to speak.

The cell phone in Bastian's pocket buzzed, but he ignored it. If the police or the wolf trackers had news on Tori, they'd been instructed to call Paul, not Bastian. Paul had a phone that could get reception absolutely anywhere, so communication on this mission was his job. Bastian needed to focus on handling the humans, and he'd guess that any shifter who'd tuned in for this broadcast—especially the Wolf Council or any other clan leader—would be calling him to threaten his life.

Suddenly Paul was out of his chair and striding out of sight. Bastian felt his heart stop, but then Nichols asked his question and Bastian answered by rote, trying to remember to be charming, funny and sincere. He had no idea if he managed. For the rest of his life, he'd never remember the next few minutes, though he'd see them often enough on television.

Paul stepped back into the room and mouthed, "She's safe."

Relief so intense it staggered him whipped through Bastian. He had to lean against the podium for support. *Thank God. Thank you, God.* She was alive. She was safe. Nothing else in his world mattered as much as that.

Paul's lips kept moving, and the words were distinct: "Ajax is going to murder you."

She'd have to get in line behind the Wolf Council. Bastian had had no illusions going into this press conference. He'd known what was coming for him, what was on the line.

He'd traded his life for Tori's.

CHAPTER ELEVEN

Three weeks later, Bastian miraculously remained alive. He still wasn't quite sure how it had happened, but he wasn't going to complain.

He was also the wolf clan Alpha.

The realization still made him break into a cold sweat. He hadn't expected to have the title for several decades. He'd always assumed his dad would die in harness, eschewing retirement to remain in power. But the world had turned ass over end in the last five weeks, and nothing was as it used to be. Nor would it ever go back. Welcome to the new normal.

The new normal in which Tori had left him. The blistering voicemail he'd received the night of the press conference allowed little doubt as to why. He hadn't believed that she could free herself, hadn't listened to her and had fucked every werekind over because of it. His actions were unforgiveable. She was done with him.

End of story.

All of his calls had been unreturned. She refused to speak to him. Which was why, after three long weeks of trying to sort out the aftermath of the big reveal, he was driving the battered Impala up a backwoods mountain highway in

Colorado. Bastian took a deep breath and did what he could to quell the trepidation and anger that surged in his gut.

The only way he'd known where to find her was that she'd called his secretary to arrange for her car to be transported to her parents' house. She wasn't speaking to him, but she cared about getting her fucking *car* back. He'd had his assistant tell Tori that the wolf clan would have someone drive the vehicle over. That someone was Bastian. Tori just didn't know that yet.

A part of him still couldn't believe she didn't understand his actions, didn't understand how desperately he'd needed her to be safe. Didn't see that he'd do anything for her.

The explosion that press conference had started was still sending shockwaves through the human and shifter worlds, but he could only deal with one catastrophe at a time.

"Honeybird Drive," he murmured, braking for the turn off Highway 82. He'd left Aspen behind miles ago and had entered bum-fuck nowhere territory about an hour before. This road was unpaved, littered with large rocks, pitted with potholes, and made his teeth clack together with each jolt of the wheels.

According to the map, he had about five miles left until he was face to face with his mate for the first time in three long, excruciating weeks. He swallowed hard and accelerated up the road. For all he knew, Tori had been hoping the Wolf Council would kill him, which would certainly end her inconvenient mating problem.

Though he'd fully expected to have the Wolf Council turn their backs on him—on his entire family—they hadn't. He'd prepared his mother and younger brothers to flee wolf territory, just in case the Council handed down a death edict. At the very least, he'd expected banishment. If it was death, Bastian was determined that it was only his father and he who would pay the price for their actions. At the time, he'd been grateful that Tori wasn't there.

Fortunately, Michael had already convinced just enough members of the Wolf Council that werekind exposure was inevitable that the vote had gone the Lykaios family's way. Mostly. The Council had demanded Michael's retirement as Alpha and condemned his actions, banishing him from clan land for the remainder of his life. If he didn't obey this edict, the sentence was turned to one of death. Bastian had scrambled to call in personal and family favors, so now Michael and Miranda were settling down in dolphin territory in Florida.

The Council had held only Michael and Hector responsible for the information leaks that led to shifters being outed. Hector was also permanently banished from wolf lands, though that was far less drastic than what happened to Michael. Frankly, Bastian had never known the Council to be so lenient. To their minds, Bastian had made the best of a bad situation, but he wasn't at the root of the problem so he wasn't punished. They had confirmed his right to ascend to clan Alpha.

Even several weeks later, he still couldn't believe it. The reality was so jarringly different from what he'd expected. He shook his head, blowing out a breath. His family was safe for the moment, but the crisis had only just begun for shifters.

And Bastian wanted his mate at his side, if he had to be the one dealing with humans' reaction to werekind while his father got to kick back on a beach in Miami. Not an entirely fair assessment, but Bastian wasn't inclined to be reasonable about his father right now.

Then he reached the final turn. "Chimera Lane. Go straight for two miles, destination on the right."

Unlike the road off the highway, this one was wide and smooth. Both were on Haida property. Bastian chuckled. Someone didn't want visitors. It seemed like just the kind of thing Tori would do to discourage anyone from finding her home—annoy the shit out of them until they went away.

When he finally reached the top of the rise and a sprawling house came into view, he braked to a stop and took in his surroundings. Drawing a deep breath, he smelled Tori for the first time in twenty-one long, frustrating, terrifying days.

Something within him loosened at that proof that she lived. But then wariness made his muscles tighten. Yes, he smelled Tori, but the overwhelming scent was the musky odor of bears. This was no passing scent. He was walking into a bear's den.

A bear's den that was Tori's family home. He frowned. He knew her mother was a swan and still living, but had she remarried a bear after Tori's father died? Tori hadn't mentioned it, but that didn't rule out the possibility. There was little documented about the Haida family—at least not much his assistant could dig up. He'd gotten the feeling Ajax knew more than she said, but since the bird queen was royally pissed about the press conference, Bastian hadn't pushed her for information on Tori.

There was only one way to find out about the Haidas. He eased his foot off the brake, coasted the car up to the front of the house and parked next to a classic Chevy pickup. Apparently, his mate came by her love of old vehicles honestly. Climbing out of the driver's seat, Bastian took another deep breath. Three—no, four—bears nearby, and the sharper tang of excitement told him they'd sensed his presence. Not good, but he stood his ground and let them make the first move.

They filed out onto the wraparound porch, eyes narrowed, fists clenched. Anger radiated off them, and that anger was directed at Bastian.

Outstanding. Just how he'd been hoping the day would go. He nodded calmly. "I'm looking for Tori."

"She doesn't want to see you," a female voice declared. The voice was honeyed with a Southern drawl, and the woman who pushed open the screen door and lined up beside the bears gave Bastian a very clear picture of what Tori would look like in thirty years. This had to be her mother. "I believe her wishes were made very clear to you."

He waved a hand at the Impala. "I came to deliver her car, as promised."

The woman smirked. "Clever, just saying it would be a member of the clan dropping it off. This task seems a bit menial for the Alpha."

There was no good answer to that one, so he shrugged and got back to his main mission. "I'd like to speak to her before I go. I drove a long way for the opportunity."

The oldest bear male growled, "You can get the hell off my property, and I might allow you the opportunity not to get your arms broken before you go."

Backing down now wouldn't get Bastian what he wanted and would put him on weak footing for any future visits here. He crossed his arms. "You can try."

Anticipation gleamed in the gazes of the younger males—Tori's brothers—and they stepped forward as a unit.

"Stop," Mrs. Haida called out, and her sons paused, tensing. She sighed. "Come into the house, Alpha."

"It's just Bastian, ma'am." He mounted the steps, keeping a wary eye on the bears, and followed the petite woman inside.

"I imagine you still look for your father when you hear the title, but you better get used to it quick," she said unflinchingly.

They walked through a comfortable living room, down a hallway, and ended up in a large, bright kitchen. The scent of Tori was stronger here, as if she'd spent a lot of time in this room, and painful longing wrenched through him. But she wasn't in the house. Her scent was too far away for that. If Bastian knew anything about her, she was out tinkering on some car or other.

"Sit down." Mrs. Haida waved him into a chair and the bears came in behind him, a looming presence that made his wolf's hackles rise.

He settled into the seat and waited. The woman had a reason for inviting him in rather than letting her sons pound him into hamburger.

She stared at him for a long moment. "She's having nightmares."

Pain clutched at his chest. He'd worried all these weeks if she was well, if she was suffering any ill effects from her captivity. He'd seen a copy of her medical report from the werebirds' doctor, a list of her injuries and treatment, but that didn't say anything about her state of mind. His hands fisted on his thighs and he swallowed hard.

Tori's father dragged out a chair and sat, glowering at Bastian. "You shouldn't tell him that, Rhea."

"Let me say my piece, Vin." She met her mate's gaze and the bear grunted, jerking his chin to indicate she continue.

The older man met Bastian's gaze, and he got the shock of his life. Tori's eyes were the exact same shape and color as this bear's. Impossible, unless he was her biological father. A bear had fathered a swan. What the fuck? He felt his jaw sag, and he stared, which wasn't the brightest move to make with a surly species of shifter.

One of the brothers snorted with derision. "Tori didn't tell him about us. He just noticed the eyes."

Meeting each gaze, he saw that all of three brothers had the same eyes. "She told me about you as people. She didn't mention species." He looked to the tallest one. "Orien." The shortest one—which was relative because they were all huge. "Krispin." The middle one, who'd been the snorter. "Miles."

Their glares told him he'd pegged them correctly. He sat back in his chair. "So, Tori's half bear. That explains a lot."

Miles looked like he fought a grin over that observation, but it was quickly masked.

Rhea brought Bastian's attention back to her. "Regardless of what my daughter shifts into, she was kidnapped on your watch, Bastian. *My baby* was kidnapped and cut up with a scalpel. Why should I trust you with her safety? Why should I let you talk to her?"

"You shouldn't," he replied. "If it were my daughter, I'd…"

He sighed and shook his head. How the hell did he convince them when he'd kick any man's ass who'd dared put his daughter in harm's way? Maybe not intentionally, but by bringing her to Tennessee, he'd made her a target. His father's actions had made it so, and Bastian hadn't been able to stop it.

"I didn't protect her." He met each Haidas' eyes in turn. "I won't give you any excuses for that. I'm her mate and it's my duty to keep her safe. I'll do better in the future." He let a breath ease out. "Whether she wants to admit it now or not, she loves me. And I love her. We're mates. It's as simple as that."

Krispin slouched against a cabinet. "She's in more danger than ever, what with you letting the cat-shifter out of the bag."

"I know."

"She's on the internet too," Miles added.

Bastian winced. "I saw."

The police had combed through the crime scene and one of the lab techs who'd examined the video footage taken of the thwarted vivisection had decided to get rich quick by selling it to the media. He'd been fired, but it didn't matter for Tori. The video of a swan shifting, chasing around, pecking at and generally kicking the asses of two evil scientists had gone viral and become the stuff of late-night comedic spoof. Tori had to be thrilled about her new cyberstardom.

"We've had reporters trying to call her." Krispin's lips twitched. "Some of the stupid ones decided to come visit without an invitation. We've had to be creative in order to get rid of them."

If her brothers were even half as wicked as Tori, Bastian almost felt sorry for those reporters. Almost.

"I'll keep her safe, if she'll give me the chance." Not that she'd needed his protection, in the end. She'd gotten free, just as she'd said she would. But that video had shown just how close she'd come to death. If Hastings hadn't hesitated with the anesthesia, Tori would never have woken. Sweat slicked Bastian's palms at the very thought, and he rubbed his hands against his jeans. If he had his way, she would never be in that kind of position ever again.

"Orien, take him out to the garage." Tori's mother tilted her head, bird-like, in a move that reminded Bastian so strongly of his mate that his chest hurt. God he'd missed her.

"What?" Miles piped up, his heavy brows draw together. "We don't even get to kick his ass for exposing shifters?"

Bastian rubbed the back of his neck. "You wouldn't be the first to try this month."

"Who else did?" The bear's eyes twinkled with unholy glee.

"A few members of the werebird Messenger Corps, a couple of mountain lions and one of the black bear-shifters from Kentucky." Luckily, they had just been ass-kicking attempts rather than assassination attempts. His father hadn't been as fortunate. They'd had to keep tight security on his parents to make sure they weren't harmed. There'd been death threats and two thwarted assassinations. He was worried because he loved his parents, but there was still a gut-churning anger at what his father and Hector had brought down on everyone. Bastian hadn't asked, but he imagined the Leonidases were dealing with similar issues with Hector. There was a lot of resentment in the shifter community right now. It was doubtful that would fade any time soon.

"Orien, don't make me repeat myself," Rhea warned.

The tallest brother groused, "Why me?"

"Because I said so."

He huffed. "That's not fair."

"Life's not fair, honey." Her voice held just a tinge of pity. "I thought I taught you better."

He grunted in response to that. Jerking his head at Bastian, he walked out the back door.

Pausing before he followed, Bastian addressed the older woman. "Thank you."

She smirked. "I sincerely doubt you're going to survive this, so thanking me is a bit premature. But you're invited to dinner if my daughter doesn't kill you first."

"I appreciate the invitation." He lifted one shoulder in a shrug. "I hope I can take you up on it."

"Smart boy." She nodded approval.

Orien reappeared in the doorway, glaring through the screen. "You coming, wolf breath?"

"Right behind you." He pushed open the mesh door and stepped out onto the porch. Without another word, the bear-shifter led him across the driveway toward a large metal structure.

Trepidation hit Bastian again, growing with each step that drew him closer to Tori's scent. A tinge of engine grease mixed with her smell. He could hear the bone-jarring blare of rock music along with the whine of power tools. Of course, she was working on her cars. He almost smiled. Almost, but the stakes were too high for him to be amused for long.

Her brother tapped a console inside the door, and the music shut off. "You have a guest, Tori."

"Tell him to go away," came a growl from under the vehicle. Her booted feet and jean-clad legs were all Bastian could see.

He glanced at the bear-shifter. "Give us a minute, would you?"

After a moment's hesitation, the man nodded and turned to leave. "Mom said he could stay for dinner, Tori, so take it up with her if you have a problem."

"Traitor," she muttered loudly as the sound of her brother's footsteps faded.

She didn't give any indication that she was going to come out from under the car, which pissed him off more than a little. Instead of snapping at her, he glanced around the garage and frowned when he saw his name written on a sketchpad sitting on the workbench. Fine, if she was going to be rude, so was he. He flipped open the notebook.

Each page was a detailed drawing of every possible angle of a car. *His* car. The one he'd asked her to design for him. Similar but even better than the sketches she'd left at his house. It was in the "nouveau classique" style she favored, with sleek aerodynamic lines and reminiscent of an old Chevy. The car was dark blue with a pinstripe on the outside, while the interior was gray with white accents. Just right for his tastes—she'd nailed it.

Well, that answered one question that he had. He'd wondered if she'd even thought about him in the time she'd been gone, or if she'd put him out of her life so completely she'd refused to look back. He traced the line of the fender on one drawing, feeling the tiny spark of hope that had brought him this far flare a little brighter inside him.

"Did you have something to say or did you just want to hang out in my garage?" The toe of one boot bounced in a rhythm that could only mean annoyance.

Did he have something to say? Where to start? "Nice sketches."

The boot froze mid-bounce and he watched the muscles in her legs tense. He couldn't help the grin that formed on his face. Her hand came out to grasp the frame of the car, and she hauled herself out from under it.

"What do you want, Bastian?"

"You. Obviously. Why else would I be here?" He set down the notebook and settled his hip against the workbench, drinking in the sight of her. Even with a smear of grease on her cheek, she was the most beautiful thing he'd ever seen.

She shot to her feet, her eyes wide and wounded. "I don't want you here."

"Why?"

"Why?" Her mouth worked for a moment. "*Why?*"

"Yes, why?"

"Oh my God," she snapped, spun on her heel and stomped over to a sink to scrub her hands and arms. "I mean, the fact that you even have to ask. *Why?* What the fuck, seriously? Did you not get my message? I thought I was pretty damned clear."

"I got it. You were clear, but there's something you didn't consider."

He received a glare for that response. "What's that?"

"We're still mated." That said it all to him. There was no escaping this, 'til death did them part. They could separate, but they could never mate with anyone else. The bottom line was, he loved her too much not to try and make this work. He loved her enough to stand by and let his father hold a news conference that sold out his entire race. He loved her so much that the very idea of a world without her in it was incomprehensible.

She sighed, sounding weary. "Trust me, I haven't forgotten that. I wish I could."

That was a knife to the gut. "Don't say that."

After yanking a towel off a stack by the sink, she dried her hands. "I can't believe you revealed shifters to humans. Were you not at the meeting where representatives from the leopards, the wolves and the birds *all* agreed on avoiding that?"

"*I* didn't reveal shifters, Tori. My father did."

"Don't try to wiggle out of responsibility." She poked a finger at his chest. "You stood there and *let* your father do it. I didn't see you tackling his ass to the ground to keep him from speaking into the mike. You were part of that mess."

"You think I haven't reconsidered my actions of that night over and over again? I have. I made the best decisions I could in a shitty situation." He threw out his arms. "Even if we'd had time to confront the dads as planned, the damage had already been done. Enough information had been leaked to those scientists that they were going to prove their point *at any cost*. If it wasn't you they'd kidnapped, it would have been Sarah Beth or Ajax or, God forbid, Ajax's daughters. I've been over their notes. Those little girls were on the list of people they considered grabbing. Maybe the birds would have reacted differently than the wolves did. We'll never know, but—"

"But those are *little girls*. I'm an adult. I said I could get myself free." She grabbed her earlobes and tugged. "You never listen. You don't trust me to take care of myself."

"They managed to kidnap you in the first place," he pointed out.

She sliced a hand through the air. "I know that. I also know I managed to get myself unkidnapped *without* your help."

True enough. He sighed. "Your family is pissed that I didn't protect you. Apparently, they think you occasionally need someone to take care of you."

"Well, *I'm* pissed that you didn't listen, that you outed our entire fucking species. I'm not worth that. No one person is worth that." She poked her thumb between her breasts. "How dare you put that on me?"

"Was I just supposed to let you die?" Inconceivable, the idea of letting his mate be murdered. His mind wouldn't even go there.

Her chin jutted pugnaciously. "Yes. If it came to that, *yes.*"

"No."

"You're not thinking rationally." She tapped her forehead. "You're thinking with your he-man alpha testosterone, like 'how dare someone touch *my mate?*' rather than with your brain that knows it wasn't worth throwing all shifters under the bus to save my skin."

"My testosterone?" A harsh laugh spilled out of him, and he felt the humiliating burn of moisture at the backs of his eyes. "No, you're right. I wasn't thinking with my head, I was thinking with my heart. It's just a fucking shame my mate can't understand that." He shoved a hand through his hair. "What the hell am I doing here?"

Her hand rose as if to touch him, but then she let it drop. "Bastian…"

"If our situations were reversed, would you have wrestled my father to the ground and knocked him unconscious? Would you have killed him to keep our secret safe? Because short of death, Michael Lykaios had made up his mind and nothing but the grave was going to stop him. Or Hector. How many members of my family—if we're getting to extended family, even Hector counts—did you want me to lose that night? Maybe it makes me a shitty person and an even shittier leader, but I'm not strong enough to be responsible for your death and both of theirs. Are you?" His gaze bored into her, daring her to respond.

"No," she whispered.

"I assumed I'd be killed for being party to that news conference. I assumed I was trading my life for yours." For a moment, she seemed to stop breathing, her hands pressed to her chest. He pushed on relentlessly. "I tried to get everyone but my father to stay home and pretend no knowledge, but they refused."

She swallowed. "I don't want you to die for me. I don't want *anyone* to die for me."

"I would in a heartbeat. If that's what it took to keep you safe."

Shaking her head, she harkened back to her main argument. "If you had just trusted me to get free, we—"

"I trusted that you would try, but I couldn't risk that you might fail." He sighed, exhausted. "Just remember the last thing I saw was you being knocked out. How was I to know when you'd regain consciousness, if ever? If they'd had their way, you wouldn't have."

"I know." She closed her eyes. "I hate—*hate*—that you did this for me. That I was the excuse Michael and Hector got to use to fuck everyone over."

"You feel guilty, and you're angry." And unless he missed his guess, she was using her fury to cover her self-blame. "The anger is totally understandable. We're *all* angry, sweetheart. But the guilt is misplaced."

She opened her mouth to retort, but all that emerged was a squeak when he reached out to wipe away the grease streak on her cheek.

"Dominic is going through this too. Blaming himself for not tracking you down in time. He was about twenty minutes too late. All he found was a rabid Cyclops scientist and a fight-tossed lab." Nothing Bastian or Paul or Tomas or Miranda had said could ease Dom's shame, so Bastian had ordered everyone to leave him alone and let him work through it on his own. Sometimes a wolf just needed to lick his wounds in private.

"The bitch deserved it." Tori's jaw jutted. "I don't care if Michael screwed her over, she had no right to try to kill *me*."

"True. Nice job too." He cradled her face between his palms as she gave a watery chuckle. Bastian wanted to deny his own sense of failure, but he'd come too far to try to hide anything from her. He'd decided before he left Tennessee to lay everything out on the table when he got here, and he wouldn't take the coward's way out now. "I hate—*hate*—that you were in danger and I could do nothing to stop it. I'm ashamed of how I failed you. I'm ashamed of how helpless I was to stop *any* of the shit that went down that night."

Pain reflected in her gaze. "We're just one big fucked-up mess, aren't we?"

"That sums it up nicely, yeah." He drew in a deep breath, and with it came the sweetness of her scent. "I've missed you. Even knowing you were out there in the world hating my guts, it was enough to know you were alive enough to be feeling anything. But damn, I missed you."

Her lips compressed and moisture glimmered in her gaze. "I don't hate you. I hate the situation we were in, I hate that I feel so guilty, I hate that I didn't keep myself from being kidnapped, I hate that you didn't believe I could save myself, I hate everything Michael and Hector did. But I don't hate you." She closed her eyes, and a tear slipped free. "I missed you too."

He caught the tear with his thumb, swiping it away. "The question is, can you get past this enough to come home to me?"

A laugh straggled out of her. "To be completely honest, it wasn't just what happened that night that kept me away. I *can't* be mated to the Alpha, Bastian. I just can't. It was hard enough to consider being mated to the Beta, but the Alpha? All the reasons I gave you before are even more valid, to like the *nth* degree. I could twist myself into knots for you, but I couldn't bite my tongue for the rest of my life. Especially not with the news cameras watching my every move now. It's not just the shifters keeping a watchful eye on clan leaders anymore."

He'd thought of this long and hard, trying to come up with a solution that would work for everyone. There wasn't one. All he could offer was a temporary compromise. "Five years."

"What?" She blinked up at him.

Smoothing a lock of golden hair away from her forehead, he offered a crooked smile. "I talked to my brothers and we think that if I stay the Alpha for five years, I can step aside and hand over leadership without making too many waves."

The air left her lungs in a rush and he could feel the jolt of shock that went through her. "I..."

He shrugged, hoping beyond hope that she could live with the plan he'd come up with. Their time apart had been a torment. "Think of it as being the First Lady while I'm elected president. You may not like it, but it's not forever."

"You'd give up being Alpha. For me." Her voice was flat, disbelieving.

"Do you really doubt it?" He arched his eyebrows. "You've already seen what I would do for you. *Anything* is pretty much on the table."

She licked her lips. "I don't know what to say."

"I do listen to you, Tori." He stroked his fingertips over her face, reveling in the feel of her soft skin. "I don't always agree with you and I'm not always going to do what you want, but I listen to what you say."

Her mouth opened and closed, more tears forming in her eyes. "I thought it was a package deal. Mating with you meant being a clan leader's mate. Forever."

A reasonable assumption, and one he would have agreed with wholeheartedly before he'd met her. Before he'd loved her. "Maybe it would be for some Alphas, but as much as I want to be a good ruler for my people, there is one thing I want even more. *You.*" He tried to smile, but didn't think it was very successful. "So, here I am, asking if you'd be willing to hang in there with me for a few years."

He held his breath, waiting for her answer. Waiting for her to decide the direction their lives were going to take. If he walked away from the clan now, it'd be a free-for-all grab for power. The situation could easily devolve into civil war, which would give humans all the excuse they needed to step in and mess with shifters. Bastian couldn't let that happen. He had to stay leader long enough for the power dynamic in the clan to settle down again. Which might mean living without his mate for five *years*. How he'd survive that, he didn't know.

His entire life hinged on what she'd say next. "Tori?"

She knew he was waiting for a response from her, but she stared at him like a halfwit. He was willing to walk away from one of the most powerful positions in the werekind world for her. She could see on his face that he was dead serious, that he'd give it all up just to keep her happy. Another tear spilled over her lashes, and she sniffled. After all the sobfests she'd had since she'd left Tennessee, you'd think she'd be too dehydrated to cry, but apparently not. She'd told her family the waterworks were some kind of delayed aftereffect from quitting cigarettes, but she doubted anyone had bought that particular lie. They'd just given her a wide berth, quiet support and a busted-up car to keep her busy.

"I'm not going to give up my cars." She raised her chin. "I'm thinking about making a business of it. The Wolf Council and everyone else will just have to deal."

"Fine." He nodded, something hopeful beginning to shine in his beautiful eyes. "I'll support your right to whatever career you want. Just agree to come back."

A snuffling little sob escaped, and she wanted to throw herself into his embrace. Being without him was like a physical ache inside her, a bruise that had just kept spreading and spreading. She didn't know how much longer she would have lasted before she'd packed her stuff and hightailed it back to Chattanooga, even without the compromises he'd offered. It was humbling to realize how much she'd have given up for him, and even more humbling to realize how much he'd give up for her. She met his gaze. "Okay."

"Okay, you'll be the Alpha's mate?" He eased closer, though only his fingers touched her.

"No, I'll be *your* mate." She pressed her palms to his sides, feeling the warmth of his skin through the soft cotton T-shirt. "As for the Alpha thing...maybe I won't hate it as much as I think I will."

Relief shone stark on his expression. "We'll cross that bridge when we come to it. Five years and then if you think you can hang in there for longer than that, we'll decide then."

Giving in to her needs, she slipped her arms around him and rested her cheek against the firm wall of his chest. She could hear the rapid tattoo of his heart, smell a hint of sweat and fear. He'd been nervous she wouldn't come back to him. She almost laughed. He had a higher opinion of her resistance than she did. Which was an excellent thing, really. She needed to keep him on his toes.

"I love you," she whispered.

His arms snapped around her like steel bands, crushing her against him. "I love you too."

Then his mouth was on hers and she almost sobbed again, it was so good. Her fingers gripped his shirt, and she thrust her tongue into his mouth. He groaned, his hands sliding up to cradle the back of her head. His lips moved over hers, a slow and reverent exploration, a tender homecoming that made moisture sting her eyes. Dear God, but she'd missed him, craved him every single second they'd been apart. Their tongues tangled, stroked together as their bodies rubbed with a subtle rhythm that mimicked what was to come.

Her body burned with the kind of desire she'd never felt for anyone but him. She welcomed it, a cessation of the pain their separation had caused her. She skimmed her hands over every inch of him she could reach, up the back of his shirt to caress his skin, and still it wasn't enough. Arching into him, she tried to communicate her need without breaking the kiss. Her sex throbbed, so damp she could feel the swollen slickness of her pussy.

But he didn't give her what she wanted, just kept up the slow, maddening seduction. He palmed her breast, his thumb circling her nipple. She felt each sweep of his digit like a lightning strike straight to her loins. Unable to take anymore, she tore at the button on his jeans, shoving her hands down his pants. They both groaned when she grasped his dick. The angle was awkward with her arm wedged between them, but she stroked him.

The kiss grew rougher, more feral. His fangs scraped against her lips, and she tasted the tang of blood, which called to the animalistic side of her. Her hips bucked in a blind seeking for contact, for surcease that only he could grant her. She was going to implode if he didn't fuck her soon.

With a growl, he jerked back, his chest heaving.

She sputtered. "Don't stop!"

"We're in a garage," he groaned, the sound almost mournful.

"So? I do my best work in garages."

The look he shot her was scolding. "Tori!"

She grabbed a clean towel from the stack, and with a quick snap, had it spread over the edge of the workbench. "Lift me up."

One dark eyebrow rose. "Not the most romantic setting for a reunion."

"All the beds are in the house. With my brothers," she emphasized.

He grinned. "It's a really nice garage you have here."

"Exactly." She pulled her shirt over her head and tossed it down next to the towel. If she got naked, maybe he'd take the hint and follow suit. Her bra went next and his gray gaze burned to pure silver as he watched her. She open her fly and worked her jeans and panties down her thighs before she remembered—*duh!*—she had to take her shoes off first. She bent to unlace her boots and tug them off. His hands bracketed her waist and he set her on the workbench. Then he wrestled the remainder of her clothes away.

"You are so beautiful, my mate."

A lot of men had said that to her over the years, but none of them had ever had love filling their expression when they said it. The emotion made all the difference in the world. She leaned back on her hands and let him look his fill, feeling more beautiful than she ever had in her life.

"You're pretty good-looking too, Lykaios." She gave a pointed glance to his attire. "I'd like to see more of you. We've both waited long enough."

His Adam's apple bobbed and something vulnerable moved behind his gaze. Even with his clothes on, she'd never seen him more naked. He let her see everything—all that he felt, all that he was. Not perfect or powerful. Just a man. Just her mate. "I love you."

"I love you." She held out her arms. "Come here."

He stripped in under a minute and then stepped into her embrace. She wrapped her arms and legs around him, holding him as close as she could. His erection was rock-hard against her belly, and he took her mouth again. She danced her fingers over his form—satin flesh stretched taut over steely strength. Touching him fulfilled a need she'd never known she had before him. The need to connect, to steep herself in the essence of another. To mate. The taste of him was hot and masculine on her tongue, and she sucked his lower lip into her mouth, sinking her teeth into its fullness.

Groaning, he reached between them to grasp his dick and guide it to her entrance. His knuckles brushed over her clit, and she whimpered in response. When he pushed into her, the whimper turned into a throaty moan. He was so big, the stretch as exquisite as ever. Her eyes drifted shut and she bit her lip, rocking her hips into his thrusts. Heat and friction, the crisp hair at his groin rubbing her clit, their gasping pants, the creak of the workbench beneath them. One sensation piled on top of the other, and she reveled in it. This was where she belonged, with this man, wherever they happened to be. All the pieces clicked into place.

He pumped into her, hard and fast, and the angle the table lent them was so fucking amazing. Each time he slammed inside her pussy, the head of his cock hit her G-spot. She fell back on her hands and arched her torso, choking at how much better that felt. Climax was rising like a tide within her, threatening to pull her under. Moans spilled from her throat, and she clenched her thighs around his trim hips. So close, so very, very close.

"Tori."

"Hmm?" She opened her eyes to look at him.

His gaze locked with hers, caught her in their silver intensity, and there were no barriers between them anymore. Just acceptance, forgiveness. Love. The kind of love that would last for a lifetime. A smile curled her lips as they both fought their orgasms, tried to drag this out as long as possible, tried to hold on to the connection. He laughed, pure joy shining in his gaze. Light glinted off his fangs, the wolf as evident as the man. She loved both sides of his nature, loved that she could always lighten the seriousness in his expression. He needed her as much as she needed him. They moved in perfect sync, faster and faster, driving each other to the very brink of sanity.

Then he dropped his hand between them and thumbed her clit. "Come for me, honey."

She could do nothing else. Goosebumps broke down her limbs as climax crashed over her in a wild rush of sensation. He fucked her hard, his hands gripping her thighs to hold her in place as he hammered deep. She exploded again, a broken cry ripping from her. Her pussy fisted around his dick again and again until she felt lightheaded and giddy with the pleasure of it.

Still, they kept the eye contact and she saw the moment orgasm took him. His gaze lost focus, and great shudders racked his big body. His hot fluids pumped into her, his claw-tipped fingers digging into her flesh as he rode her through his climax. They were shaking when it was done, the experience even more powerful than the ones they'd shared before. They may have already marked each other, but this time they'd committed to each other. This time it meant more. His head fell forward and his arms cradled her close. Sweat glued their skin together, but she ignored the slight discomfort.

She slumped against his chest, breathing hard. He buried his face in her shoulder and cuddled her for long moments. She heard him swallow, and his voice was rough when he spoke. "There were times I was scared I'd never get to do this again. Hold you."

"Bastian." Her heart turned over. The man was usually confidence incarnate. In the days they'd been together, he'd always been one step ahead of her, so accepting of their mating, their love. So certain of their future. "I was scared too."

"You?" His fingers drifted down her spine. "Why?"

She turned her nose into his hair and breathed in his scent. "I was scared I couldn't be what you needed. That we'd make each other miserable just by being who we are. In private, we fit so well, but you have a very public life."

"For now." He pulled back and looked at her, his gaze fierce. "Don't ever leave me again, Tori. *Ever.*"

"I couldn't." She'd barely managed it this time. She might have to kick his ass occasionally if he got a little *too* Alpha on her, but she didn't think she could leave. She loved him too fucking much.

"I'm glad." His embrace tightened, crushing the breath out of her. "I've been dying without you, but I couldn't get away sooner. Things are still too unstable for me to be gone long."

"I know." She ran a soothing hand down his back. "Meetings with the president, protecting shifter rights. I've been glued to the news keeping tabs on you."

His laugh was little more than a huff of air. "All you had to do was call. Email. Send up a smoke signal. Anything. I would have answered."

"I was too mad." Too busy going over every nanosecond of her abduction, second-guessing every move, playing the blame game that nobody won. Least of all her.

His fingers squeezed the back of her neck. "Forgive me. Forgive yourself."

"I don't think I can ever forgive your father or Hector."

"That's okay." He hesitated. "You may have to tolerate Dad during the occasional family visit though. Maybe Hector too, if we're visiting Celeste and Lyra. He's gone back to Arizona."

She flicked her hand dismissively. "Lots of people have in-laws they don't like. I'll deal."

He crooked a finger under her chin, forcing her to meet his gaze. "You're an amazing woman."

Her nose wrinkled as she made a face. "If I were that amazing, I wouldn't have gotten kidnapped in the first place."

"Stop that," he ordered gently. "If it hadn't been you, it would have been someone else. Maybe a child who couldn't have escaped. The blame rests on Hector's and Michael's shoulders. No one forced them to betray their kind. The blame rests on Powell's and Hastings's shoulders. No one made them abduct you. You have nothing to feel bad about. You made the best decisions you could under bad circumstances. That's all anyone can expect. They can agree or disagree, but they weren't there and can never really know what they would have done in the same situation. We can only move forward from here."

He was right. It was going to take some time to internalize it though. But it would be easier with him around to remind her, to understand what she'd been through and why she felt the way she did. Then again, considering what he'd said about feeling ashamed of himself for not saving her, he might need some reminders occasionally too. She gave him a wry smile. "How'd you get so smart?"

His smile was sardonic. "I had a good teacher—my dad—even if I'm still unhappy with him. He did what he thought was right."

"I can't understand *why* he thought exposing us was the right thing."

"Me neither, but to his mind, it was."

She sighed. "Now we just pick up the pieces he left behind."

"Yep." His broad shoulder lifted in a shrug.

"Five years." She nodded. "Longer if I can handle it."

He swept a hand through her hair, his expression tender. "I'm in if you are."

"As long as you're with me, I'm all in." Everything inside her settled, all the bullshit and worry fading. She'd spent so much time stressed that Bastian's job would change her that she hadn't recognized how much their love had already changed her. For the better, she thought. They were both strong, hardheaded people, but they'd learned to bend. Compromise was part of relationships, and knowing she wasn't trapped as the clan leader's mate forever would go a long way toward helping her cope with whatever problems came because of it. She had an out, if she wanted it. She'd have the career of her choosing, and he'd have her back if anyone ever challenged her for that choice. He'd made sure she had what she needed, which was all she could ever ask for.

He hadn't tried to cage her—he'd given her space to fly.

ABOUT THE AUTHORS

Crystal Jordan is originally from California, but has lived and worked all over the United States as a university librarian. An award winning author, Crystal has published paranormal, futuristic, and erotic romance with Kensington Books, Harlequin Books, and Entangled Publishing. Visit her at ww.crystaljordan.com.

Loribelle Hunt is a beach bunny at heart, but in a pinch she'll settle for a pool. An Atlanta native, the Army relocated her to southern Alabama more years ago than she cares to remember. Since it only snows once every two decades or so, she decided to stay. She lives with her husband of twenty years, their three kids, and way too many English Springer Spaniels. She writes science fiction and paranormal romance often with a Southern drawl. Visit her at www.loribellehunt.com.

In case you missed the first volume of *Forbidden Passions*...

Turn the page for a sneak peek at the first chapter!

Forbidden Passions

Love is the most dangerous game of all…

Stolen Passions by Crystal Jordan

Lyra Marcus is a werewolf left for dead in enemy territory, but she's not going down without a fight. Leopard-shifter Zander Leonidas wants the little she-wolf the moment he sees her--he'll keep her safe no matter what it takes. In fact, he'll just keep her, period.

Passions Recalled by Loribelle Hunt

Celeste Lykaios is a dead woman. At least that's what her mate, Jason Leonidas, was told after a plane crash no one walked away from. When she shows up a year later, alive and well, he vows to protect her from all comers…a hurricane, a killer, and the werewolf family that kept them apart.

Fleeting Passions by Crystal Jordan

Cleo Nemean is a lioness on the run from an abusive ex, and she takes a job with the Leonidas family hoping for protection. A night spent toasting her newfound freedom lands her in bed with Adrian Leonidas--her new boss, and her new accidental mate. But then her ex tracks her down…

Renegade Passions by Loribelle Hunt

Ajax Petros is leader of the eagle's elite Messenger Corps, heir to the throne, and not ready to settle down. But when Nico Leonidas enters her territory searching for answers about the plane crash that killed his father everything changes.

CHAPTER ONE

It was the heat that woke her.

Something rough rasped against her cheek, and sweat slid in slow beads down her face. It stung her eyes when she opened them to see the blazing sun overhead. Sand. It was sand scraping the skin on her face. From the smell of it, she was in the desert, no longer in the humid air of New Orleans. She was so hot, she felt as if her blood was boiling. Exhaustion sapped at her strength, willing her to return to oblivious slumber, but questions nagged at her, buzzing around like insistent gnats.

Where was she, and how had she gotten here? Why was she outside?

When she tried to lift her head to get a better look at her surroundings, every muscle in her body screamed in protest. Oh, God. She remembered now. She'd been attacked after she'd finished a late shift at the clinic in New Orleans—a clinic just for people like her. Shape-shifters. Wereanimals.

The last thing she remembered seeing was a gloved fist slamming into her jaw—and it packed the kind of strength behind it that a human couldn't manage. It had to be another shifter. The physician in her began cataloguing injuries even as the wolf wanted to rip someone's throat out for doing this to her. Multiple lacerations and contusions, possible fibular fracture and a serious case of dehydration. If she didn't get to water soon, she was so screwed.

The anger whipping through her made it easier to ignore the shrieking agony that threatened to make her collapse back to the sand. It didn't matter if it hurt—she was going to die if she stayed here. She wiped sweat and dried blood from her face, pushing her long black hair back over her shoulder.

Lifting her nose to the wind, she inhaled and tried to catch the scent of civilization…or water, whichever was closer. West. The faintest aroma of people came to her, so she turned in that direction. Her gait was a broken stagger, but she was moving. She stumbled again and again, crashing hard to the ground and scraping skin from her palms and elbows.

A hopeless sob was wrenched from her chest, but she forced herself to get up, to keep going. She didn't want to die. She didn't want to give the son of a bitch who'd done this to her the satisfaction. The wide expanse of rocky desert terrain stretched before her endlessly, broken only by stark mountains rising to the north. Sweat burned the cuts on her face. Gritting her teeth, she pushed on. If she gave in to the pain, she'd never get to see them punished. A grim smile pulled at her cracked lips. Revenge was a great motivator.

When her ankle twisted and gave out from under her, she tumbled down a short ravine, landing on her back. Squinting against the glare of the sun, she saw a large bird pass in front of it. Probably a buzzard coming to pick her bones when she died. Groaning, she braced her hands on the ground and tried to force herself up again, but her arms collapsed, and her head slammed down to the ground. Her ears rang with the force of the impact.

It was almost funny that she, Doctor Lyra Marcus, fastidious to a fault and niece of the most powerful werewolf Alpha in America, was filthy, bloodstained, lying in the dirt and couldn't do a damn thing about it. A giggle that bordered on hysteria bubbled from her throat. Well, at least she remembered her own name. That was something. She clamped a hand over her mouth to stifle the laughter.

Get a grip, Lyra.

Digging down deeper inside herself than she ever had before, she used the side of the ravine to pull herself upright, to stand, to lean against as she shuffled along again. The farther she walked, the more her thoughts grew fuzzy around the edges, and that wasn't good. No, not good at all. Eventually the ravine ended, and she staggered out into an arid wasteland. It wouldn't be much longer before she couldn't get up if she fell, couldn't go any further. And then the scavengers would have their turn at her. The thought didn't scare her as much as she knew it should, and time slid away as she put one foot in front of the other.

She lifted her head as she smelled something worse than death on the wind, and the horror of her predicament finally hit home.

Wereleopard.

The sworn enemy of her kind. She was in the desert, which meant that if she was still in the United States, she was deep into the western territory the cats claimed for their own. A place where no sane wolf would ever go.

She couldn't see it among the scraggly brush and broken rock, but she knew it was there. The way her wolf senses screeched danger was no lie. She picked up her pace, tried to run, tried to escape. To where, she didn't know, but she wasn't being taken in enemy territory without a fight.

And there it was, all tawny fur and dark spots—huge, sleek, and undeniably male. His gaze locked on her as he pursued her at a ground-eating pace, hunting her. She snarled, more the wolf now than woman. Her fangs erupted from her gums, but she didn't have the energy left to shift into full wolf form. Too weak to defend herself.

Weak, and probably dead before the vultures ever got a piece of her. It was her last thought before she tripped over a sunken boulder, and the ground came rushing up to meet her.

The world went dark, and she knew her life was over.

Zander slowed to a lope to circle the unconscious woman. Confusion and anger had flooded him the moment the scent of werewolf had reached his nose. Someone was trespassing on his family's land, and he'd needed to investigate. This wasn't what he'd expected to find. His claws dug into the loose sand as he paced around her, looking for a trap. The desert was eerily silent. He hadn't seen anyone else out here, couldn't smell anything but her on the wind. It was distracting, that smell. Titillating in a way that he shouldn't allow it to be. Still, it didn't answer the most important questions. What the fuck was going on here? Who was she, and how had she gotten here?

He nudged her shoulder with his muzzle, pushing her limp body over on to her back. Whoever she was, she was in bad shape. Blood caked her nostrils and the corners of her mouth. Ugly bruises mottled her creamy skin. Horror and rage fisted his belly as he saw distinct handprints on her flesh. Someone had done this to her deliberately—beaten this woman until she collapsed. He fought the urge to track down the bastard and return the favor. Every muscle in his body locked as he got a stranglehold on his temper. It was unlike him to react so violently, and he shook his head hard.

She sucked in a quick breath, her eyes flaring open for a moment. The unusual liquid silver color snared him, fascinating the cat within him. Her lips moved, but no sound emerged. She growled a warning at him, her fangs baring. But he read the fear and desperate helplessness under the fierceness in that gaze. He wanted to reassure her, let her know that she was safe, that he would never allow anyone to hurt her again. But then she was gone, her eyes closing and her body relaxing against the ground as she passed out.

Some emotion he couldn't name gripped his chest as he stared down at her. Whoever she was, she was his responsibility now. She was his now. A shudder of foreboding ran through him, but he pushed that aside the way he had his unexpected anger. He had more vital matters to deal with, like saving this woman from dehydration under the blazing sun.

He stretched, his body shifting from leopard to human form. The spotted fur retracted until he was left crouching naked beside her. He gingerly scooped her up and cradled her slim form to his chest. Protectiveness flooded him as he felt how delicate she was compared to him. He could get all his questions answered about her after he got her out of the desert heat. Sweat already slid in rivulets down his back and stuck his skin to hers.

After only a few steps, the hot sand managed to scorch and blister his very human feet. He bit back a curse as he started the long trek home.

Over twenty-four hours later, he sat by her bedside while she slept fitfully. Her silver eyes rolled back for a moment before she opened them fully to meet his.

"Welcome back." Zander dropped the financial report he was reading to the bedside table and leaned forward in his chair. It looked like his uninvited guest was finally awake.

Neither he nor his brothers had been able to figure out who she was or how she'd ended up on their land. He did know that if he hadn't had a meeting and needed to cut short his daily run around his family's extensive property, he never would have found her. If he hadn't taken that shortcut, she'd be dead.

And that would be a damn shame. A woman this lovely shouldn't have to die that way. Once he'd cleaned her up and the natural healing ability all shifters possessed kicked in, he could see the fine bone structure, the full lips, the lovely face framed by a pool of inky black hair against the white pillowcase. Those locks had trailed to her waist when she'd run from him. As beat up as she'd been, he had no idea how she'd managed to run at all. The way she'd bared her fangs showed a predator's nature. Her strength impressed the hell out of him, and his reaction to her on every level made her unlike any woman he'd ever known before, regardless of species. She'd been in and out of consciousness, and he'd forced liquids down her throat every time she came to.

His brothers had offered to take turns sitting with her, but he'd refused. The first moment Zander had seen those gray eyes focus on him, he'd been caught by something more powerful than he'd ever experienced before. It hadn't relaxed its grip on him since. The leopard in him wanted her, the animal as intrigued as the man. He couldn't walk away. So here he sat, alert to every breath she took as her body rapidly restored itself. She appeared to be completely healed, so he watched and waited for her to awaken and not just resurface briefly as she had before.

Her gaze was blank and glassy as she returned to awareness by degrees. "W-where am I?"

That low voice reminded him of chicory and hot, humid nights on the bayou.

"The infirmary at Refuge Resort." Leaning farther forward, he caught a lock of her silky hair between his fingers and slid it away from her face. Her scent came to him the way it had that first moment in the desert, sweet, rich and all woman. He sat back with a jerk, pushing away the errant thought.

"Refuge? That's in Arizona." She blinked hard, raising herself onto her elbows. Her movements made the narrow cot squeak. The thin sheet slipped down to bare a dusky nipple. His gaze dropped to it, to the slight, firm curves of her body, and his body reacted, cock going rock hard. She lifted a hand and covered herself without haste. Not a scrap of embarrassment shone on her face when he met her gaze. He arched a brow, and her mouth quirked at the corners. "Sorry, kitty cat. I'm not shy. I'm a doctor, so nudity doesn't bother me."

"Good to know." He let a lascivious smile curl his lips as his gaze swept over her body. The sexual response he had to her was outside of his control, but what he did with it wasn't. And he always kept the upper hand.

But...kitty cat? As if a leopard could be compared to a

domestic house cat. He snorted. The woman was more than bold.

It was too bad he liked that in his women.

Look for these series
from the authors of Forbidden Passions:

Crystal Jordan

<u>Wereplanets</u>
In Ice
In Heat
In Smoke
In Mist

<u>Twilight of the Gods</u>
Viking Fire
Viking Desire

<u>In the Heat of the Night</u>
Total Eclipse of the Heart
Big Girls Don't Die
It's Raining Men
Crazy Little Thing Called Love

<u>The Night</u>
Embrace the Night
Night Games
Edge of Night

Loribelle Hunt

<u>The Elect</u>
Protector
Guardian
Warrior

<u>Delroi Connection</u>
Invasion Earth
Leaving Earth
Stolen Earth
Claiming Earth

<u>Delroi Prophecy</u>
Freedom
Irresistible
Redemption
Absolution

<u>Delroi Warrior</u>
Shadow Warrior
Dark Warrior
Star Warrior